SKULL MOON

TIM CURRAN

PART 1: AFTER THE NOOSE

1

A full moon. Big, bloated, obscene.

Its pallid light filters down on the craggy, shadow-pocketed landscape of the northern Wyoming Territory. Black surreal clouds roll in the sky. A cool wind howls and shrieks, the dark pines bend and sway.

A lone, crooked oak claws at the sky, its stripped limbs creak and moan. From one blasted fork a body hangs, strung by the neck with a coil of frayed rope. The body swings and turns with a gentle tenebrous motion, urged by the night winds.

With a sound like dry lips parting, the eyes open.

2

The Indian was old. His burnished face was a map of the rocky, gouged landscape around him. He wore a faded gray army shirt and a tattered campaign hat with the crossed silver arrows of the scouts. On his knotted feet were black moccasins, the soles threadbare. Wrapped around him was a stained blanket. He carried an oil lantern that hissed and sputtered, casting grotesque shadows over the rocks and leafless, stunted trees.

He was very old. Even he couldn't remember just how old. He only knew that in his youth he had fought the beaver trappers in the mountains. And much later, had been with them when the mountain men had their final rendezvous in 1840. And he had been old then, nearly forty years before.

His name was Swift Fox and he was Flathead.

He knew this just as he knew some of his tribe called him Old Fox or Sly Fox behind his back. Just as he knew he'd first fought, then befriended the whites, even serving in their army in campaigns against the Dakota.

He kept walking.

He mounted a rise, the cool November wind blowing dust in his face. He saw the big oak in the distance and made for it. He stepped carefully, a lifetime of navigating such terrain teaching him the value of patience. He'd seen too many men scramble over the rocks and slopes in a rush only to catch their boots in a yawning crevice and snap their ankles. This had never happened to him and he planned on keeping it that way. Old men's bones, he knew, didn't mend so well.

The temperature was in the mid-forties.

Seasonable for that time of year in Wyoming Territory. Yet, the chill dug into him, laid on his skin like frost, clotting his old, sluggish blood with ice. This more than anything told Swift Fox in no uncertain terms he was an old man.

At the big oak, he stood motionless for some time, watching the hanged man.

The breed, Charles Goodwater, had told him of this. He'd seen the hanged man from a distance as he stalked a deer and had quickly returned to camp to report it. Swift Fox had come, knowing if he didn't cut the body down no one else would. Not Indian nor white. And in his way of thinking, there was something blasphemous about letting a man hang in the wind until he rotted and dropped to bones.

So he had come.

Holding the oil lamp with a steady fist, Swift Fox studied the hanged man. He was dressed in a long midnight-blue broadcloth coat with black pants, scuffed Texas boots, and a dark flat-crowned hat. He wore a white cotton shirt that was brown now with dried blood.

Swift Fox wetted his lips and set the lamp down. The flickering light threw huge, leaping shadows. The body hung only a foot or so off the ground so Swift Fox only needed to climb up a few feet. He slid a long, curved skinning knife from the sheath at his hip and sawed at the rope. The blade was sharp enough to take off a finger with a single slice, but the rope was stubborn. It took him a few seconds to cut through it, the blade winking back moonlight and steel.

The body hit with a thud.

Slowly, patiently, Swift Fox climbed down and sat next to the man. His old bones creaked in protest. The man's hands were tied behind his back and Swift Fox cut them free. The arms were not stiff as he worked them free and rolled the man over. He hadn't been dead long.

Swift Fox pushed aside a strand of white, blowing hair and brought the lantern closer to the man's face. He had the dark skin of an Indian, yet his features were European. A half-breed maybe or just a white who'd spent his life in the wind and sun.

The wind howling like the spirits of the dead in this lonesome place, Swift Fox checked the man's pockets. He carried no weapons, no identification. Just inside his coat, Swift Fox felt metal beneath his fingertips. He turned the flap of material out.

A badge.

The hanged man had been a deputy U.S. Marshal.

There would be hell to pay for this, the old man knew. The murder of a federal marshal meant nothing but trouble and a lot of it. Swift Fox looked into the dead man's face.

And the eyes opened.

3

For the next four days, the many daughters of Swift Fox cared for the hanged man. They wrapped him in buffalo blankets and fed him a hot broth of deer blood. While they did this, the old man kept watch and smoked his pipe. On the morning of the fifth day, the hanged man regained full consciousness.

He looked at the old man's daughters and then at the old man himself. He asked for water in a dry, dead voice. The old man sent his daughters away and let the hanged man drink all he desired from a jug fashioned from the bladder of a buffalo.

"My throat burns," he finally said, his eyes blue and icy.

"It is not broken," Swift Fox said. "By the grace of the fathers, you live."

"You speak good English."

The old man took this as a fact, not a compliment. "I was a cavalry scout."

"Did you bring me here?"

"Yes."

The man nodded painfully. He looked around. "Flathead?" he asked.

"Yes. I am called Swift Fox."

"Joseph Smith Longtree," the man said. "Where am I exactly?"

"You are in a camp on the north fork of the Shoshone River. Less than a mile from where I found you, Marshal."

Longtree coughed dryly, nodding. "How far are we from Bad River?"

"Two miles," the old man told him. "No more, no less."

Longtree sat up and his head spun. "Damn," he said. "I have to get down to Bad River. The men I'm hunting...they might still be there."

"Who are these men?"

Longtree told him.

There were three men, he said. Charles Brickley, Carl Weiss, and Budd Hannion. They'd ambushed an army wagon in Nebraska that was en route to Fort Kearny, killing all six troopers on board. The wagon had carried army carbines which, it was learned, were sold to Bannock war parties. That was a matter now for the army itself and the Indian Bureau. But the killing of soldiers was a federal offense which made it the business of the U. S. Marshals Office. Longtree had trailed the killers from Dakota Territory to Bad River. And in the foothills of the Absarokas, they had ambushed him. They jumped him, beat him senseless, strung him up.

"But you did not die," Swift Fox reminded him.

"Thanks to you." Longtree was able to sit up now without dizziness.

Swift Fox was studying him. His hair was long and dark, carrying a blue-black sheen foreign to whites. "You are a breed?" he asked.

Longtree smiled thinly. "My mother was a Crow, my father a beaver trapper."

Swift Fox only nodded. "When do you plan on hunting these men?"

Longtree rubbed his neck. "Tomorrow," he said, laying back down and shutting his eyes.

4

The wind was blowing when he got to Bad River.

It wasn't much of a town. A rutted road of dirt and dried mud meandered between rows of peeled clapboard buildings. What signs hung out front had been weathered unreadable by the elements. There was a livery, a blacksmith shop, and a graying boarded-up structure that might have passed for a hotel. There was no law, no jailhouse. What Longtree had come to do, he would do alone.

Dust and dirt in his face, the wind mourning amongst the buildings, he hitched the horse Swift Fox had loaned him outside the livery barn. The horse—an old gray—wasn't too happy about being left in the wind.

"This won't take long," Longtree promised him.

He broke open the short-barreled shotgun the old Flathead had given him, fed in two shells, and started down the rotting, frost-heaved boardwalk. His army spurs jangled as he walked. Swift Fox had done some checking and found that the men Longtree was looking for often frequented the Corner Saloon in Bad River.

This is where Longtree went now.

He had his neckerchief pulled up over his nose and mouth so he wouldn't be breathing grit. The shotgun was held firmly in his fists, his eyes narrowed. His dark clothes were gray now with dust and wind-blown debris. Outside the saloon, he paused. It was a decaying structure, single-story, its boarding warped and peeled, the doorway askew with an old army blanket tacked to the frame.

Longtree went in with a slow and easy pace, the shotgun ready in his hands. It was dim inside, lit only by sputtering lamps. The floor was uneven and covered in layers of pungent sawdust. The stuffy air stank of cheap liquor, smoke, and body odor. Beaten men lounged at the bar. A few more in booths. An obese, toothless bar hag slicked with sweat and grime grinned at Longtree with yellow gums.

"What'll ya have?" the bartender asked. He was bald and had but one arm, an empty sleeve pinned to his side.

Longtree ignored him, keeping his neckerchief up over his face so the men at the back table wouldn't recognize him.

They were all there.

Brickley, thin and wizened, hat pulled down near his eyes. Weiss, chubby and short, grinning at his partners. Hannion, a muscled giant, a knife scar running down one cheek.

Longtree went to them.

"You want somethin'?" Weiss asked, a single gold tooth in his lower jaw.

"I have a warrant for the arrest of you men," Longtree said. "Murder."

They looked up at him with wide, hateful eyes.

Longtree flashed his badge and pulled down the neckerchief.

"Oh God," Weiss stammered. "God in Heaven...you're dead..." He fell backwards out of his chair as Brickley and Hannion went for their guns. Longtree shot Brickley in the face, his head pulping in a spray of blood and bone. Hannion pulled his gun and took his in the chest, hitting the floor and flopping about, pissing rivers of red.

Longtree broke open the shotgun, emptied the chambers, and fed in two more shells. He stepped over the corpses and towered above Weiss. Weiss was trembling on the floor, his crotch wet where he'd pissed himself, bits of the other two men sticking to him.

"Where's my horse?" Longtree asked him. "My guns?"

Weiss shuttered, unable to talk.

Longtree kicked him in the face, the boot-spur slicing off the end of his nose and dumping the man in the wreck of Hannion. Weiss screamed, left arm sunk up to the elbow in the bloody crater of Hannion's chest. Longtree grabbed him by the hair and pulled him to his feet.

"My things," he said in a deadpan voice. "Now."

Barely able to walk, Weiss led him out of the saloon and through the screaming wind to the livery stable. A lamp burned in there; a grizzled old man oiled a bridle. He saw the blood on Weiss. Saw Longtree's badge and fled.

Weiss pointed to Longtree's horse and saddlebags, his bedroll and weapons lying in the corner. Then he fell to his knees, crying, whimpering, drool running down his chin.

"Don't kill me, Marshal! Oh, God in Heaven, don't kill me!" he rambled in a broken, lisping voice. "Please! They made me do it! They made me!"

Longtree kicked him in the face again and the man howled in agony.

Sighing, Longtree turned to his things and went through them. Everything was in order, save the warrants and wanted fliers of the men—they were missing. His gun belts and nickel-plated Colts were untouched. His Winchester rifle had been emptied of cartridges. Nothing else had changed.

Behind him, he heard Weiss make a run for it.

Longtree turned quickly and let him have both barrels. The impact threw Weiss through the doors, his midsection pulverized. He hit the ground a corpse. Only a few ripped strands of meat held him together.

The killing done, Longtree sat down and smoked.

5

Later, after he'd hauled the corpses to the undertaker's and arranged for their burials using the outlaws' horses and guns as payment, Longtree hit the trail. He rode up to the camp of the Flathead and gave Swift Fox the horse and gun back, thanked the man.

And then he was gone.

Longtree didn't like Bad River. It had a stink of death and corruption about it. And if the truth be told, there were few frontier towns that did not. And the reality of this brought a bleak depression on him.

So he rode.

He headed east to Fort Phil Kearny where orders from the U.S. Marshals Office would be awaiting him.

And that night, the air stank of running blood.

6

The switchman was a big fellow.

He went in at nearly three-hundred pounds and though some of that was fat, much of it was hardened lanky muscle accrued from a lifetime of hard work. His name was Abe Runyon and in his fifty years, he'd done it all. He'd driven team and rode shotgun on a stage in the Colorado Territory. He'd been foreman for the Irish gangs that laid track from Kansas City to Denver for the Kansas Pacific Railroad. He'd logged some. Trapped some.

Of all things, he liked railroad work best.

And tonight especially. A storm was hitting southwestern Montana with a vengeance. The sky was choked with snow, propelled with gale-force intensity by winds screaming down from the Tobacco Root Mountains. Already some six inches had fallen.

He was sitting in a signalman's shack, playing solitaire before the glow of a lantern. Outside, the wind was screaming, making the little shack tremble.

Runyon cursed under his breath, knowing he'd have to spend the night out here. Knowing he'd been a damn fool to be inspecting track with the clouds boiling in the first place.

There'd be no whiskey tonight.

It would be just him and the cards and the little wood stove that kept him warm.

"Damn," he said.

He bit off the end of a cigar and lit it with a stick match, spitting out bits of tobacco. Snow was beginning to drift in the corner, forced by the wind through any available crevice. Runyon stuffed a rag in there. It would serve for a time.

Swallowing bitterly at his luck this night, he wiped his hands on his greasy overalls and sat back down to his card game.

And this is when he heard the sound.

Even with the howl of the wind and the rattle of the shack, he heard it: someone out back rifling through the woodpile.

Runyon knew who it was.

Getting up, he grabbed his light Colt double-action .38 and opened the door. Snow and wind rushed in at him. And despite his size and strength, he was pushed back a few feet. Gritting his teeth and squinting his eyes, he forced himself out, pounding through drifts that came up to his hips at times. Out back, he caught the thieves in the act.

"All right, goddammit," he shouted into the onslaught of wind and snow. "Drop them logs!"

The thieves were three scrawny-looking Indians dressed in raggedy buffalo coats and well-worn deerhide leggings. They dropped the wood, staring at him with wide, dark eyes. A lean, starving bunch, slat-thin and desperate.

"Please," one of them said in English. "The cold."

His English was too good for a redskin and this made the bile rise in Runyon's throat. He had no use for Blackfeet and Crow savages and especially those that considered themselves civilized enough to use a whiteman's tongue. Runyon, a well-thumbed catalog of intolerance, hated Indians. Raised in an atmosphere of anti-Indian sentiments, he was born and bred to hate anything just this side of white. They'd never actually given him any personal grief but he knew that a raiding party of Cheyenne had killed both his grandparents in Indian Territory and that his father had watched the bastards scalp the both of them from his hiding place.

"Cold, are you?" Runyon said.

The one who spoke English nodded. The other two just stared. And Runyon knew what they were thinking, knew the hatred they felt and how the sneaky, lying devils would sooner slit his throat as look at him.

"We were caught in the storm," the injun said. "We need wood for a fire. In the morning we will replace it."

"Oh, I just bet you will. I just bet you will."

"Please." The voice was sincere and had it been a white man, even the lowest murdering drifter, it would've touched Runyon.

But these were savages.

And he knew the moment you showed them any mercy, any compassion, was the moment they laughed in your face. And that they'd come back and kill you first chance they got. The heathen red devils didn't respect compassion; they saw it as a weakness.

"If you're cold, injun," Runyon said, leveling the .38 in his face, "I can warm you up with some lead right fast."

"Please," the Indian said and seemed to mean it. Hard-won pride cracked in his voice; it was not easy to beg for a few sticks of wood.

"Get out of here!" Runyon cried. "Get the hell out of here before I kill the lot of you!"

The three of them backed away slowly, not taking their eyes off the white, knowing it was not a good idea to do so. Too many times had members of their tribe been murdered by turning their backs on armed whites.

"We will die," the one said. "But so will you." With that, they were gone.

But they weren't moving fast enough for Runyon's liking.

Spitting into the wind, he took aim on the stragglers and sighted in on the one who thought himself the equal of white men. He drew a bead on the savage's back and pulled the trigger. The chamber explosion was barely audible in the shrieking, biting winds. Visibility was down, but he saw one of the savages fall just as a wall of snow obscured him.

"Damn heathens," Runyon cursed and made his way back.

Sitting by the wood stove and warming his numbed hands, he grinned, knowing he'd freed the world of a few more thieving redskins.

The bastards would freeze.

Runyon smiled.

7

It was much later when the scratching began.

Runyon had been dozing in his chair, a game of solitaire laid out before him, the .38 still in his fist. He'd been dreaming he was down in Wolf Creek, warm and toasty, having a drink and eating a good meal. Then he opened his eyes. He wasn't in Wolf Creek. He was out in the goddamn signal shack waiting for morning.

Rubbing the sleep from his eyes, he set the Colt down and listened. He'd heard *something*. Some unknown sound. He wasn't one to wake without reason. Cocking his head, he listened intently. The wind was still shrieking, the snow still dusting the shack and making it tremble.

But something more now.

A low, almost mournful moaning noise broken up by the winds.

And scratching. Like claws dragged over the warped planks of the shack.

He swallowed, a trickle of sweat ran down his back. It was the injuns. It had to be the injuns. Somehow, they had survived the subzero temperatures and had come back now. Maybe with a raiding party. At the very least with guns, knives, and evil tempers.

What had that injun said?

We will die...but so will you.

Runyon shivered.

He shouldn't have shot that one...*he should've shot them all.* He should've tracked the bastards through the snow and killed them. Shot them all down and saved himself a hell of a lot of trouble.

But now they were back.

Runyon lit his cigar back up. He wished he'd brought more bullets for the Colt, but, hell, he hadn't expected any trouble like this. He should have known better. Those savages were always on the lookout for a lone white man they could murder and rob.

They were circling the shack now. Moving with quiet footfalls. He could hear them scratching at the shack. But what he heard then made no sense: growling. A low, bestial growling. No man made sounds like that. Maybe they had brought a dog. He could hear it sniffing, pressing its nose up against the boards, growling low and snorting like a bull.

He aimed the .38 at the door.

The first one in was a dead man.

The door began to rattle, to shake as someone pulled at it. The boards were shuddering, groaning beneath great force. Nails began popping free. The entire shack was in motion now, swaying back and forth as something out there clawed and tore at it. It wasn't built for such stress. The roof was collapsing, snow raining down as planks fell in.

The lantern went out as it was engulfed in snow.

With something like a scream in his throat, Runyon began kicking at the rear of the shack, knocking boards free. Just as he pulled a few planks clear and squeezed his bulk through, the door was shattered to kindling.

He plowed through the drifts, his ears reverberating with the deafening howls of the thing that could not be a man. He ran through the swirling, blowing snow, tripping, falling, dragging himself forward. Behind him, there was an awful low evil growling and something that might have been teeth gnashing together.

He turned and fired twice at a blurry, dark shape.

A huge shape.

He could smell the beast now. It came on with a stink of decay, a reek of rotting meat and fresh blood.

Runyon screamed now, a high insane screech that broke apart in the wind.

And something answered with a barking wail.

Down in the snow, breath rasping in his lungs, fingers frozen stiffly on the butt of the Colt, he saw a great black form leaping at him. Much too large to be a man. A giant. Runyon fired four more bullets and the gun was knocked from his hand.

But the wetness.

It steamed from his wrist.

In the numbing cold he hadn't even felt it, but now he saw— the thing had sheared off his hand at the wrist. And as these thoughts reeled in his head with a quiet madness, the black nebulous shape attacked again.

Runyon saw leering red eyes the size of baseballs.

Smelled hot and foul breath like a carcass left to boil in the sun.

And then his belly was slashed open from crotch to throat and he knew only pain and dying.

Runyon was the first. But not the last.

8

By dawn, the storm had abated.

The wind was still cool and crisp, but only a few flakes of snow drifted from the clear, frigid sky. In the Union Pacific Railroad yards in Wolf Creek, it was business as usual. Just before nine a flagman discovered the wreck of the signal shack. Searching around out back, he saw a single blood-encrusted hand jutting up from a snowdrift.

Within the hour, the law was there.

"What do you make of it, Doc?" Sheriff Lauters asked. He was rubbing his gloved hands together, anxious to get this done with.

Dr. Perry merely shook his head. His hair was white as the snow, his drooping mustache just touched by a few strands of steel gray. He was a thin, slight man with a bad back. As he crouched by the mutilated body of Abe Runyon, you could see this. His face was screwed tight into a perpetual mask of discomfort. "I don't know, Bill. I just don't know."

"Some kind of animal," the sheriff said. "No man could do this. Maybe a big grizz."

Perry shook his head, wincing. "No." Pause. "No grizzly did this. These bite marks aren't from any bear. None that I've ever come across." He said this with conviction. "I've patched together and buried a lot of men in the mountains after they ran afoul of a hungry grizz. No bear did this."

Lauters looked angry, his pale, bloated face hooking up in a scowl. "Then *what* for the love of God?" This whole thing smacked of trouble and he did not like trouble. "Dammit, Doc, I need answers. If there's something on the prowl killing folks, I gotta know. I gotta know what I'm hunting."

"Well it's no bear," Perry said stiffly, staring at the remains.

Abe Runyon was missing his left leg, right hand, and left arm. They hadn't been cut as with an ax or saw, but *ripped* free. His face had been chewed off, his throat torn out. There was blood everywhere, crystallized in the snow. His body cavity had been hollowed out, the internals nowhere to be found. There was no doubt in either man's mind—Abe Runyon had been devoured, he'd been killed for food.

With Lauters' help, Perry flipped the frozen, stiffened body over. The flannel shirt Runyon had worn beneath his coveralls was shredded. Perry pushed aside a few ragged flaps of it, exposing Runyon's back. There were jagged claw marks extending from his left shoulder blade to his buttocks.

"See this?" Perry said.

He took a pencil from his bag and examined the wound. There were four separate claw ruts here, each ripped into the flesh a good two inches at their deepest point. On the back of the neck there were puncture wounds that Perry knew were teeth marks. They were bigger around then the width of the pencil, and just about as deep.

"No bear has a mouth like that," Perry told the sheriff. "The spacing and arrangement of these teeth are like nothing I've ever come across."

"Shit, Doc," Lauters spat. "Work with me here. Dogs? Wolves? *A cougar?* Give me *something.*"

Perry shrugged. "No wolf did this. No dog. Not a cat. You know how big this...*predator* must have been? Jesus." He shook his head, not liking any of it. "Hell, you knew Abe. He wasn't afraid of man nor beast. If it was wolves, they'd have stripped him clean. And he got off five shots from his .38, so where are the dead ones?"

"Maybe he missed," Lauters suggested.

"He was a crack shot and you know it." Perry stood up stiffly with Lauter's help. "Well, I'll tell you, Bill. No bear did that, no way. Those teeth marks are incredible. The punctures are sunk in four, five inches easy." He looked concerned. "I don't know of anything in these parts that could do this. And I hope to God I never meet it in the flesh."

"You saying we got us a new type of animal?"

Perry just shrugged, refusing to speculate.

Lauters spat a stream of tobacco juice into the snow and looked up towards the mountains. He had a nasty feeling things were about to go bad in Wolf Creek.

9

When Joseph Longtree rode into the quadrangle of Fort Phil Kearny, the first thing he saw was bodies. Eight bodies laid out on the hardpacked snow and covered with tarps that fluttered and snapped in the wind. They were all cavalry troopers. Either wasted by disease or bullets. Both were quite common in the Wyoming Territory. He brought his horse to a halt before the bodies and followed a trooper to the livery.

He had been to the fort before. But like all forts on the frontier, its command roster was constantly changing. During the height of the Sioux War of '76, this was especially true. Troopers were dying left and right. And now, two years later, that hadn't changed.

His horse stabled, Longtree made his way to the larger of the blockhouses, knowing it contained the command element of the fort. It was warm inside. A great stone hearth was filled with blazing logs. A few desks were scattered about, manned by tired-looking officers, their uniforms haggard and worn from a brilliant blue to a drab indigo. They watched him with red-rimmed eyes.

"Can I help you, sir?" a stoop-shouldered lieutenant asked. He had a tic in the corner of his mouth, his amber eyes constantly squinting. A habit formed from long months chasing Sioux war parties through the blazing summer heat and frozen winter wind.

Longtree licked his chapped lips, pulling open his coat and flashed his badge. "Joe Longtree," he said in a flat voice. "Deputy U.S. Marshal. You have some orders here for me from the Marshals Office in Washington, I believe."

"One moment, sir," the lieutenant said, dragging himself away into the commanding officer's quarters. He came back out with a short, burly captain.

"We've been expecting you, Marshal," the captain said. He held out his hand. "Captain Wickham."

Longtree shook with a limp grip. "The orders?"

"Don't have 'em," the captain apologized. His cheeks were full and ruddy, his hairline receding. Great gray muttonchop whiskers rode his face like pelts. "There's a man here, though, to see you. A Marshal Tom Rivers. From Washington."

Longtree's eyes widened.

Rivers was the Chief U.S. Marshal. He was in charge of all the federal marshals in the Territories. Longtree hadn't seen him since Rivers had appointed him.

"Tom Rivers?" Longtree asked, his face animated now.

"Yes, sir. He's come to see you before riding on to Laramie. I'm afraid he's out right now with Colonel Smith." Wickham frowned. "One of our patrols was ambushed by a Sioux raiding party last night. We lost eight men. Eight damn men."

Longtree nodded. "I saw the bodies."

"Terrible, terrible thing," Wickham admitted.

"Sure it was Sioux?"

Wickham looked insulted. "Sure? Of course we're sure. I've fought them bastards for ten years, sir." He quickly regained his composure. "We still have trouble with isolated bands. Most of 'em don't even know Crazy Horse surrendered. And until they do...well you get the picture, Marshal."

"When do you expect them back?"

"Before nightfall, sir. I've heard you went after the fugitives who robbed that wagon in Nebraska. Murdering thieves. How did you fare?"

Longtree shrugged. "Not as well as I'd hoped." He scratched his chin. "Had to bury all three of 'em. Would've liked 'em alive."

"It's what they deserve, sir." Wickham patted Longtree on the shoulder. "It seems you have some time before the colonel and his party return. You've had a long hard ride, sir, might I suggest you take advantage of our hospitality?"

"It would be welcome," Longtree said, the burden of the past few days laying heavy on him now.

"Lieutenant!" Wickham snapped. "Find a bed for the marshal. He'll be wanting a hot meal and a bath, I would think."

The stoop-shouldered lieutenant took off.

"If you're a mind to, sir, I'd be pleased to join you for a hot drink."

"Lead the way, Captain," Longtree said.

10

The interior of the groghouse was dim and dark and smelled of pine sap and liquor. There were tables arranged down the center and knotty benches pushed up to them. Longtree and Wickham each got a mug of hot rum and sat down. There was no one else in the house but them.

Longtree hadn't been to Kearny for some time, but it hadn't changed very much. In '68, it had been abandoned due to pressure from warring Indians as had Forts C.F. Smith and Reno, all located along the old Bozeman Trail. Only Kearny had been re-opened, back in '75.

"So tell me of your exploits in Bad River," Wickham asked in his typically robust manner. He could discuss a woman's frilly pink underthings and make it sound masculine with that voice.

Longtree sipped his drink. "Not much to tell."

"They put up a fight, did they?"

Longtree laughed without meaning to do so. "You could say that." In a low voice, he described the events that had transpired. "If it hadn't been for that Flathead...well, you get the picture."

Wickham furrowed his eyebrows. "A strange turn of events, I would say. Very few men survive the noose. I've known but one and he spent the remainder of his days with a crooked neck."

"My throat doesn't feel the best," Longtree admitted, meeting the captain's gaze, "but nothing's damaged. A week or so, I'll be fine."

"Odd, though."

Longtree had the distinct feeling Wickham didn't believe him. He loosened the top few buttons of his shirt, revealing a bandage wound around his throat. Carefully, he unwrapped it. There was a bruised, abraded, and raw-looking wound coiled on his neck.

Wickham's eyes bulged. "My God... how could you survive that? *How?*"

Longtree wound the bandage back up. "I don't know. Luck? Fate? The grace of God?" He shrugged. "You tell me."

Wickham had nothing to offer. He downed his rum. "Well, back to work, Marshal. I'm sure we'll see each other before you leave. Good day, sir."

Longtree watched him leave. No doubt he was going back to gossip about the hanged man to his fellow officers. Longtree supposed it *had* been a bit dramatic showing the wound, but he detested a look of disbelief in another man's eyes. And after everything he'd been through, he figured he could be excused a bit of drama.

He ordered another rum and waited.

Waited and thought about Tom Rivers.

11

The room wasn't bad.

There was a bed and blankets and a little firepot in the corner. A few logs blazed in it. A washtub had been filled for him with steaming water. A cake of soap and a couple towels were set out.

"Just like home," Longtree said, kicking off his boots and clothes.

After his third hot rum, the lieutenant had come for him and brought him to the officer's mess. He stuffed himself on tender buffalo steaks, roast potatoes, and cornbread washed down with ale. He hadn't eaten a meal quite so good in some time.

As he scrubbed a week's worth of dirt and sweat off, he thought about Tom Rivers. Why would the Chief U.S. Marshal come all the way from Washington to the Wyoming Territory to bring him his assignment? It just didn't wash. Maybe Rivers was out visiting his marshals—something Longtree had never heard of him doing—and had just decided to serve Longtree's papers in person.

Could be.

But Wickham had said that Rivers wanted to see him before riding down to Laramie. What was so important that Rivers would wait around to see him in person? There had been no set time for the arrival of Longtree; it could've been today or next week or next month for that matter.

Longtree reclined in the soothing, steaming waters and wondered about these things. Thoughts tumbled through his head in rapid succession.

There was always the possibility that Rivers had come in person to tell him that his appointment as a federal marshal had been revoked. It had happened to others. But it seemed unlikely. Longtree had been with the Marshal Service since '70 and in that time, of the dozens and dozens of wanted men he'd hunted down, only a few had eluded him. His record was very impressive. If he was being turned out, then it wouldn't be a matter of job performance.

The drinking? Was that it?

Also unlikely.

He hadn't allowed himself to do much drinking recently. And the only time he did was between assignments. And lately, there'd been no time between them: one assignment came right on the heels of the last with no break in-between. It had always been the boredom before, waiting around with nothing to do, no constructive purpose, that set him going on one of his drinking binges or indulgences in other vices.

No, Rivers coming had nothing to do with that.

But just what the reason was, Longtree couldn't guess.

The next thing he knew, the water was cold and there was someone knocking frantically at the door.

"I'm coming," he mumbled.

12

"Let me guess," Longtree said. "I'm fired."

"Of course not, Joe," Tom Rivers said, plopping himself down in a chair by the fire. He warmed his hands. "In fact, we need you more than ever now."

Longtree, dressed only in a red union suit, pulled his shoulder-length dark hair back and tied it with a thong of leather. He reclined on the bed.

"Tell me of your expedition with Colonel Smith," he said, changing the subject.

Rivers grinned, smoothing out his mustache. He was a thin man, corded with muscle. His face was lined and pocketed with shadow, eyes the misty green of ponds. He had an easy way about him and there were few who didn't warm to him almost immediately. It was rumored that years ago when he had been a marshal in Indian Territory, he'd charmed many a white and redskin outlaw into handing over their weapons. He was a natural diplomat. People just seemed to want to do good by him.

"We didn't see a thing," he admitted. "Not a damn thing. The only injuns we came across were a beaten, pathetic lot, half-starved." He shook his head. "I never cared much for the Sioux. You know that. Give me a Shoshone or a Pawnee or a Flathead any day. But to see them reduced to what they are now...well, it's a sorry sight to see a once proud lot like them begging for a few crusts of bread."

Longtree rolled a cigarette. "The buffalo are disappearing fast and with them, the Plains Indians. I think we're about to see the death of an entire people."

"It pains me some, I must admit," Rivers said.

Longtree lit his cigarette. "I never loved the Dakotas either." It was a truth that didn't require elaboration. Longtree had been a scout in the army and had fought the Sioux, Cheyenne, and Commanche back in the sixties. He developed a hatred for the Sioux Nation not only for their campaigns against whites but for the brutalities and indiscriminate slaughter of other tribes. "Still, it's a shame to see this happen. When the buffalo are gone...well, they won't be far behind."

"I'm afraid that was the plan, Joe."

Longtree nodded.

In 1874, he knew, a group of Texas legislators had proposed a bill limiting the slaughter of the buffalo herds. It would've imposed restrictions on how many animals hunters could kill each day and limited the range in which they could be taken. It sounded like a good idea. But the army jumped all over it. The sooner the buffalo were gone, they argued, the sooner the backs of the Plains Indians would be broken. It was logical and during the height of the Indian Wars, no one really opposed such thinking. The army had found it almost impossible to pin down and defeat the swift-moving nomadic tribes of the plains—the Blackfoot, Sioux, Cheyenne, etc. But once the buffalo had been decimated, these peoples would no longer be able to feed, clothe, and house themselves. And an army cannot survive without raw materials.

It was sound thinking, if somewhat cruel.

But it worked.

"There must be a few bands out there still, though," Rivers said. "It'll probably take a few more years to clean them out."

Longtree nodded. "Why don't you tell me now why you've come."

"I'm just visiting my marshals. It's something I've been planning on doing for awhile; I just haven't gotten around to it." Rivers paused, pulled out a clay pipe and filled it. "As for you, Joe, I have a special assignment."

"Which is?"

"I need you to go up to Wolf Creek in Montana Territory and look into some killings up there."

Longtree exhaled a column of smoke. "Wolf Creek. I know of it, near Nevada City. But that's John Benneman's territory," he reminded Rivers. Benneman was the deputy U.S. Marshal operating in southwestern Montana.

"Benneman's on a leave of absence, Joe. He got shot up pretty bad bringing in a couple road agents. He'll be out of commission for months." Rivers looked unhappy about this. "Besides, this is a special situation. We need more than a lawman on this. We need someone with investigatory skills."

"Go on."

"There's been five murders in and around Wolf Creek," Rivers explained. "Vicious, brutal killings. It appears to be the work of an animal. The bodies have been devoured. But...well, you'll see for yourself."

"So hire a hunter, Tom. If it's some marauding grizz that's your best bet. I've been hunting men for too long now to be going after an animal."

Rivers sighed. "Word has reached us that it may be a *human being* doing this. Nothing concrete, just rumor."

Longtree lifted his eyebrows. "What are we talking here?"

"I don't honestly know what's going on, Joe. Something strange, that's all. I want you to go up there and have a look. That's all. Poke around a bit, see what you find out."

"This is all pretty sketchy."

Rivers looked him in the eye. "You've done more on less."

"Maybe. Still, not much there."

Rivers nodded. "I know. Just take a week or so and nose around. If you think we got an animal, fine. We'll put a bounty on it and bring in the hunters. If it's a man...well you know what to do then."

Longtree still didn't care for it. "What makes this government business, Tom? Sounds like a local matter to me. Doesn't seem like our jurisdiction at all."

Rivers found and held him with those crystal green eyes. "Shit, Joe, you know better than that. I can make just about any goddamn place the province of my marshals if I so choose."

"Sure, Tom, I know. But humor me."

"Well, we've got an ugly situation there, Joe. First off, Wolf Creek sits at the foot of the Tobacco Root Mountains and I don't have to tell you what that means—silver. And lots of it. Some people back in Washington, some of whom I work for, don't like this business at all and you can't rightly blame them: they own interest in the mines. Secondly, we've got a camp of Blackfeet in the hills outside Wolf Creek on reservation land. They've been crying foul to the Indian Agents about how the law has been treating them up there." Rivers mulled it over. "What we're afraid of is these murders getting hung on the Blackfeet and the locals taking matters into their own hands. And you know the Blackfeet. You know 'em well as any—they get pushed, they'll push right back. They won't tolerate whites raiding into their territory."

"They're a proud bunch," Longtree said, nodding. "They don't particularly care for whites and you sure as hell can't blame them."

"And that's where you come in, Joe. You're half-Crow."

"Crow ain't Blackfoot, Tom."

"No, and a pecker's not a pike, but you're all we've got, my friend. Just go on up there, nose around. See if you can get friendly not only with the townsfolk but the Blackfeet, too. They might accept you. We need somebody in there who can play both sides of the fence before this gets uglier than it already is."

Longtree nodded. "Okay, I'll do it. What they got for law in Wolf Creek?"

Tom Rivers sighed, chewed his lower lip. "Sheriff name of Lauters. He's a hardcase, Joe. I never heard anything good about him. You might have trouble with him."

"Oh, I'm sure I will. You always manage to stick me into some spot like this."

Rivers laughed. "It's why I keep you around."

After Rivers left, Longtree sat and thought about it. Usually, he had a man to go after. Something tangible. Not this time.

It would be a challenge.

13

Early the next morning Longtree set out for Wolf Creek.

He took to the trail at a leisurely pace. He was a bit skeptical about any of the killings being done by a man once he learned the details. But if it was an animal, then it was like none he'd ever heard of. Few animals were brave enough to venture into a town. And none that he knew of would kill like that once they did and make a habit of it.

It had all the markings of a damn strange investigation.

14

Nathan Segaris sat in a copse of trees and waited.

He was watching the west bluff that separated Carl Hew's grazing lands from those of the Blackfoot Indian reservation. Hew had about four-hundred head and if things went well, before morning, he'd be down about fifty.

Segaris grinned.

It wasn't a pleasant sight: he had no teeth, just mottled gums.

There were several broken sections of fence along the west bluff that Hew and his men hadn't gotten around to repairing just yet. With a little help, these could be widened up nicely.

Segaris climbed back up on his brown and steered the gelding back down towards Wolf Creek. Tonight would be a good night. The others would meet him around midnight and, with luck, they'd get the steer off of Hew's land and into the next valley by morning.

It was a plan.

Segaris grinned and lit a cigar.

It was after sundown by the time he reached his little place outside of town. He made himself a meal of corn cakes and what remained of the smoked ham from yesterday. It wasn't much, but it would suffice. And by this time next week, he'd have some real money for food.

He sat down and re-lit his cigar.

Life was grand, he thought, life was surely grand.

Outside, his horse whinnied.

He sat up. It was too early for the rest of the boys to show. He listened, cocking an ear. He could hear the wind out there, skirting the barn with the wail of widows.

Nothing else.

But Segaris was a careful man. He took his shotgun off the hook above the hearth, broke it open, and fed in two shells. If someone had come to pay a call, they'd best be wary.

The door rattled in its frame like someone had shaken it.

There was a scratching at it now. That and a hoarse, low breathing. Segaris stood up again and took aim, closing the distance to the door with a few light steps.

The door shook violently again and then exploded in with an icy gust of wind that carried a black, godless stink on it. He was thrown to the floor. He came up shooting, not knowing what it was he was shooting *at.*

Then he saw.

"Jesus," he muttered.

His screams echoed into the night.

15

Nobody in Wolf Creek particularly cared for Curly Del Vecchio.

He of the striped coats and trousers, gold watch chain, and immaculately brushed derby hats. He was a conniver and con man, gambler and self-styled ladies' man who'd spent ten years in prison for his part in a horse-rustling ring. He fancied himself a champion pistol-fighter, but anyone with a real draw would've killed him before his hand even slapped leather.

The only thing Curly was really good at was drinking. This night he'd swallowed eight bottles of beer and was halfway through a pint of rum by the time he got to Nathan Segaris' spread outside town. It was a cool night, a light snow falling, but Curly felt none of these things. He felt very good, very drunk. He was celebrating—prematurely—the theft of fifty head of Carl Hew's steer.

He knew Nate Segaris and the others wouldn't be too happy with him getting boozed up and all. But a man had a right to celebrate from time to time.

Especially one that was about to come into a good bit of money. Fifty head of old Hew's cattle at fifty bucks a crack. That would be a nice chunk of change for the lot of them, being that five of their member were now gone. Five-hundred U.S. Treasury Greenbacks to a man. Nothing to sneeze at.

"Rest in peace, boys," Curly said to himself.

Five of us gone, he thought, five of us left.

Coincidence. That's all.

Curly gave his old mare a little taste of the spurs—a nick in the sides, nothing more—and she picked up speed a bit, galloping over the hard-packed snow. She brought him over a little rise and there was Nate's place. It looked inviting. A trail of smoke drifting from the chimney, a lantern glowing in the window.

I surely hope he has a bottle of something warm, Curly thought.

He tethered his horse in the barn and drunkenly made his way up to the front porch, stopping only once to urinate. He was on the top stair before he realized something was wrong.

The door had been ripped asunder, shattered into so much kindling. Only a few jagged sections clung to the hinges, the rest were spread out over the floor in a rain of shards and split fragments.

Curly reached down for his old Army .44.

The metal was like ice in his trembling hand.

"Nate?" he called in a weak voice.

Getting no answer, he mounted the final two steps and stopped just inside the door. Tables were overturned and broken. Shelves collapsed, their contents strewn everywhere. A bag of flour had been ripped open and another of sugar. There was a dusting of white everywhere. A sudden chill gust kicked up, making the old house creak and sway, churning up dust devils of flour.

There was blood everywhere.

Curly's stomach turned over.

It was pooled on the floor, sprayed on the walls, beading the old sheet iron cooking stove. The stink of it hung in the air with a ripe, raw insistence. It was in Curly's nose, on his skin. He could taste it on his tongue.

He didn't wait to see a body.

He didn't need to.

He set off at a run, pounding through the snow, falling, slipping, but finally making the barn. He was cold stone sober as he unhitched his mare and climbed on.

The storm was starting again, snow flying in the air.

The horse began to whinny, to pace wildly from side to side. It would move off in one direction, snort, and start off in another.

"Come on, damn you!" Curly cried, the smell of violent death everywhere. He pulled on the reigns and gave the mare the spurs. "Get up!"

The barn door slammed open in the wind and then shut again. Nate's horse was whinnying and pulling madly at its tether in there. Something was wrong and both animals knew it.

The lamp in the house flickered and went out.

A cold chill went up Curly's spine and it had nothing to do with the screaming, bitter wind. And then there was another sound in the distance: a low, horrible howling, an insane baying that rose up and broke apart in the wind. Curly went cold all over, his hackles raising. That sound…the roar of a freight train echoing through a mineshaft.

The howling sounded out again.

Closer.

With a scream, Curly yanked on the reins and the mare took off down the road, nearly throwing him. It galloped crazily in the wrong direction and Curly couldn't get it under control. His face went numb from the cold, his eyes watering. Terror rattled in his heart and in his ears—the howling.

Closer.

And closer still.

16

"Big" Bill Lauters dismounted his horse and waited for Dr. Perry to do the same. It took the old man a little longer.

"Damn cold," Perry said. "My back's really acting up."

Lauters rubbed his hands together. "Let's go," he said. "Might as well get it over with."

He went in the house first. He saw pretty much what Curly Del Vecchio had seen the night before. The house was trashed, looking much like a small tornado had whipped through it.

Furniture was shattered. Dishes and crockery broken into bits that crunched underfoot. Bottles were smashed. Everything seemed to be ripped and splintered. And over it all, flour, sugar...and blood.

"Mary, mother of God," Perry gasped. "What in the hell happened here?"

Lauters surveyed the scene. He was disgusted, angry, but his features never changed; he always looked pissed-off. "What do you *think* happened here, Doc?" he said sarcastically.

They both knew what they were facing. They knew it from the moment word reached them that Nate Segaris hadn't shown up at the Congregational Church that morning. Segaris never missed. He was a thief and a cheat, as everyone knew, but he never missed Sunday services. His mother had given him a strict moral and religious upbringing. And although he had managed to shake off the morality, the religion in his soul clung on tenaciously. Or had.

"What sort of animal does this?" Lauters asked for what seemed the hundredth time. "What sort of creature busts into a man's house and does a thing like this?"

Perry said nothing. He had no answers. The killings were more than acts of hunger, but violent acts of mutilation and mayhem. And what sort of creature murders people for food like a savage beast and then destroys their lodgings like a crazy man?

Lauters looked at the blood everywhere. "He's gotta be around here somewhere."

Together, they stepped through the carnage and hesitated before the door to the rear parlor. There were claw marks in it running a good three feet. Perry examined them. The gouges were dug into the wood at least half an inch.

He swallowed dryly. "The strength this thing must have to do that."

Lauters pushed through the door.

The parlor was wrecked, too. Segaris had kept all the belongings of his late wife in here. Her frilly pillows were gutted, feathers carpeting the floor. Her fine china serving sets pulverized in the corners. Her collection of porcelain dolls were broken into bits. One severed doll head stared at them with blue painted eyes. Her dresses which had been hanging from a brass rod, were shredded into confetti. Even the walls were scathed with claw marks, torn flaps of wallpaper hanging down like Spanish Moss.

"No animal does this, Doc," Lauters said with authority. "No goddamn beast of the forest comes into a man's home and wrecks it."

Perry looked very closely at all he saw, scrutinizing everything with an investigator's eye. He checked everything. He held a fold of wallpaper in his nimble fingers and examined it as though it were a precious antiquity. He mumbled a few words to himself and extracted a bit of something that was wedged between the wallpaper and baseboard.

"But no man leaves this behind," he said, holding out what he found.

The sheriff took it, rubbed it between thumb and forefinger. It was a mat of gray coarse fur. "Some dog maybe," he muttered to himself.

"Think so?"

Lauters scowled. "I don't know what to think. I've got five dead men on my hands and what looks like possibly a sixth...what the hell am I supposed to say? What the hell do you want from me?"

"Easy, Sheriff."

Lauters dropped the fur and stalked back into the living area. Cursing, with one hand pressed to the small of his back, Perry stooped and picked it up, sticking it in his pocket. Groaning he stood back up.

"Look here, Doc."

Lauters was squatting down next to a collapsed end table. There was a shotgun beneath it. It had been snapped nearly in half, the barrels bent into a U. Lauters sniffed them and checked the chambers. "Nate got off two shots with this before it got him. And what," he asked pointedly, "walks away from a shotgun blast?"

"Whatever made this track does," Perry interjected.

Lauters was by his side now. There was a track in the flour, slightly obscured, but definitely the huge spoor of some unknown beast. "What in Christ has a foot like that?" he wondered aloud.

Perry just shook his head. "Not a man. We know that much."

The print was over two feet in length, maybe eight inches in diameter. Long, almost streamlined, whatever left it had three long toes or claws in front and a shorter, thicker spur at the rear.

"Like the track of a rooster almost," Lauters said.

"No bird left this," Perry was quick to point out.

"Jesus, Doc. The print of a giant."

Perry moaned and stooped down.

"Ought to see someone about that back," the sheriff joked out of habit, but there was no humor in his voice.

Perry ignored him. He was digging through the mess. His fingers found an iron loop. "Root cellar."

With Lauter's help, he pulled it up and threw it aside. The root cellar was a five-foot hole with walls of earth that had been squared off. Lying on the frozen mud of the floor was what remained of Nate Segaris.

"Shit," Lauters said quietly.

Segaris was a mess. His guts had been cleaved open, the organs torn free, the body cavity hollow as a drum. His arms were broken in several places, smashed and bitten. The fingers of his left hand were missing, save for the grisly nub of a thumb. His right leg was hacked off beneath the knee, leaving a knob of white ligament to mourn its passing.

Lauters swore beneath his breath and lowered himself down there. He thanked God it was November. Had it been the warm months...well, he didn't want to think about the stink and the flies.

"It must've killed him and threw him down there," Perry suggested.

"No shit, Doc."

The sheriff wasn't in the mood for Perry's bullshit speculation. He wasn't in the mood for anything these days. He searched around and could find no sign of the man's missing appendages.

Above him, Perry stared down at the ruin of Segaris' face.

His left eye was gone, as was most of the flesh around it. But his other eye was wide and staring with an accusatory glare. His mouth was frozen in a scream. The top of his head was bitten clean open—even from five feet above, Perry could see the teeth marks sunk into the skull. The brains had been scooped out and, it would seem, the gray splatter in the corner was what remained of them.

Lauters looked up with pleading eyes. "God help us," he uttered.

"I hope God *can* help us, Sheriff, I really do," Perry said. "But if he can't, then we'd better start thinking about helping ourselves."

Grumbling, Lauters pulled himself up out of the root cellar, ignoring Perry's outstretched hand. He stood and brushed himself off.

"It would be interesting to know the turn of events," Perry mused. "In what order they occurred."

Lauters glared at him with watery gray eyes. "What possible use would that be? A man's dead. Murdered. *Half-eaten for the love of Christ.*"

Perry nodded patiently. He brushed a silky wisp of white hair from his brow. "What I mean, Bill, is that it would help us to understand our killer if we knew a few things."

"Like what for instance?"

"Well, for starters, I'd like to know if Segaris was killed before or after this place was torn apart. If it was after...well, then we're talking about an act of hateful, willful destruction here, an act of vengeance. Hardly an animal characteristic."

Lauters shook his head. "You look too deep into things."

"And you," Perry said, "don't look deep enough."

Lauters ignored him. "Let's get back to town. We've got to get Spence out here with his wagon to cart this body off."

"His wagon?" Perry said. "Hate to be the one to tell you, Bill, but Spence is a woman."

"That's your opinion." Lauters sighed and sipped from a pocket flask of whiskey. "Sooner we get that body into the ground, sooner folks'll stop speculating about it."

Perry followed him outside and mounted.

"Yes," the sheriff said, finishing off his flask and stuffing it in his saddlebag, "I see trouble on the horizon, Doc."

Perry said nothing. His eyes, however, looked to the mountains for an answer. There was none. Only wind and cold.

17

Later, standing outside his office and listening to the relative calm of a Sunday evening, Lauters kept drinking. He didn't even feel the cold that swept down from the mountains. In his mind he saw only blood, death, and a forecast of more dying.

Wolf Creek was almost peaceful this night.

The ranch hands had stayed home. The miners remained up at the silver camps. Few people ventured out of doors. Maybe it was the frigid temperatures or the blowing snow. But maybe it was something else. Something that killed people for sport as well as food. Maybe this is what kept people behind locked doors.

Lauters took another pull from his silver flask.

Even the old Blackfoot beggars were nowhere to be seen. Come to think of it, he hadn't seen any injuns around for some time. Since the killings began, it seemed. This stopped the flask at his lips.

Was that worth considering? he wondered.

Could the Indians have something to do with the murders? Maybe. Maybe not. The local Blackfoot tended to steer clear of town for the most part, being that a lot of folks tended to harass them for no good reason. And when a major crime like a murder or robbery came down, they were nowhere to be found. Again, because if a scapegoat was needed, an Indian was always a good bet.

Thinking of this, made the sheriff remember the time that Blackfoot was hanged.

He scowled and took another drink.

The Blackfoot's name was Red Elk. He was being held in connection with the rape and murder of a local white girl, name of Carpenter. The girl had no family. She was new to Wolf Creek. Red Elk had supposedly surprised her one night as she left the dry goods store she worked at, forced himself on her and then cut her throat.

The second night he was in jail, the vigilantes came. They wore black hoods with eye and mouth slits. Nine of them pushed their way into the jailhouse.

"We want the injun," the leader said. "And we plan to have him."

"You boys better clear out of here," Lauters had told them.

The vigilantes all carried guns and they were all on the sheriff.

"You don't understand," the leader said. "We want that murdering redskin and we'll kill you if need be to get 'em."

Lauters had gone for his gun, but the men were already on him. They knocked him senseless with the butts of their rifles and tied him to a chair. When he came to later, it was all done with. His deputy—Alden Bowes—had returned from delivering a prisoner to Virginia City and untied him.

Red Elk was hanged from an Oak in the square across the street.

There were a few questions after that, but none Lauters couldn't answer. The men had worn masks, he couldn't identify them. They had overpowered him and he had the bruises to show for it. And why had he sent his deputy away to deliver a prisoner to Virginia City with a volatile situation brewing and anti-Indian sentiment running high? He'd thought no one would try such a thing.

The questions were answered to everyone's satisfaction.

Besides, the man they'd strung up was just an Indian, a Blackfoot. And he'd killed a white. Case closed. The only ones really concerned were the Blackfoot people and they didn't count.

Everyone else believed Lauters.

They never guessed he was lying about it all.

Knowing this, Lauters drank more. It was a year ago this week that Red Elk had been lynched and duly swung. In his mind, he could hear the creaking of the limb the noose was strung over.

It made him shiver.

18

The blizzard had been threatening for several days. On around midnight of the day Nathan Segaris' body was discovered and carted away in Wynona Spence's funeral wagon to be plucked and polished in secret, it hit. It came down out of the Tobacco Root Mountains, urged forward by shrill, squealing winds that forced the mercury well below freezing. Several feet of heavy, blowing snow were dumped over Wolf Creek, the wind sculpting it into four and five foot drifts that looked like frozen waves crashing ashore on some alien beach.

Around four, the storm passed.

The world was white. Drifting, swirling, frozen. In the foothills of the mountains, Curly Del Vecchio waited in an old abandoned mine shaft wondering when death would come. His horse threw him the night before, a short distance away, breaking his leg in the process.

Now it was night again.

He was alone.

Thankful only that he found the old shaft. Thankful there was a firepot in it and a heap of kindling left behind when the miners sought greener pastures. Enough wood to burn for three, maybe four days. Maybe by then, he hoped, someone would find him.

Maybe not.

Curly fed the fire only when he had to. This way the blaze would last for days, he figured. The only other thing he did was look at his leg and the bloody knob of bone that had burst through the skin. If he moved too much, the pain was so intense he lost consciousness.

So he sat and fed the fire.

The rest of the time was spent in a feverish half-sleep in which shadows mulled around him. Shadows with claws and teeth that reached out for him as the moon brooded above…a yellow and dead winking eye.

He didn't even move to relieve himself. He pissed his pants and his crotch steamed with spreading warmth. If he moved his head just a few inches, he could see the mouth of the shaft and the world beyond. A huge drift had insinuated itself there now and he could see only a few feet of the world. He saw parting, rolling clouds and cold stars, a sliver of moon growing fat by the day like a spider gorging on flies.

Long before dawn, a savage, primal baying rode the screaming winds. Curly wondered again when death would come.

Then, before sunup, with the decayed stink of an old slaughterhouse, it did.

19

It was two days later when Joseph Longtree approached Wolf Creek.

He came from the southeast, across the Madison River on a night of blowing snow and subzero winds. He paused astride his black on a ridge outside town, looking down at the sprawl of houses, buildings, and farms below him. Wolf Creek was a mining town, he knew, its blood running rich from transfusions pumped in from ore veins. There were miners here and ranchers. That and a lot of hatred between the whites and the local Blackfoot tribe. Tom Rivers had told him this much.

Not that he needed to be told.

Whites hated most Indians as a rule.

And the Blackfoot, he knew, were a hostile bunch. They'd fought whites and, before them, other Indians with a vengeance next to which even the Dakotas often paled. But Longtree knew the Blackfoot weren't a bad lot. Not really. Just fiercely territorial and unrelentingly proud.

He held no prejudices against them.

In his line of work, he couldn't afford to. Such things blinded a man's judgment. And the last thing he ever wanted was to arrest a man and see him brought to trial (and possibly the gallows) simply because of his skin color.

He accepted long ago, that although he might've been a lot of things, no one would ever accuse him of not being fair or honest. Because if a lawman didn't have that going for him, he was no better then the criminals he hunted.

20

Joseph Smith Longtree was born in 1836, the son of William "Bearclaw" Smith, a beaver trapper, and Piney River, a Crow Indian. His father died fighting Comanches in 1842. Longtree had barely known him. In 1845, a Sioux raiding party attacked his family's village on the Powder River, killing everyone but himself and a few others that had scattered. His mother was among the dead. He was taken away by a local missionary priest to a mission school in Nebraska. After seven years of strict Catholic upbringing and schooling, he left.

He ran away, making his way west.

He fell in with a reformed gunman named Rawlings who was canvassing Wyoming and Montana Territories in his new profession as a Baptist preacher in search of a congregation. Rawlings still carried a gun; only a fool didn't in the Territories. During their months together, Rawlings, very impressed with Longtree's knowledge of the Bible and other spiritual matters, taught him how to shoot. Getting the boy an old .44 Colt Dragoon, he drilled him every day for hours until Longtree could knock an apple out of a tree from forty feet with one swift, decisive movement.

In southeastern Montana, Rawlings and Longtree went their separate ways. Longtree sought out his Uncle Lone Hawk, who'd been away on the day the Sioux raided their village and hadn't returned until well after Longtree had been carted away to the mission school. Lone Hawk and his family had a cabin on the Little Powder River and it was here that Longtree spent the next five years.

His mother's brother was a practical man.

He knew the old ways were dying fast and a new world was beginning for the Indian. He himself lived more like a white man than a red one. He knew a young man needed a trade, a skill with which to eke out a living. But he also believed one should be acquainted with and be proud of one's ancestral heritage. He found a way in which he could bestow both upon young Joe Longtree—he would train him in the time-honored ways of the Indian, he would school him as a scout.

For the next five years, under Lone Hawk's tutelage, Longtree learned how to "read sign": tracking animal and man, learning a wealth of information from such subtle clues as footprints, hoof marks, and bent blades of grass. He learned the fine art of pathfinding. He learned how to doctor wounds with expertise. He learned how to live off the land—what plants and roots could be eaten, which could not, and which could be used as medicines; how to locate and stalk game; how to find water and dozens of other tricks. He was taught how to hunt and fight with a knife, a hatchet, the bow and arrow, the lance. He received advanced instruction in shooting and navigation by the sun and stars. He was taught the arts of stealth and concealment.

All in all, everything the Crow had learned in thousands of years of survival were imparted to Longtree in just a few years. It was then he left and signed on as an Indian scout to the army. For the next six years he fought with the whites against the Comanche and Cheyenne.

Afterwards, his belly full of blood and death and atrocities committed by Indian and white alike, he drifted to San Francisco. Where, among other things, he made a name for himself (Kid Crow) as a barefisted boxer. He made a good run of it until an Irish hothead named Jimmy Elliot gave him a thrashing he wouldn't forget this side of the grave. Restless, tired of hitting and being hit, he headed into Arizona Territory where he turned his skill as a scout to tracking men as a bounty hunter. After six years of that, with a record boasting of tracking thirty men and bringing them all in (dead or alive), he was appointed as a deputy U.S. Marshal in New Mexico Territory and later, Utah Territory, and finally, a special federal marshal.

And now after all the killing he'd done, all the men he'd tracked, all the convicts and murderers he'd brought in, he was going after something a little different.

A killer that acted like a man.

But sported the hungers of an animal.

21

It was late when Longtree found the body.

He was just making his way down a slope of scrub oak towards the outskirts of Wolf Creek when he saw what might have been an arm covered with a light dusting of snow. Bringing his gelding to an abrupt halt, he dismounted and fought through the snowdrifts to what he'd seen. The wind was blowing with fierce raw-edged gusts that whistled through the hills. His long buffalo coat flapped around him as he bent down and began to dig through the drifts to expose the rest of the corpse.

He got his oil lantern out and lit it.

The corpse wasn't worth revealing.

Especially on a night of black, howling wind and bitter flurries. Longtree judged the man to be in his mid-forties and this was about all he could tell. The body was mutilated, chest and belly gouged open. The flesh clawed and shredded to the point that it and the ripped garments it wore were knotted into each other. Both legs were snapped off below the knees, skin stripped free. The head was twisted around so it was face down in the snow. Both arms had been pulled off. One was missing, the other nearby, mangled and punctured with teeth marks, a Colt pistol frozen in its red fist.

Longtree tried to turn the remains over, but they were frozen into the earth. He poked and prodded gently in the snow with his gloved fingers. There was very little blood around, most of it frozen into sparkling crystals.

Not enough for a slaughter of this magnitude.

He surmised from this that the man had been killed somewhere else and dragged here, gutted and dismembered on the spot.

He looked around for the remains of the cadaver's legs, but they were gone.

He studied the body again in the dancing light.

It was hard to say exactly how the man had died, such was the nature of the carnage. His throat was torn out. Little remained of it but a twisted spiral ladder of vertebrae and hacked ligament. He had been opened up in countless places and could've bled to death from any of a dozen wounds. Longtree figured the attack must've been sudden and vicious. But not too sudden; the man had drawn his gun, precious little good it had done him.

The initial attack must've been savage. Brutal beyond comprehension. The man was dead long before he was dumped here and cannibalized.

Longtree examined the wounds the best he could in the flickering light.

From the teeth and claw marks there was no doubt in his mind: Only an animal could have done this. A huge and powerful beast with iron hooks for claws and jaws like razored bear traps. No man possessed the strength. No insane mind, regardless how fevered, could've summoned up the strength to pull a man literally apart. And the tools that would've been needed to create such injuries would have been complex beyond reason.

The killer in Wolf Creek was an animal.

Type: unknown.

Clenching his teeth and sucking in icy air, Longtree picked up the severed arm. It was much like handling a frozen leg of lamb. Wedging the limb between his knees, he began the grisly task of pulling the fingers free of the gun. He had to know if it had been fired. Rigor mortis and the freezing temperatures had turned the hand into an ice sculpture. The fingers snapped like pretzel rods as he forced them away from the Colt. Two popped off completely and fell in the snow.

It was gruesome work.

But it wouldn't be the first time he had done such things. A man in his line of work spent a lot of time urging the dead to give up their secrets.

The gun had been fired; only three bullets remained in the chambers.

He set the arm and weapon next to the body.

Mounting his horse, he rode into a little arroyo that was protected by a wall of pines. He tethered the black to a tree and gathered up some firewood with his hatchet. The wind was reduced to a gentle breeze in the gully and he got the fire going right away. He would spend the night here. In the morning, he would drag the body into Wolf Creek and begin the job he'd come to do.

He unhitched his saddle from the black and jerked the saddle blanket off, stretching it over some rocks to let it dry; it was damp with the horse's perspiration. He curled up before the blazing fire and chewed some jerky from his grub sack.

He dozed.

22

He didn't sleep long.

Sometime after midnight he heard horses coming up the trail that cut down the slope below him and led in the direction of Wolf Creek. He heard at least a half dozen of them come within three-hundred yards of his position, the riders dismounting. They must've seen the smoke from his fire.

He pulled himself free from his bedroll and swigged from his canteen.

In silence, he waited.

He heard them coming, stumbling through the snow to the pines that sheltered his arroyo. They were a noisy lot. Had to be whites. They stomped forward, chatting and arguing.

Longtree strapped on his nickel-plated Colt .45 Peacemakers and drew his Winchester from the saddle boot. Then he waited. They were coming down now. He positioned himself away from the glow of the fire, leaning against a shelf of rocks, hidden in shadow.

They came down together, six men in heavy woolen coats. They sported shotguns and pistols and one even had an ancient Hawken rifle. They plowed down, packed together. Very unprofessional. It would've been easy killing the lot of 'em.

"You got business here?" Longtree called from the darkness.

They looked startled, hearing a voice echoing, but unable to pinpoint it. They scanned their guns in every which direction. Longtree smiled.

"Identify yourselves or I'll start shooting," he called out.

The men looked around, bumping into each other.

"Bill Lauters," a big man said. "Sheriff, Wolf Creek." He tapped a badge pinned to his coat.

Longtree sighed. He knew who Lauters was.

He stepped out of the shadows and moved noiselessly to them. He was almost on top of them before they saw him and then their guns were on him.

"Who the hell are you?" one of them said.

"Easy, Dewey," Lauters said.

"Longtree, deputy U.S. Marshal," he said in an even tone, showing his own badge. "You were wired about—"

"Yeah, yeah, I got it all right. I know who you are and why you're here." Lauters said this as if the idea were beneath contempt. "You can just ride right back out again far as I'm concerned. We don't need no damn federal help."

"Regardless, Sheriff, you're going to get it."

"Where the hell's Benneman?" the one called Dewey asked. "He's the federal marshal in these parts."

"John Benneman got shot up," Longtree explained. "He'll be out of action a while."

Lauters spat a stream of tobacco juice in the snow. "And we're really lucky, boys, cause we got us a *special* U.S. Marshal here," he said sarcastically. "I guess we can just hang up our guns now."

Longtree smiled thinly. "I'm not taking over your investigation, Sheriff. I'm just here to help."

"My ass you are," one of them muttered.

"Nothing but trouble," another said.

Lauters nodded. "We don't need your help."

"Don't you?"

"Ride out," Lauters said. "Ride the hell out of here."

"Never happen," Longtree assured him.

The guns weren't lowered; they were raised now, if anything.

"I'm here to help. Nothing more." Longtree fished out a cigar and lit it with an ember from the fire. "Course," he said, "if you boys would rather stand around and argue like a bunch of schoolboys while more people are killed, that's your own affair."

"Who the hell you think you're talking to here?" Lauters snapped, taking a step forward.

Longtree stood up, pushing aside his coat and resting his hand on the butt of a Colt. They all saw this and he wanted them to. "I think I'm talking to a man with a strong like of himself."

Lauters' face went slack and then tight in the blink of an eye. "Listen, you sonofabitch!" he barked. "I don't need your goddamn help! I'm the law in this town! Not you, not the U.S. Marshals Office! If you're coming into my town, then you do what I say when I say to do it! Understand?"

Longtree remained impassive. "All I understand, Sheriff, is that you've got five dead men on your hands and if you keep this up, you'll have more. Maybe if we work together, we can stop these killings."

There was no arguing with that.

"You just keep out of my way, Longtree. I don't need your damn help."

Longtree nodded. "That's fine, Sheriff. That's just fine. I'll do my own investigating. But I sure would appreciate your help."

Lauters gave him an evil stare. "Forget it. We don't need outsiders making any more of a mess of this."

"Sheriff," the one called Dewey said. "We got six murders here for the love of God. If he can help—"

"Shut up, Dewey." Lauters turned his back on all of them and started up out of the gully.

"Who's the sixth?" Longtree asked.

"Nate Segaris," one of the men replied. "Got killed right in his house."

"Ripped to shreds," another said.

Longtree took a drag off his cigar. "Before you boys head back," he said, "you ought to know there's a seventh."

Everyone stared at him.

And in the distance, a low mournful howling rose up and died away.

PART 2: OLD RED EYES

1

The good Reverend Claussen, scarf wrapped around his throat, fought through the biting wind to the undertaking parlor. He paused in the street outside of a peeling gray building. A wooden, weathered sign read: J. SPENCE, UNDERTAKER. It was barely readable. Too many seasons of harsh winters and blistering summers had faded the black lettering to a drab leaden color.

Clenching his teeth against the elements, Claussen went in.

He went directly into the back rooms where the bodies were prepared.

In there were Wynona Spence, Sheriff Lauters, and Dr. Perry.

The reverend eyed them all suspiciously. "Why is it," he said in his New England twang, "that I wasn't told of another death? Why must I learn these things by word of mouth, by rumor?"

"Keep your shirt on, Father," Lauters said. "I—"

"I'm not a Catholic, sir. Please address me accordingly."

Lauters scowled, fished a plug of tobacco from his pouch and inserted it in his cheek. "What I was *trying* to say, Reverend, was that this here is Curly Del Vecchio. Or what there's left of him. Curly wasn't what you'd call a religious man."

Claussen, his close-cut steel-gray hair bristling, said, "The dead are granted certain considerations, Sheriff. By the grace of God let me give this poor man spiritual absolution."

Dr. Perry, standing next to the sheeted form on the table, shrugged and pulled the sheet away.

Reverend Claussen paled and averted his eyes.

"Not very pretty, is it?" Wynona Spence said, her pursed lips pulled into a thin purple line which might have been a smile. "But beauty is in the eye of the beholder."

Claussen glared at her. He saw no humor in death.

Wynona Spence inherited the business from her ailing father. Being a female, she was a rarity in the business. But truth be told, she was the perfect undertaker. God molds men and women for certain tasks in life, the reverend knew, and she could have been nothing but what she was. Cadaverous, tall, bony with tight colorless flesh and bulging watery eyes, she was the very image of her father. Only the drab gray dresses and the tight bun her colorless hair was drawn into marked her as a woman. Her voice was deep and velvety, her face hard and narrow. Unmarried, she lived in rooms above the funeral parlor with another woman…and the gossip took off from there.

Claussen went through the ritual over the body almost mechanically.

The words flowed from his lips like wine with the perfect intonation and breath control, but he was not aware of them. He saw only the plucked, slit, and hacked thing laid out before him staring up with blanched, bloodless eyeballs.

He completed the ritual with a few prayers and an "amen". He turned and faced Lauters with a bizarre species of contempt on his rosy features. "The members of my congregation want something done, Sheriff. They demand resolution."

Lauters stared at him with unblinking, dead eyes. "We're doing all we can."

"Do more! Do it in the name of our Lord!" the Reverend exclaimed piously. "The dead deserve justice! The living, protection!"

Dr. Perry folded his arms and turned away, hiding a smile.

Wynona leaned forward, her lifeless eyes intrigued as if examining a new type of insect.

"We're doing our best," was Lauters' only comment. He was visibly trembling, not the sort of man who liked to be told his job.

"One would think your best isn't good enough," Claussen said.

Lauters face went red. "Now, listen here, Reverend. My mother taught me to respect the clergy. God knows I do my best. But don't you dare tell me my goddamn job," he said, finger stabbing the air. "I don't tell you how to pray, so don't you tell me how to run the law around here."

The reverend, electric with religious zeal and self-imposed holiness, stepped forward. "Perhaps someone should."

"*Listen,* you little sonofabitch! I've had all I'm going to fucking take—"

"Your profanities fall on deaf ears. Such talk is the work of a weak mind."

Lauters grabbed him by the arm, but not too roughly. "That's it, Claussen. March your holier-than-thou butt right out the door before I kick your teeth so far down your God-loving throat that you—"

"Sheriff," Perry said, flashing him a warning look.

Claussen, his eyes bulging in fear, rushed out the door like something was biting his backside.

Wynona giggled. "My goodness."

Perry sighed. "Not a very good idea, Bill. If you make him angry he could turn his whole congregation against you."

Lauters bellowed with laughter. "He's already turned one of them against me—my wife."

With that, he turned and left.

"My, what excitement!" Wynona exclaimed as best she could. "We never have this much excitement here. I feel as though I've stepped into a dime novel. Tsk, tsk."

Perry said, "You're a strange one, madam."

And she was. Perry could never understand a woman wanting to be an undertaker. But he honestly couldn't picture her doing anything else. Even her movements—the slow stiff motions of her skeletal fingers, the slat-lean face pulling into a skullish grin—bespoke a worker of death and graves. She looked much like the bodies she prepared for burial and was only moderately more animated. Whereas most women were scented with perfume, Wynona always smelled vaguely of chemicals and dry flowers.

"I still don't understand what attracts you to this profession," Perry said, shaking his head. "But I suppose, given your particular *talents,* you're well-suited."

Wynona smiled as if it was a compliment. "The sheriff really should control his outbursts," she said with all sincerity. "Not good for a man his age."

Perry lifted his eyebrows. "He's not even fifty yet, madam."

"He looks seventy," Wynona observed. "One of these days, I fear he'll be here as a customer." She sighed, looking at the corpse of Del Vecchio. "Well, we'll be glad to have him, won't we?"

Perry scowled. "He's not in the best of health. In the past year he's gone downhill. Must be the job."

"Stress. It takes the best of them. You can take my word for that."

"Ever since they lynched that Indian," Perry said, "he just hasn't been the same."

2

Joe Longtree came to the undertaking parlor less than an hour later.

Wynona saw him come in and her first thought was that the man was a shootist. He wore a black flat-crowned hat and a long midnight blue broadcloth coat, unbuttoned, that went to his knees. He carried a buffalo coat over one arm. The spurs on his black, scuffed and scraped Texas boots rang out with each step. There were twin Colt pistols slung low on either hip like a gunman would wear them.

"Can I help you?" Wynona asked.

"Joe Longtree," he said, turning the lapel over his heart inside out. There was a badge pinned there. "Deputy U.S. Marshal."

"Ah, yes. The Sheriff said you'd be coming."

Longtree smiled. "I'll just bet he did."

Wynona was unsure what was meant by that. Lauters said a federal man would show up and begin nosing about. He also said to beware of him. Longtree, he'd said, was pushy, arrogant, and mouthy. Wynona was expecting the very worst. She had no earthly intention of opposing this man in any way; he was, after all, a federal marshal and carried a certain amount of weight because of it. Besides, Longtree looked dangerous. His eyes were a deep, fathomless blue. Very intense. They were the eyes of a man that killed for a living. Had she been moved by such things, she would have found him exciting.

"I'll be glad to help the law in any way," Wynona told him.

"I'd appreciate that, Miss Spence...you are J. Spence, aren't you?"

"No, unfortunately not. J. Spence was my father, Joshua, dead these past seven years. I'm his daughter, Wynona," she explained in a flat voice. "Do you find it strange for a woman to occupy herself in such a profession?"

Longtree shrugged. "Family business, I guess. Most natural thing in the world for your father to want his kin to carry on things. As long as you're happy with it."

"Oh, I am."

"Then you don't need my approval."

Wynona found herself staring at him, finding him a remarkably enlightened man. It only added to his air of mystery, made him seem exotic somehow. Interesting. She figured she would've fallen in love with him years ago. But not now.

Longtree said, "I don't know what Sheriff Lauters told you, but I can assume it wasn't good. He's taken an instant dislike of me. I'm only here to look into these murders, not take over his job or bully anyone into confessing to the crimes."

Wynona sighed. "Of course not." Longtree had an easy way about him. He seemed well-spoken as if he were educated, sincere, honest. He seemed to be the kind of man it would be easy to like, easy to trust. "Would you like to see the body?"

Longtree shook his head, pulling up a chair. "No, I got my fill of that last night. I want to talk about the others."

Wynona sat down near him. "Very well." She seemed almost disappointed.

Longtree lit a cigar, pulling out a little notebook and pencil.

Wynona watched his every movement, somehow fascinated by him. He was maybe an inch under six feet, muscular without being stocky or massive. His face was clean shaven, rugged, handsome, the skin nearly as dark as that of an Indian, yet the features were clearly European in origin. His hair was long, black, a lustrous tinted indigo like that of an Indian. It was pulled back tight and tied with a leather thong.

"My mother was a Crow," Longtree said, reading her thoughts.

Wynona blushed a bit. "My Lord...how did you know I was thinking that?"

"In my profession, mind-reading comes in handy."

She swallowed. "Yes, I imagine it would. So you are an Indian, then?"

Longtree smiled. "Not too many people ever guess. They think my skin is dark from too much time spent in the sun and wind."

The glow faded from Wynona's cheeks, her skin was sunless again. "No, I don't imagine too many do. The study of physiognomy is something of a hobby of mine. I often try to guess from skin coloration, features and the like where a man's point of origin in the world might be. Do you know, Marshal, that the Indian has dark skin not only because of heredity but because of his lifesytle? If the white race were suddenly to take to the plains and live out in the elements like the Indian, within a few hundred years or so we'd probably look much like them."

"I don't doubt it. My father was English. In the summer he was dark as any Indian. Only in the winter did his skin pale."

"Fascinating," Wynona said.

"Did you examine the other bodies?"

Wynona nodded. "Yes, sir, I did. In some depth."

"Tell me what you found."

Wynona told him all she knew, giving him very detailed information not only on the physical remains and their condition, but on the men themselves. Their habits and lifestyles as best as she knew them.

"Abe Runyon, Cal Sevens, Charlie Mears, Pete Olak, George Rieko, Nate Segaris, and finally Curly Del Vecchio," Longtree read from his notebook. "All men. Odd that this beast hasn't gotten a woman or child. It's almost like its killing selectively."

Wynona raised an eyebrow. "I doubt that. We're dealing with a beast here, Marshal, not a reasoning being."

"I'm not so sure of that."

"You don't...I mean, you don't think a *man* is responsible for any of this?"

"No, not a man. Not exactly."

"You mean a beast which...*reasons?*"

He would not comment on it.

Wynona considered it. Yes, the victims were all men...but it had to be a coincidence. The idea of a creature that *selected* its victims...now that was frightening. She'd never even contemplated such a thing. But now that she had, she feared it would never leave her mind.

"Well," she said, "you've certainly given me food for thought. Dark food, at that."

Longtree thanked her for her help and left.

Wynona shrugged and went back to the cadaver of Nate Segaris. "Well, Nate, back to work. Did I ever tell you that I was well-acquainted with your mother? No? It was when you were off fighting the war..."

3

Longtree next did what he dreaded the most: he went to the Sheriff's office.

He'd dealt with countless local lawmen in his tenure as a federal marshal. They came in all varieties as did all men. Some were kind and friendly, glad for his assistance. Others were suspicious, yet helpful. Still others were like Lauters: arrogant, hateful, self-serving. They saw the advent of a federal man in their territory as an insult, the government's way of saying they weren't doing their job. And nothing could be farther from the truth.

Longtree fought through the vicious winds and entered the jailhouse. As he feared, Lauters was there. Without the heavy coat on, he was still a large man, earning his nickname of "Big Bill". He was a powerful fellow, Longtree decided, both physically and psychologically, but well past his prime. He was fat, bloated almost, having the look of a man who drank heavily on a daily basis. His face was puffy and white, the eyes bloodshot, blood vessels broken in his nose.

He was a veteran alcoholic. There was no doubt of this. Longtree, a man who'd battled the bottle himself, knew a drunk when he saw one.

"Morning, Sheriff," he said.

Lauters just glared. His pale lips spread in a frown. They didn't have to go very far. "Well, well, well, the Marshal has come to save the day."

Longtree suppressed a grin. Lauters was drunk. "I need a little information on the murdered men."

"Well, you won't get it from me."

"C'mon, Sheriff. What's the point of this? You know the law; you have to cooperate. Help me out here and I'll do my best to stay out of your hair."

"Yeah, I know the law, mister," Lauters said, his eyes not quite focusing. "I know the goddamn law and I don't need no yellow sonofbitch like you to tell it to me. Damn breed."

Longtree sighed and put his hat on the desk. "You got a deputy?"

"None of yer fucking business."

Longtree sat down and stared at the man. Obviously, he'd been doing some checking to know that Longtree was a half-breed or "breed", as he called it. That meant that he probably knew everything there was to know. Not that it mattered.

"You're wrong there, Sheriff, it *is* my business. I'll ask you again: Do you have a deputy?"

"Goddamn breed. You know how many injuns I've killed? Do you?"

Longtree grinned sardonically. "Know how many white men I've killed?"

Lauters stood up, swaying a bit. "I oughta take yer sorry ass out back and teach it a lesson."

"Nothing you can teach me, Sheriff. Nothing at all."

"Wanna slap leather, boy? You wanna—"

"Sheriff." The voice was stern, authoritative. It belonged to a white-haired man with a drooping gray mustache. "That'll be enough now. We got enough problems around here without you being put in your own jail."

Lauters grimaced and staggered into the back room. Another man came out, shutting the door behind him. He was tall and thin, not more than thirty, wearing a deputy's badge.

"I'm Doctor Perry," the old man said. "This here's Alden Bowes. We're pleased to meet you."

Longtree shook hands with both of them.

"What you're seeing there," Perry said, stabbing his thumb at the back room, "is the wreck of a good man."

"Too bad," Longtree said.

Bowes shrugged. "He never used to drink, mister. Maybe a drop or two on Saturday night, never more. I swear to God."

"I believe you," Longtree said. "The fact remains that he's in a bad way now. He's a menace. A man in his position can't go around in a drunken stupor. He'll kill someone eventually."

"He wouldn't do that," Bowes affirmed.

"You don't think so?"

Neither Perry nor the deputy bothered arguing the point.

"I gotta get back," Perry said, tipping his hat. "Marshal."

Longtree took out his tobacco pouch and rolled a cigarette. "I don't know what you might think of me, Deputy, or what the Sheriff has filled your head with, but—"

"I draw my own conclusions on a man, Marshal."

Longtree nodded, lighting his cigarette, a cloud of smoke twisting lazily away from his face. "We've got us a major problem here, Deputy. We've got a slew of killings and they ain't gonna stop the way Lauters is doing things. You and I, we'll have to work together on this."

Bowes leaned back in the chair behind the desk, knowing, as all did, it would soon be his chair. He scratched at his thin beard. "I'm all for that, Marshal. But where the hell do we start? Folks around here are all for putting up a bounty on this animal. You know what that would mean? Every drifter with a gun who fancied himself a hunter would be crawling out in those hills, shooting any damn thing that moved and each other in the process."

"Yeah, I figured they'd be thinking that way." Longtree smoked and was silent for a moment. "We've got to think this thing out carefully. There's no room for mistakes here. We're dealing with something much more dangerous than any animal I've ever come across."

"What the hell is it, Marshal? What kills like that? What sort of beast kills like it...*enjoys* the act of killing?"

Longtree shook his head. "Something's going on here. Something the likes of which neither of us have ever seen."

"Like what?" Bowes asked.

"I'm not sure," Longtree admitted. "Not just yet."

Bowes looked irritable. "If you've got some idea, let me in on it. Christ, this is madness."

"I'll keep my thoughts to myself for now," Longtree said. "No point in going off half-cocked or making myself look foolish."

Bowes didn't look happy. "Okay, have it your own way."

Longtree would have liked to share his thoughts. But as yet, they were just thoughts. Half-formed ideas with no basis in reality. *Yet.* They were dealing with something horrible here. Something unknown. Something that didn't follow the rules, but set new ones. A beast that killed like an animal, but seemed to be almost following some indecipherable pattern. Once Longtree could figure out what that pattern was, they would be close to finding out what sort of killer they were dealing with.

"What's our first step, Marshal? Can you tell me that much?"

"I need to know about these men that were killed," Longtree said.

"Why? They were just men."

"I need to know about them," Longtree maintained. "If there was anything they might have had in common."

"You aren't suggesting that this beast *picked* these men to kill, are you?"

"Could be. I just don't know yet. I won't overlook anything at this point."

Bowes shrugged and talked at some length about the victims.

He covered a lot of the same ground as Wynona Spence had. Abe Runyon had been a railroad man, quick with his temper and fists. Not well liked. Cal Sevens had worked at the livery where he was killed. He was a newcomer to town, been there only a few years and kept mostly to himself. Charlie Mears lived at the

Serenity Motel. He was a miner and had been fired from the mines for drinking. But he always seemed to have plenty of money and some suspected he was a highwayman. Pete Olak was a woodsman who cut firewood for a living. He had contracts with a few hotels and the railroad. He had been married with two kids and was well-liked. George Reiko was little better than a drunk. He lived with the Widow Thompkins and never seemed to do much but drink and gamble. Nate Segaris had a little spread outside town and had gone to seed since the death of his wife. He had a few horses. Gambled a bit. Drank with the miners and ranch hands on Saturday nights. Curly Del Vecchio was an ex-con, a veteran gambler and drunk, and pretty much just a plain nuisance.

Longtree mulled this all over. Despite the fact that a few of them tended to drink and gamble, there was no thread that tied them together. And drinking and gambling hardly made them members of an elite club.

"Nothing more?"

"Well...they all hated the local Indians. I know that much. Most folks around here do," Bowes said, unconcerned. "I didn't know all of them that well, but I've dealt with them in my job. None of 'em really seemed to associate together. I've heard all of 'em talk about what they'd like to do with the injuns more than once." Bowes shrugged. "But there's a lot of folks around these parts with the same leanings. Those men were just like a lot of 'em."

"There's a Blackfoot reservation outside town, isn't there?"

"Yeah, but I wouldn't advise going up there. They don't like white folks much. Especially ones that carry badges."

"I'll keep it hidden."

"You're crazy, Marshal."

"Maybe, but I'm going."

"Well don't expect me to drag yer body out come morning."

Longtree just grinned.

4

Dewey Mayhew looked down on the sheriff. "Had yourself a good toot, did ya?" he said.

Lauters grimaced. "What the hell do you want?"

"To talk. Nothin' wrong with old friends talkin' is there?"

The sheriff tried to sit up but his head was pounding. An oil lamp was going in the corner. Darkness was pressed up against the little window. God, how long had he been out? Hours? Last thing he remembered was some run-in with that Longtree fellow.

"What do you want to talk about?" Lauters grumbled.

Mayhew looked very solemn, scared almost. "About the murders."

"Ain't nothing new to say."

"There's been seven killings, Sheriff. Seven killings."

Lauters rubbed his eyes. "I'm aware of that."

"Those men—"

"I know."

"There's only three of us left," Mayhew said. His voice was desperate.

"Keep your voice down."

Mayhew was trembling. "That thing won't stop till we're all dead."

"That's enough, Dewey."

"Tonight it'll come for me or you or—"

"Enough," the sheriff said with an edge to his voice. "You just keep quiet about things. If you don't, I'll kill you myself."

5

Longtree rode into the hills with only the vaguest of directions from Deputy Bowes as where to find the nearest of the Blackfoot encampments. The wind had died down from what it was earlier in the day and the temperature was above freezing. Longtree'd experienced things like that before in Montana and Wyoming. Blizzards and freezing winds followed by a brief warming trend, a thaw that would turn everything to slush and then to ice a week later when the temperature took another dive below freezing.

The country above Wolf Creek in the foothills of the Tobacco Roots was beautiful. Brush and scrubby cedar on open slopes gave way to snowy peaks, twisted deadfalls, and thick stands of pine and spruce. The mountains were huge and jutting above the timberline, barren and majestic.

But dangerous.

This whole country was like that, he knew. It was almost a religious experience viewing it, but the reality was sobering. This was a place of sudden landslides. Blizzards that kicked up with no warning. Frozen winds that seemed to rise up out of nowhere. Starving wolf packs. Marauding grizzlies that were anxious to pack extra meat and fat in their bellies before hibernation. It was also the home of the Blackfoot Indians, considered by some to be the most bloodthirsty nation on the upper Missouri.

Coming up over a ridge, Longtree saw the camp. He had no doubt he was being watched and probably had been for some time.

6

He rode into the Blackfoot camp unmolested, accompanied by barking dogs.

There were about twelve buffalo skin lodges, most painted with geometric designs and huge, larger than life representations of birds and animals. A few weathered faces poked out of the flaps of tipis and withdrew at what they saw. Around twenty people were formed up in a camp circle around a vast blazing fire.

Longtree dismounted and tethered his horse to a pine. He approached the band cautiously, making it known he was no threat.

The Indians seemed intent on ignoring his very presence.

The men remained seated, dressed in buffalo hide caps with earflaps and buffalo robes with the fur next to their bodies. A few wore hooded Hudson Bay blanket coats and heavy moccasins. The women were dressed pretty much the same in robes and trade blankets covering their undecorated dresses. Babies poked out of the furry folds of their robes. A few women were nursing older children.

Longtree tried to communicate with a few via sign language and a bastard form of Blackfoot Algonquian he'd learned many years before.

No one paid any attention.

Finally, a young woman in a knee-length buffalo coat and black buffalo hide moccasins approached him, stopping a few feet away. She was beautiful in a wild, savage sort of way. Her eyes were huge brown liquid pools, the cheekbones high, the lips full, the skin lustrous. She had a raw, unbridled sexuality about her that you rarely saw in white women. And she had a look about her that told Longtree very clearly that she was tough as any man.

"I am Laughing Moonwind, daughter of Herbert Crazytail. What do you want here?" she asked in perfect English.

Longtree cleared his throat. "I need help. I wish to speak with the tribal chief."

Longtree knew that, this being a small group, it would have only one chief. Larger tribes had several, but only one was considered the acting chief and his position was really that of a chairman of the tribal council. Many whites thought the chief was something of an executive officer in the tribe, but this wasn't so. His rank was of little importance save during the summer encampment. The Blackfoot were very democratic and most major decisions were reached by the tribal council acting with the chief. Most chiefs were the leaders of the hunting bands, the basic political unit of Blackfoot culture.

"Who are you?" she asked.

"Joe Longtree. I'm a federal marshal."

"I will ask Herbert Crazytail if he will speak with you."

Longtree stood waiting and watching as she disappeared into a lodge. It was larger than most of the others, the hide covering painted with wolves in deep, rich reds. There were also numerous skulls, gruesome things with huge eye sockets and sharpened stakes for teeth. Longtree knew the wolves signified that the owner of the tipi considered the wolf to be the source of his supernatural power...but the skulls, who could say? Along the bottom, the lodge cover was red with unpainted discs. Along the top, it was painted black with a large Maltese cross.

Many of the Indians were watching him now, wondering what his business could possibly be. Children gawked at him, but were silent as only tribal children could be.

There were long racks of buffalo meat drying and hides staked out to cure and bleach in the sun. A few of the women were eating, chewing bits of pemmican mixed with sarvis berries. The men sat smoking from gray shale tobacco pipes, clenching ash pipe stems in their fists. Horses were corralled out near the treeline, pawing away at the snow to reach the grasses below. A few dogs lapped from rawhide troughs.

Moonwind finally returned. "My father will see you. Come."

He followed her to the lodge just as three other women departed it. Longtree assumed they were Crazytail's wives.

Inside the cavernous lodge, a small fire burned in a pit. It cast crazy, dancing shadows everywhere. The air smelled of smoke, tobacco, and dried meat. Moonwind by his side, Longtree sat across from an old man wearing a buffalo fur headpiece with horns intact. He was wrapped in a blanket, his left shoulder covered, his right arm and shoulder uncovered. His face was shadowy, the skin a leathery seamed brown, the eyes dark and unreadable. He smoked a long pipe ornamented with beads and eagle feathers.

Longtree knew it to be a medicine pipe, a sacred object.

Moonwind chatted in low tones with her father, then turned to Longtree. "My father wishes you to know that Chief Ironbrow is ill. He will speak in his place. What is it you wish here?"

"I need help. There have been killings in Wolf Creek. Brutal slayings that seem the work of an animal."

Moonwind relayed this. Crazytail blinked, nothing more. Then he spoke.

"My father is aware of the killings. He can tell you only that they will continue."

Longtree expected as much.

Long experience with Indians had taught him that you couldn't take what many of them said at face value. Crazytail saying the killings would continue meant nothing. It wasn't an admission of guilt; merely something the man had probably seen in his visions or dreams.

"Does Crazytail know what this beast is?" Longtree asked of her.

She relayed the information. "Skullhead," she said.

Longtree shifted uneasily on the buffalo hide bedding beneath him. "Ask him who or what this Skullhead is."

Moonwind did.

The old man talked at some length, finishing with a shake of his head.

"Many, many years ago, long before the dog days, Crazytail's great ancestor, Medicine Claw, a member of the Skull Society, spent twelve days on a mountain plateau," Moonwind said, "calling up the spirits of sky, earth, and water. He fasted for ten days and drank water but once. His guide spirit, the Wolf-Skull spirit, came down to him and taught him many things. He taught Medicine Claw the ways of the Skullhead, his sacred ways and rituals. The enigma of the Blood-Medicine. It has been passed down through a hundred generations of the Skull Society."

Longtree stared at her, hoping there was more. Crazytail said it was before the "dog days." The dog days, Longtree knew, was the period before the Blackfoot were using horses, when they only had dogs to move camp with. This was before white men had come into contact with them. And Crazytail had said it was before this time, a "hundred generations" ago. This would mean that Longtree was hearing a tribal memory, something handed down for hundreds of years if not more.

"When Crazytail was a young man," Moonwind went on, "he, too, spent many days fasting on a mountainside as all men of the Skull Society must do. The Wolf-Skull spirit came to him saying the Skullhead was always near, close enough to touch. But that Crazytail must be cautious, for the Skullhead was fierce and voracious, a force of nature like thunder and wind. To contact Skullhead he must use the sacred Blood-Medicine, but this medicine was holy and not to be used foolishly. For the Skullhead, once summoned, could not be sent away until its appetite was satisfied with the blood of tribal enemies. Two months ago, in the sweat lodge, Crazytail was again visited by the spirit Wolf-Skull. The time of the Skullhead is at hand as it was in ancient times."

Longtree felt a chill go up his back. "Who is the Skullhead?"

Moonwind shook her head. "My father will speak no more. No white man may know of this. The Blood-Medicine is sacred to the Skull Society. The Skullhead has been summoned. He is among us now," she said, her eyes shining, "and getting closer."

Longtree felt a certain uneasiness worm through him. His skin had gone cold now, his stomach stirring sickly. There was a veiled threat in her words.

He was half-white, yes, and that half wanted to laugh at all this nonsense. Nothing but injun gobbledegook, ghost stories, old wives' tales. Crap handed down generation by generation. Just shit that had been dreamed up by some injun shaman blown clear into dreamland by peyote. But Longtree was also half-Crow. And that part of him was concerned. It knew better than to scoff at the medicine of the tribes. And it was commonly known that the Blackfoot were possessed of a very powerful medicine.

He left Crazytail, knowing he'd get no more this night. He mounted his black and looked down at Moonwind.

She watched him, her lips forming words silently. Under her breath, she said, "Beware, Joseph Longtree, for the Skull Moon grows full."

Longtree rode off into the dead of night, shivering.

7

At around ten that night, Lauters—not drinking for the moment—decided to pay a visit on Dr. Perry. Anna, Perry's housekeeper, answered the door and led the sheriff through the maze of the surgery to the little study at the back of the house.

"Didn't expect to see you this late, Bill," Perry said.

"Couldn't sleep," Lauters explained. "I can never sleep worth a damn anymore."

Unless you're dead drunk, Perry felt like saying, but didn't. He was sitting behind his desk, a brass microscope set out before him along with a box of slides, a few dark corked bottles, several jars, an array of metal instruments. A dissection kit stood open, a scalpel and forceps missing from the felt-lined case. There were several tufts of fur laid out as well.

"What are you doing, Doc?"

Perry stroked his mustache. "A little detective work." He motioned to the tufts of fur. "You know what these are?"

"Bits of animal fur," Lauters said, examining books in oak shelves, most titles of which he couldn't pronounce.

"Not just any, though. I have pelts from grizzlies, foxes, coyotes, wolves. In fact, from all the known predators in this area," he explained. "I'm examining hairs from each with those of our mysterious friend here."

Lauters sat down across from him. "And?"

"And I've concluded what we already know. This tuft of fur is not from any of those creatures. Though," Perry confided in a low tone, "it shares similarities with human hair. But much more coarse."

"So what does this tell us?"

Perry cleared his throat. "Do you know what a mutation is, Sheriff?"

"Haven't the foggiest."

Perry studied him closely. Lauters' fingers were trembling. He was bloated and pale. The tip of his nose was purple from ruptured blood vessels and capillaries. Liver spots were numerous on his hands. He licked his lips constantly. These were the signs of the chronic alcoholic.

"Doc?" Lauters said.

"Oh yes, sorry. Getting old. My mind wandered."

Lauters fixed him with a cold stare. "I'll just bet it did."

"Anyway, Sheriff, a mutation is simply a variation in a known species. A physical change that occurs suddenly or slowly, either from environmental factors or hereditary or any number of reasons that science has yet to determine."

"What does this have to do with anything?"

Perry smiled. He knew Lauters understood very well what he was getting at. But the sheriff was a man who liked things explained to him in very clear language so there was no possibility of misinterpretation.

"What I'm saying, Bill, is that we're dealing with a new life form here, an animal unknown to science."

"I thought we already figured that."

Perry nodded. "Yes. But what sort of animal walks upright like a man?"

8

Longtree made it back to his camp around midnight.

He had originally been planning on spending the night in a hotel in Wolf Creek, but the warming trend changed his mind. Tonight would be a good night to sleep out under the stars by the fireside. He rode down into the little arroyo and tethered his horse for the night. After getting the fire going, he had himself a little supper of beans and salt pork from his grub sack and washed it down with coffee.

He had a lot of thinking to do.

Sprawled out on his bedroll by the blaze, a cigarette between his lips, he did so. First off, only the facts. *Fact.* There were seven murders in and around Wolf Creek. *Fact.* Same method used on all victims—they were torn apart as if by some wild beast, eaten, mutilated. *Fact.* All evidence would suggest the attacker to have been some large and powerful predator. *Fact.* Nearly all the victims had been armed and had shot at their attacker, either missing (which seemed unlikely given that two of the men had shotguns and they *all* couldn't have missed) or their bullets simply had no effect. *Fact.* Though supposedly an animal, the creature attacked with an almost human rage.

The facts pretty much ended there.

He took a long, deliberate pull off his cigarette.

Now for the speculation.

Speculation. The attacker is an unknown form of animal. *Speculation.* The attacker is somewhat intelligent. *Speculation.* The attacker seems to be targeting a certain group of people, but what their connection might be is unknown. *Speculation.* The attacker is tied up with the local Blackfoot tribe.

That pretty much did it.

Once the facts and speculations were done with, there were only more problems. If the Blackfoot were involved, then how were they directing the attacks of this wild beast? And what of Herbert Crazytail and his Skull Society and this mysterious other called Skullhead? Was it just a bunch of bull? Was the crazy old Indian allowing a bunch of savage murders to justify his own mythologies and visions?

Longtree had no idea whatsoever.

His mother was a Crow. He had Indian blood in him and as a boy in the Crow camp before the Sioux raiders had murdered everyone, he'd witnessed the spiritual and mystical side of Indian life. But he'd forgotten most of it in the Catholic mission school as Christianity was rammed down his throat. And later, with Uncle Lone Hawk, there'd been little mysticism. Lone Hawk was a Christian. He was a practical man, having little use for the supernatural. Yet, despite the fact that Longtree knew very little of Indian spiritualism and the assorted, complex myth cycles and legendry of the tribes, he wasn't above believing there were mysteries in this world. Things unknowable, things dark and ancient that white man's science or religion couldn't hope to explain.

The world was a wild place.

And though there was no one better than whites at collecting information and dissecting it for truths, there were some things in the world that defied rationality and scientific realism.

Longtree winced, knowing he was thinking like a superstitious man.

But all men were superstitious at their core; it was the nature of the beast. Men thought certain rifles and knives were lucky. That wearing a particular coat or pair of boots would bring them good fortune or, at the very least, keep them alive in this hard country. In the army he'd known officers that were highly-educated men who would only put their boots on a certain way or carried lucky coins or pictures of their children as talismans.

Superstition was everywhere.

And that was the same now as it had been two hundred years before or would be two hundred years in the future.

Longtree was confused about this thing with Crazytail, this talk of the Skullhead. Something was slaughtering people, something that left huge prints like those of a monster.

Crazy?

Perhaps. But he would've liked to have known something of this Skull Society and particularly this Blood-Medicine. It was, according to Moonwind's translation, the medium through which this Skullhead was called up like some Christian demon out of hell. But...*Christ*. Monsters? Demons?

You're a lawman, he told himself.

This was true. A lawman. A peace officer. A deputy U.S. Marshal. A special federal officer. He was a man of facts, not fantasy. He didn't deal in Indian superstitions or half-forgotten folklore.

Yet, he was scared.

He would never have admitted it, but he was. A deep-rooted fear was growing in his belly. After all the things he'd done, all the danger he'd faced, this scared him. He was frightened like he'd never been before.

(beware for the skull moon grows full)

The import of that unnerved him. Devils. Monsters. Primal beasts. There were names for things like this, for beasts that prowled the lonely countryside. Longtree was well-read, he knew something of folklore. Knew that even white European culture had their bogeymen, their haunters of the dark, their atavistic horrors. Bogarts and ogres and assorted flesh-eaters. Things with claws and teeth that stalked the dark forests.

Enough, he thought, enough.

And then out in the moon-washed countryside he heard it. The low, awful, evil sound that perfectly punctuated his thoughts: a mournful, drawn-out howling. He bit down on his lower lip, his head suddenly filled with nightmare imagery, terrible things that stalked the wind-swept shadows of cemeteries and burial grounds. Impossible, red-eyed horrors with long claws and sharp teeth that waited on frosty, forgotten lanes for wayward travelers...

He shook it clear from his head.

A monster of Indian myth given life, hunting enemies of the tribe. That was insane.

But as the night went silent, even Longtree's horse dared not breathe. An eerie abnormal hush had taken the world now, enclosing it in folds of midnight satin. A heavy breathing stillness.

Then the howling began again.

9

Sheriff Lauters was on his way back to his office when he heard the screams.

He had half a bottle of rye in his desk drawer and the thought of it warming his belly and lulling him into an easy sleep was all he cared about. He didn't pay any attention to the miners he saw fighting in the streets outside the saloons and gambling halls. He ignored the lewd behavior exhibited by a few ranch hands outside the parlor houses.

He saw nothing but the bottle and the sweet release it offered.

Then he heard the screams.

They stopped him dead.

He'd heard men cry out after being shot, knifed, and even scalped. But this was different. This was a bloodcurdling screech that went right up his spine like spiders, giving him about the same sense of aversion. It sounded again. Weaker now. It was coming from behind the smithy's shop.

A few others were running in that direction now, guns drawn.

Lauters raced by younger men and elbowed aside men and women alike. There was no time for courtesy here. When he rounded the shop and made it to the alley out back, people were already turning away in disgust. Rikers, the blacksmith, had a lantern going and what it revealed was a horror.

Lauters knew it was Dewey Mayhew.

Somehow, in the back of his mind, he'd suspected it.

Mayhew was lying in the hard-packed snow, blood sprayed out in every possible direction. He was curled up, fingers trying to press his internals back in through the ragged incision in his belly. He was open in half a dozen places and blood ran from all of them. The left side of his face was stripped clear down to the meat. His legs were broken and twisted out at odd angles, bone pushing through the tears in his pants. The left side of his neck was ripped open, a great chunk of flesh missing. He bled from the nose, mouth, ears—too many places to count.

But he wasn't quite dead yet.

He was trying to talk.

Lauters kneeled next to him, trying to hear what he said. Blood gurgled from his mouth, his lips shuddering, his remaining eye staring off into space.

"What?" Lauters said softly. "Tell me."

Mayhew kept trying to talk. Lauters put his ear to the man's bloody, torn lips.

"...those eyes..." Mayhew sputtered. "...those red eyes..."

His body shook with spasms for a moment and went still.

"All right, goddammit," Lauters said, climbing to his feet. "The man's dead. All of you clear out of here. Now."

Slowly, the onlookers vacated the scene, leaving only Rikers and Lauters. Lauters went up to the man who, despite his powerful physique and girth, was trembling, the color gone from his usually ruddy face.

"You find him?" the sheriff asked.

"Yeah," Rikers said. "I...I heard the screaming...lit the lantern and came out... Jesus, oh sweet Jesus..."

Lauters turned him away from the body. "What did you see?"

"Something...something running...I don't know..."

"Think man, dammit," Lauters commanded. "This is important."

Rikers swallowed. "It happened so fast...I'm not sure..."

"What? Tell me." He was shaking the man now.

With a look of anguish, Rikers broke free. "A shape...a shadow...*gigantic*...Christ, I don't know...something moving away fast, down the alley. A giant."

"What did it look like?"

Rikers' eyes were glassy, staring. "The Devil."

10

The body was loaded into a farm wagon and taken over to Wynona at the undertaking parlor. She was her usual cadaverous self, not disappointed in the least that a new customer had arrived despite the hour.

Always room for one more, she was fond of saying.

"I seem to be seeing a lot of you, Sheriff," she said. "I never really thought I would until—"

"Shut up, Wynona," Lauters snapped.

"Ah, well," the undertaker said, pulling the tarp back from the ruin of Dewey Mayhew, "life goes on. Unfortunately." She smiled at her morbid joke as was her habit and gave the body a cursory examination. "And whatever did you get into?" she asked the cold, staring face. "Don't worry, I'll fix you up."

"You give me the willies, Wynona."

Wynona lifted one eyebrow. "Simply because they're dead doesn't mean they're not people, Sheriff. I'm sure they enjoy my chit-chat in their own way. People treat them like bags of meat, sides of beef. I treat them like people. I offer them the same social graces I would in life. Isn't it what you would want?"

"Just get on with it, you damn ghoul."

Wynona inspected the corpse with more attention now. Checking each wound and abrasion. She shrugged. "There's nothing I can tell you that you don't already know, Sheriff."

"Which is?"

"This man has died from massive loss of blood. He appears to have been attacked by some sort of animal."

She looked up as someone came in. The corners of her thin lips twisted in a smile. "Reverend Claussen," she said, expecting trouble and relishing the idea.

"In the flesh," Claussen said.

Lauters rubbed his eyes. He looked disgusted. "Evening, Reverend."

"But what sort of evening, Sheriff?" Claussen asked. He'd brought a cross and prayer book along with him. "An evening of murder and mayhem, I would think. An evening not fit for decent folk to walk the streets without fear for their lives—"

"That'll do, Reverend."

Wynona was still smiling, enjoying the exchange to no end. Carefully, she snipped the bloody garments away from the body.

Claussen held his prayer book over his heart. "Oh, dear Lord," he said, "an evil is amongst us. A savage and unholy beast. We pray for your guidance, for your deliverance from—"

"Oh, shut the hell up," Lauters snapped.

Claussen looked as if he'd been slapped. "You, sir, are a heretic."

"No, I'm just dead tired and don't want hear any of that Jesus-crap right now."

"How dare you, sir!"

Wynona stopped snipping.

"You know where I'll be if you need me, Wynona," Lauters said, stomping off. "I better get out of here before I make the dear reverend here into another customer for you."

"At the jailhouse?" Wynona asked.

"No doubt the nearest tavern," Claussen said with some bitterness.

Lauters clenched his teeth. "Shut your goddamn mouth."

"Your words, sir, again fall on deaf ears. The Lord will protect me from violent men with weak minds."

But Lauters was already gone. Weak mind or not, there was a lot on it.

11

The moon was up now—a fat, yellow orb that painted Wolf Creek in grim, pale illumination that reflected off snow and ice and hard earth. Wynona Spence stared out the window at the town from her rooms above the undertaking parlor. She was thinking of Joe Longtree and what he had said, wondering, wondering.

Could any of that be possible?

A beast with the mind of a man?

Unthinkable.

She turned from the window. Candles were lit, spread out almost strategically. They cast a sickly orange light and fed shadows into flesh. As she moved, they danced and swayed and stalked. She had a bottle of whiskey set out. Good whiskey, too, all the way from Baton Rouge, imported via Ireland. The label was even written up in Gaelic. Not the cheap swill they served up in Wolf Creek. Fermented goat piss is all that was. Good enough for the ranch hands and hardrock miners who only wanted to get drunk, fight, and fuck, but hardly satisfying to the discerning palate.

A love of good whiskey, like mortuary science, was something Wynona had inherited from her father. The dead did not frighten her. They were old friends and childhood playmates. She'd grown up with their staring, gray faces and empty eyes. Spent hours at her father's side while he stitched and sewed, gummed and glued, snapped and twisted bodies back into something vaguely human that could be cried over at a funeral. In a town like Wolf Creek, there were always plenty of dead bodies. Plenty of shootings and knifings and beatings and the occasional hanging. Then there were the mines, the inevitable quarrels between rival ranching combines. None of that even took into account death by natural causes. Yes, in the end, all roads led to the mortuary.

Those who had spurned Wynona in life always came around to her in the end.

It made her smile.

When she was young and first felt the stirrings of love, of desire for the opposite sex, the boys shunned her. She was never what you would've called physically attractive, there was more of the skeleton to her than the seductress. She was thin and bony by nature. Her flesh was cold to the touch. And she was the undertaker's daughter. The boys picked up on that, of course. They had no more use for her than the girls. Had she been a leper she could have been no more alone, no more shunned, no more banished from their social circles.

Without the benefit of male or female companionship—even her mother had passed on before her tenth birthday and Wynona remembered her father painstakingly preparing her for the worms—Wynona withdrew more and more until by age sixteen, she was little more than a hermit, spending most of her time with her father and his work. The cadavers became her friends. She developed secret relationships with them, named them. She would sing songs to them and play games with them. Tell them stories, secrets. She was always sad when it came time for them to go.

And in the dark recesses of her brain, an evil seed was planted: One day, perhaps, she would select a special friend. And that friend she would keep with her. That friend would not be surrendered to dank earth and feasting worms.

Wynona had something else in common with her father: She robbed the dead.

Call it desecration if you must, but to Wynona it was merely a way of supplementing her income. Watches, jewelry, silver buttons. She sold them to a jeweler in Nevada City who did not ask questions. Gold teeth went to a goldsmith who melted them down and fashioned them into settings for rings and chains for necklaces. Some might have called Wynona ghoulish, but ghoulish or not, she was not wasteful. Now and then she found money on her customers. Usually it was already purloined by the time the body came under her care. But when it hadn't, she rejoiced. Fringe benefits. Even a fine pair of boots or an undamaged hat could fetch a handsome price.

And why, she often thought, should such treasures languish in the ground?

She filled a glass goblet with whiskey and began slowly blowing out candles until the only illumination was the yellow glow of the fireplace and the anemic moonlight which filtered in with ghostly fingers.

She unlocked her bedroom door and sat on the bed, on the purple velvet coverlet, her head reclined against an avalanche of feather pillows.

There was a shape in the bed next to her. It did not stir.

Wynona sighed. "Oh, what a day I've had, Marion. What a most interesting and unusual day," she said, sipping whiskey. "More murders. More business. And a most interesting man. A deputy U.S. Marshal named Joseph Longtree. A fascinating man. What? Oh, don't act like that, I assure you he means nothing to me…"

12

Deputy Bowes watched the sheriff come in and was glad to see the man was sober for a change. "Another one?" he said.

Lauters sat behind his desk. "Dewey Mayhew."

Bowes set a cup of coffee before him. "No point in asking the particulars, I guess. I know 'em all well enough by now."

Lauters nodded. "Same three-toed prints in the snow, spur at the heel. Goddammit."

"Should we try tracking it?"

Lauters didn't answer. He stared off into space, his lips moving with silent words. He sipped a third of his coffee away and opened the bottom drawer. He took out a fifth of rye, pulled the cork with his teeth, and poured some in his coffee. "Any excitement tonight?" he asked, wincing as the liquor settled in his belly.

"Not too much. Got a miner by the name of Ezra Wholesome in lock-up."

"Wholesome?"

Bowes scratched his beard, grinning. "Yeah. Lost five hundred to the house over at Ruby's. Wouldn't pay. Pulled his iron."

Lauters looked up. "Any shooting?"

"No, I talked him out of it."

Bowes was good. You had to give him that. Lauters never once regretted signing the man on. He had an innate gift for soothing the savage beast, cooling hot blood with carefully-chosen words. He could talk sense to gunmen and crazy injuns with equal ease. Lauters figured he could've charmed the habit off a nun.

"You wanna tell me about it?" Bowes said.

The sheriff nodded. "Mayhew was alive when I got there."

"What did he say?" Bowes asked this intently.

Lauters told him. Then told him what the blacksmith, Rikers, had seen. "Devil, he said. Looked like the Devil." Lauters drank straight from the bottle now. "Goddamn Devil. What the hell is that supposed to mean?"

Bowes shrugged. "You think there's anything to it?"

Lauters shrugged. "Hell if I know. Tomorrow, I'm gonna have Johnson over at the paper print up some bounty posters. It'll draw some professional hunters in. Couldn't hurt."

"It didn't make any moves against Rikers?"

"Not a one. He came out there with his lantern, frightened it off. Lucky to be alive, I suppose."

Bowes sighed. "Longtree," he said carefully, "thinks these killings are related. That the beast is going after certain people."

Lauters took another drink. "You believe that?"

"I don't know what to believe anymore."

"Longtree don't know his ass from an umbrella stand, son."

"He seems like a smart fellah, though."

Lauters did not comment on that.

There was no point: He knew Longtree was smart. Knew it well as any man, but he'd never admit to it. Couldn't bring himself to. Federal intervention had always been a sore spot with Lauters. And now here comes this big-mouthed deputy marshal and he was a goddamn breed to boot. And a crafty, smart sumbitch, too. Lauters didn't like a guy like that poking around. There were too many skeletons in too many closets and the last thing this town needed was some breed rattling them loose.

Besides, dammit, how was it going to look if that wily, hotshot bastard solved these goddamn murders while the sheriff, a *white man,* was running around in circles scratching his fat ass? Not good, that's what.

But the murders.

Jesus. Those bodies. Despite himself, Lauters wouldn't have been one bit surprised if Rikers was right and it was old Satan himself. Those tracks…

Lauters gulped off the bottle again. Rye ran down his chin. He didn't bother to wipe it off. He just stared into space with wide, bloodshot eyes. His lips trembled with a tic.

"Something the matter, Sheriff?"

"Yeah," Lauters said, staring into the amber depths of the bottle. "I'm scared shitless."

13

It was getting on around two when Longtree heard the horse approaching.

He'd been sleeping an hour or so and started awake at the sound. Years of hunting and being hunted by dangerous men made him a light sleeper. He woke at almost anything. Sometimes a good wind stirring the trees was enough.

He pulled himself free of his bedroll. His horse snorted.

The rider stopped in the treeline surrounding his little gully. "Come on in," Longtree called, pistols out now.

The rider came down the trail slowly, the horse's hoofs crunching the snow with gentle, timed steps. Longtree fed a few logs into the dying fire and it blazed with flickering orange light. The rider was an Indian. There was no doubt of this. A long buffalo robe was pulled over his head and he sat astride a rawhide saddle.

But it wasn't a "he." It was Laughing Moonwind from the Blackfoot camp.

She wore buffalo mittens and carried an old Kentucky rifle. She tethered her horse and sat by the fire.

"I guess you were the last person in the world I expected," Longtree said, putting his pistols away and sitting by her side. He rolled a cigarette from his tobacco pouch.

"You came to ask us questions," she began, "and now I've come to do the same."

He nodded. "Fair enough. Who sent you? Crazytail?"

She fixed him with her huge brown eyes. Fire was reflected in them. It seemed to belong there. "I said *I* was asking the questions," she said sternly, then softening a bit, "I came of my own accord."

"Your English is good," Longtree commented, not bothering to ask her where she learned it.

"I was schooled by whites."

He nodded. "Me too."

"Why are you here?" she inquired. "Why does this matter involve the U.S. Government?"

"People are being killed. I was sent here to find out why." He briefly sketched out for her the trouble all this could cause, what with the mines and the reservation lands and the general hatred existing between white and red man.

"And you think you can solve all these problems?"

"No, but I can try." The flickering firelight fanned his face with jumping shadow. "Somebody has to. This is way out of control. Keeps up, people are going to start pulling out of Wolf Creek. That may be a good thing for your people, Moonwind, but not for the white man."

She had no reaction to this. "And you won't leave until you're finished?"

He shook his head. "Can't."

"Even if it means dying?"

He shrugged. "I'll take my chances. It's what I'm paid for."

"You're very stubborn. Very foolish."

She slipped the buffalo robe off, letting it fall to the ground. The fire was throwing off a lot of heat. Longtree was down to his shirtsleeves now, too. He sat smoking and watching her, letting her direct things here. She knew something and he wanted to know what.

"The buffalo herds are thinning," she said. "Soon my people will be starving like the rest of the Plains tribes. We are a dying race." She studied the ground with sadness, a sadness not so much learned, but bred. The sadness of her race. "Of all the indignities forced on us by the whites, this is the worst. They are taking away our ability to feed and clothe ourselves. We will be reduced to a race of beggars just to feed our children. We have never liked the whites. But we could even have forgiven them of this if it was an accident. But it is no accident." She stared into the fire, solemn and proud. "The army is directing the slaughter of the buffalo and as they die, so do we."

Longtree said, "I think the army wants to stop the Sioux and the Cheyenne. So the Indian Wars will end."

"And what of us?" Moonwind asked. "Must we perish with them?"

Longtree sighed. "I wish I had an answer for that."

"Your people, the Absaroka, the Crow, have fought with the Flatheads against us—"

"We also fought the Dakotas, the Sioux."

"You fought against us," she maintained.

He dragged off his cigarette. "Did the Crow have a choice? The Blackfoot raided and killed them without mercy. Moonwind, the Blackfoot are a warring tribe. They are not an innocent race."

She ignored this. "The Crow fought with the whites against us, against others. And where did it get them? They were forgotten and tossed aside when their usefulness to the whites had ended. The Crow are few now, Joseph Longtree. They are a starving, beaten race, riddled with white man's diseases."

"I know what's happened," he told her. "I'm not ignorant of any of this."

"The whites are treacherous."

"Not all of them."

"Your mother was a Crow. How can you say this?"

"And my father was a white. None of this has anything to do with why I'm here," he explained. "I didn't come to run Indians. I came to stop some killing or at least find out why it's happening."

"This matters so much to you?"

"Yes," he said flatly. "Now I'm going to ask questions and you're going to answer them. Tell me about the Skull Society."

She shrugged. "They are a men's society. We have many as do most tribes. There are others—the Bear, the Wolf, the Beaver. The Beaver is the most spiritually powerful it is said. The Wolf and Bear produce the finest hunters and warriors. But the oldest, the most secretive is the Skull Society. It is also the most feared."

"Why?"

"Because…" she pursed her lips as if what she revealed was taboo and it probably was. "Because they have the power to call the Skullhead."

"And what is this Skullhead?"

"A supernatural being. Nothing more. According to tradition, the Skullhead is a righter of wrongs."

Longtree stared at her, knowing she knew more than she was saying. She avoided his eyes. "Tell me what this is all about."

She continued staring in the fire for some time. Then, "It has been said that those of the Skull Society have the ability to change shape, to shift themselves into other forms." She let that lay with him. "It is a fairly common belief with my people. The Bear Society believes they can assume the shape of their spiritual guide, the great bear. The Wolf Society believes they can become wolves."

"Do you believe in this?"

"I believe many things."

"But do you believe in this? The whites have a name for shapeshifters. Do you know what it is?"

"Werewolf," she said. "A European belief."

He nodded. "A legend."

She seemed unconcerned with his label. "It has been said the ancients were in league with many creatures. Some no longer walk this land. Some are distant memory. That they hunted with them, *as* them. That they could reverse their skins. Beneath their flesh were the pelts of wolf, bear. This was accomplished with the Blood-Medicine my father spoke of."

Longtree tossed his cigarette into the fire. "Okay. That's fine for the Wolf and Bear Societies. I don't ridicule their beliefs. But what of the Skull Society? What is it they claim to become with this Blood-Medicine?"

"With the Blood-Medicine, men of the Society could become the Skullhead."

"What else?"

She went silent again. Then she turned and looked at him, her eyes drinking him in, making him shiver. Shadow and light played over her face. "It was said my grandfather was a shapeshifter.

That he often hunted in the form of an animal. That his father was one and his father's father."

"And Crazytail?"

"Yes, he too."

Longtree licked his lips. "Are you telling me your father is killing these people in the form of an animal? Some primal beast? This Skullhead?"

She looked angry. "No. You wanted to know about the Skull Society. That's all I'm telling you."

But was it? Was she laying it all out for him? No, he decided, she was spinning tribal tales, nothing more. People didn't turn into animals. There were no werewolves. Or Were-bears. Or Skullheads. If he started believing garbage like that then it was time to turn in his badge. It was madness.

"One year ago," she said, "a local white girl was murdered in Wolf Creek. Her name was Carpenter. She was raped, then stabbed. My brother, Red Elk, was arrested for the crime."

"Did he do it?"

"No, he wouldn't do such a thing." She seemed to believe this. "He had too much honor. He was found stooping over the body, so, of course, being an Indian, the whites decided he was guilty." Her lips tightened down like a vise. "He was arrested and put in jail. Two nights later, vigilantes stormed the jail and hanged him." She laughed dryly, without emotion. "At least, this is the story Sheriff Lauters told."

"And you think he was lying?"

"Yes. I don't know why he would, but I think it was to protect someone." Moonwind had planted the seed of uncertainty, now she nourished it. "In recent years, the local ranchers have been plagued by a cattle rustling ring. Red Elk told me he thought he knew who the members of that ring were."

"So he was arrested and lynched to shut him up?" Longtree asked.

"Yes, I think so. But there's more to it than that. A rumor circulated after he was hanged, mainly among the whites, that Red Elk didn't kill the woman. That he came upon her as she was dying and she told him who her attacker was."

"One of the ring?"

"It would seem...*logical,* don't you think? Red Elk knew who her killer was and he knew who the rustlers were."

Longtree sighed. "You're just guessing."

"Am I? I visited Red Elk in the jail the day before he was lynched. He told me he knew who the killer was. That in the courtroom he planned on pointing the finger at not only the killer, but at the entire ring."

"But he didn't tell you who this person was?"

She shook her head. "He said it was too dangerous for me to know."

Longtree thought about it. It made a certain amount of sense. If Red Elk knew who the real killer was and who the rustlers were, then certain parties would have every reason in the world to have him jailed and lynched before he came to trial. But what of Lauters? What was his part in this? Logic dictated that he was one of the ring, that the killer was another. Lauters didn't want this killer going on the stand because, facing the noose, he'd have told everything. Red Elk was seen stooping over the body, a very convenient surrogate. Everything fell into place after that. The ring must've have known Red Elk knew about them. It made sense...it answered many questions...but was it *true?*

Longtree rolled another cigarette and lit it with an ember from the fire. "Who," he said, "saw Red Elk bending over the body?"

"Sheriff Lauters."

Longtree winced. Damn. It was all too obvious now. Or was it? He couldn't jump to conclusions here. He would have to proceed slowly. Check out all this as quietly and covertly as possible. If Lauters was involved and he discovered Longtree nosing into the affair...it could get ugly. Still, none of this explained the series of killings.

"I'll look into it," he promised. "But my first consideration is still the murders."

"Maybe if you solve one crime, you'll solve the others."

He looked at her. Moonwind knew much more than she was saying, but she was fiercely stubborn. She would tell no more than she wanted to. A woman like her couldn't be coerced into talking. He had to gain her confidence and the only way he could do that was by investigating her brother's lynching and what led to it.

One step at a time.

"If I didn't know better," Longtree said to her, "I'd say you were suggesting these killings were done as revenge."

She shrugged. "You'll have to find that out yourself."

He let it rest. He'd suspected a connection between the murdered men and now one was offered him—they had to be the rustlers, the same ones who'd lynched Red Elk.

Take it easy, he cautioned himself. Be Careful. She could be lying about all this.

But he'd made no decisions yet. He would investigate it all and then draw his conclusions.

He found himself staring in her eyes and she into his. He arched his head toward her and she took him in her arms, kissing him passionately. She pulled away, slipping free of her calico dress. Longtree followed suit. Her taut body was bathed in orange light. He kissed her breasts, her belly, everything. She drew him on top of her and guided him in. And even as he pushed into her with powerful thrusts and stared into her savage, hungry eyes, he saw the face of Lauters.

But not for long.

Some time later, they lay together before the fire, covered in Longtree's blankets. The night was cold, but they were sweating and filled with the pleasant afterglow of their act. They didn't speak, not for the longest time. There didn't seem to be a need to. The breeze was crisp, yet gentle in the arroyo beneath its wall of pines. The stars overhead were brilliant.

Sitting up on one elbow, Moonwind said, "You were raised in a mission school?"

"Partly." He told her of the Sioux raiders that had destroyed his village, his family. "You could say, I was equally schooled by the Crow and by whites."

"The whites often place things in categories. Have you noticed this?"

"Yes."

"Everything must be labeled and organized and separated into appropriate boxes. A strange thing."

Longtree laughed. "They find life easier that way."

Moonwind said, "My father, Herbert Crazytail, is a very wise man. When I was young he was friends with many whites. When they built the mission school in Virginia City, he sent me there so that I could learn the ways of the whites. That I would speak their tongue and know their god. He said that the whites were possessed of a strong medicine."

"He was right," Longtree admitted. "It's something I've learned and sometimes the hard way."

"Yes, my people as well. Crazytail wanted me to know the ways of whites and to understand that, although their medicine was strong, they misused it. I learned this. He wanted me to know that their god and his teachings were wise, but that the white man did not follow them. This also, I learned. The white man is wasteful, Joseph Longtree. He destroys what he does not understand and laughs at that which he cannot fathom. He has a god, but he profanes him, ignores his teachings."

Longtree couldn't argue with any of that. White religion, unlike red, was generally a matter of convenience. It was practiced only when it did not interfere with other aspirations or needs.

"The white man separates the natural and the supernatural. But my people—and yours—do not. We have no words to divide them. They are one and the same," Moonwind said, her eyes sparkling and filled with fire. "If the whites believed this, they would accept us and us, them."

"You might have a point there," Longtree said. "What you have in this land is a collision between cultures."

"Answer me this," she said to him, holding his face in her long, slender fingers. "Since you are half-white, do you believe in the supernatural or only that which you can touch, can feel, can hold in your hand?"

It was not an easy question to answer.

And the only way he could was to tell her about Diabolus. "It was in the Oklahoma Territory along the New Mexico border. Many years ago. I was a bounty hunter at the time. A man paid me to bring him a body…"

14

He rode almost 200 miles to collect the body, and all the way the demon wind was blowing. It came out of the north, screaming over the dead, dry land with the wail of widows.

When he finally made it to Diabolus, he knew there would be trouble. The town was a desolate place, a typical failed Oklahoma/NewMexico border town with skeletons lining the street: closed-up, boarded-down buildings weathered colorless by the winds and heat. He saw no one and he didn't like it at all. In another year, this place would be another ghost town, blown away by the desert dust. And after he got what he'd come for, it could do just that.

"Shit and damnation," he cussed under his breath, steering the wagon down a black, lonesome street. The thud of the horse's hoofs was like thunder on the hardpacked clay, echoing through abandoned buildings and thoroughfares.

A few tumbleweeds chased each other down the road.

He had two lanterns hung on long hooked poles to either side of him and they did little to light up the ebon byways. It was like creeping through the dark innards of a hog.

Up ahead, there was light and people. Horses were hitched up before a sagging single-story saloon and there were fires lit in the street, groups mulling around them.

He stopped the wagon a reasonable distance from them and dismounted.

Indians. He saw that much.

But this was the Oklahoma panhandle. These were not his people, not his mother's people. She had often told him that the Crow were not the same as other tribes. That the Sioux and Ute and Flathead and Bannock were all separate peoples. That they had only the stars and moon and sun in common, but nothing else. But Longtree's white teachings had told him that all Indians were the same—they were all heathen savages, no more, no less.

And in those dark days after his tenure as an Indian scout for the army and time spent beating men in the ring, he had little use for anything but money. Men, white or red, were all savages to him. He thought of himself as truly belonging in neither world so he hated equally.

He watched the Indians and they watched him.

A beaten, lean lot they were, all bundled up in rags and moth-eaten blankets. Zuni, he figured. They studied him with hateful, mocking eyes sunk in burnished skins. And who were they to look on him like that? These pathetic, hopeless sonsofbitches who begged for crumbs in a white town and warmed themselves around a buffalo shit fire?

He despised them.

He tethered his horses so the thieving redskins wouldn't make off with them and, gathering up his shotgun and saddlebags, went inside.

There was a fire burning in the hearth and a few depressed and drunken men slouched over shots of whiskey or forgotten card games. The place smelled of piss, sickness, and misery.

There was a Mex behind the bar, a greasy little thing missing an eye.

Longtree set his shotgun on the bar. "Gimme a shot of something," he told the Mex.

The Mex poured him whiskey.

Longtree looked around surreptitiously. "You know a guy named Benner?"

Someone walked up behind him and he turned around real fast, hand on the butt of his Navy Colt.

"I'm Benner," a man said. He was so ravaged by the climate he could've passed for an Arapaho. "You here for the body?"

"Yeah," Longtree said. He was listening to the commotion out on the street. The injuns were chanting and pounding gourds and rattling beads. Commingled with the moan of the wind, it all took on a very eerie, haunted sound.

"Heathen Halloween," Benner croaked.

Longtree eyed him up to see if it was a joke. Benner's face was forbidding. "Since when do redskins celebrate that?" Longtree asked. "Halloween's a whiteman's—"

"It don't belong to any Christians," Benner said in a low, guarded voice. "Halloween's a pagan ceremony, my friend."

"Halloween...out here? That's crazy. Out east, maybe, but not here."

Benner shrugged. "That's what we call it. Heathen Halloween. They celebrate it this night every year." He seemed disturbed by the idea. "Now, we'd best get you what you came for."

Longtree downed his shot and followed Benner into a claustrophobic back room. A match was struck and a lantern ignited. There was a wooden box sitting atop a heavy table. It was about six feet in length and looked much like what it was: a coffin. Benner pried open the lid and held the lantern close.

"Christ," Longtree muttered.

It was some sort of Indian chieftain done up in skins and beads and necklaces of animal teeth. The face had the texture and color of tanned animal hide, the skin just barely covering the ridges of the leering skull beneath. The eyes were empty, grizzled pits, the teeth broken and pitted like deadwood. A beetle crawled out of one eye socket and Benner brushed it aside.

"Almost two-thousand years old," he told Longtree. "Been baking in the sun and drying in the wind since before white men ever set foot here…"

Longtree shrugged and thought of the money they promised him in San Fran for it. A smile brushed his lips. "Some people'll pay good money for anything, I reckon."

But an Indian chief, is what he was thinking. *I'm taking money to deliver an Indian chief. That's what it has come down to.*

"Those Indians out there," Benner said in a whisper, "usually have their October heathen service out in the hills where we can't see. But they brought it to town now that *he's* here. They're mighty ornery about me having stolen him. They want him back. Some sort of god to them, I guess."

"Don't look like a god to me," Longtree said.

Benner was staring at him. "You're kinda dark yourself friend…you ain't got no injun blood in you, do you?"

"No," Longtree lied.

"That's good. I can trust you then, I guess."

Longtree grunted and looked down at the chief and couldn't help shuddering: the old boy looked angry. His leathery, crumbled face was hitched in a sneer, it seemed. And there was something slightly off-kilter about it, almost as if his bones weren't laying quite right. His face had a narrow, inhuman cast to it, the eyes too large, the jaws exaggerated. It was reptilian somehow, suggestive of the skull of a rattlesnake.

"We'll have to take him out the back way," Benner told him. "Those injuns'll be angrier than a fistful of snakes if they know he's gone and you're taking him."

Longtree nodded.

Benner suddenly took a step backward, one trembling hand grasping his temples. He was whiter than flour in a sack. His eyes were lunatic, rolling balls shifting in their sockets.

"What the hell is it?" Longtree asked.

Benner shook his head, mouthed a few unintelligible words and then seemed to calm down. For one awful moment he looked as if he'd seen something Longtree hadn't. "I'm okay," he said.

"You accustom to spells?"

"No, I'm fine. Just this place, I guess. Gets to a man after a time. Nothing here but injuns and sand and the wind. Goddamn snakes everywhere." He mopped his forehead with a discolored bandanna. "I wish them redskins would take that damn heathen ceremony somewheres else."

Benner put the lid back on the crate and opened the rear door. The wind slammed it violently against the outer wall and both men started. Longtree brought the wagon around. The box didn't weigh much and it was a simple matter to load it.

"Where did you find this, anyway?" Longtree asked him in the whispering darkness.

"Out in the hills," Benner said hesitantly. "Out in some burying ground the injuns call Old God Hollow. Lot of curious things out there. I'm probably the only white man who has ever been to that awful place. It's an ancient place and an evil one, friend. Only in your nightmares will you ever see such a thing. Must be ten or fifteen other scaffolds there with injun corpses drying out on them, injuns with devil-faces like his. There's faces carved into the rocks and bones everywhere, piles of 'em. And scalps...Christ. Must be thousands strung up on poles and not recent ones either, but old things tanned by the wind into leather." He paused, lowering his voice. "This old chief and the others I saw, there's something not right about 'em. I've heard stories about an older race...shit, I don't know. But somebody had to teach them injuns how to scalp folks."

"A fellah down in Tucson told me white folk started that," Longtree said.

Benner grinned. "You believe that, do you?"

"Nope. Just mentioning the fact."

"If you coulda seen them scalps in the Hollow, you'd think different."

"Where is this place?" Longtree asked.

"About ten miles, due east." That crazy look was in Benner's eyes again. "I heard about it from an old Kiowa name of Hunting Lizard or Hopping Lizard, can't remember which. He wasn't much then, just some old rummy who'd sell his soul for a bottle, but I guess in the old days he was some big shot medicine man. He called it the Snake Grounds. Told me there was gold up there, more than a man could carry away in a week. I fell for it. He got a bottle out of the deal and sent some white fool to his death, that being me. No gold there, of course, just them mummies and scalps and other things meant to drive a sane man crazy."

Longtree nodded with disinterest. "Gold, you say? Maybe you didn't look too good."

"Maybe not. I just wanted out. Goddamn place."

"So, you took one of these dead ones instead?"

Benner was brushing the palms of his hands against his pants as if he were trying to rub off some old stink. "Yeah. I was hoping I could sell it to a carnival or something. Damn. The wind was howling like nothing I'd ever heard before and there were snakes everywhere, biguns, coiled around them scalp poles and hiding in the rocks. Rattlers bigger than anything you'd want to see. Must've killed a dozen, barely got out of that devil-yard alive."

Longtree said, "Country's full of snakes."

"Not like these, friend, not like these." Benner was grinning like a desert-stripped skull. "If you coulda seen 'em, seen what was in their demon eyes..."

"I'd best be on my way," Longtree told him, wanting nothing more than to get out of that damn town.

"I hope God rides with you, son."

Longtree paid him and unhitched his horses.

"Good luck," Benner said and was gone.

A few of the injuns were eyeing up Longtree and what he had under the tarp in the back of the wagon. He set out his shotgun and Navy sixes on the seat next to him.

If it's killing you want, it's killing you'll get, Longtree thought at them. This old boy's going to a museum, Heathen Halloween or not.

The Indians' chanting took on a raw, expectant tone, the lot of them dancing in crazy circles, shaking bone and feather talismans and waving skulls about.

Longtree urged the horses around facing the way he'd come in and started to make his run. He'd barely gotten them up to a trot before the Indians made their move. They came on foot, brandishing knives and ceremonial spears.They were a howling pack of crazy men, their eyes bulging. If he had ever seen true religious fervor reach its ugly, insane climax before, he would've known what this was, but he never had. He only knew they stood between him and freedom, him and a lot of cash.

He left them behind in a cloud of dust, laughing to himself.

It was a long, hard ride through the desert at night. Somehow, somewhere, he'd gotten turned around. There was heavy cloud cover so he couldn't see the stars, had no true way of navigating. It was just him and that wagon and the body in the box. The horses started acting funny right away. They moved with starts and jerks, pulled the wagon in circles. Even the bite of the whip could not convince them to do his bidding.

After a time, he just stopped them completely.

The desert had gone cold and lonely and silent as the crypt.

There was something in the air: heavy, ominous, and enclosing. It was thick, suffocating, hard to pull into his lungs. He could actually *feel* it laying over his skin like a tarp. It smelled funny—like spices and age and things shut up for too long.

He stepped down off the wagon and could not get his bearings.

He had been a scout and it had once been said of him that he could track a pea through a blizzard…but now he was blind, his senses—always so preternaturally sharp—were completely shut down. Had he been dumped on the desolate plain of some alien world he could have been no more helpless.

He thought: What gives here? What is this about?

It was so dark suddenly it was like being sewn-up tight in a bag of black velvet. The horses were snorting and neighing and pawing at the earth. A breeze had picked up, carrying a horrible stagnant odor on it. Not natural in the least. He had never smelled anything like it before, but it made his skin go cold, wrapped icy fingers around his heart.

He wanted to run.

Something in him was demanding it, screaming it in the blackness of his brain: *Run! Run, goddamn you! Take flight while you still can! Before, before—*

The wind kept picking up, adding to his disorientation.

His own breathing seemed loud, almost deafening.

The wind was beginning to make a low, moaning noise that dragged fingernails up his spine. Distant, was that sound, but getting closer by the second and sounding like voices mourning in unison and coming from every direction.

Longtree uttered a strangled cry and pulled his Navy six.

The mesa and towers of black rock seemed to rise up higher and higher, reaching into the sky and…and then leaning out, pressing together, drawing over him like fingers trying to clutch and hold him.

The wind became gale force and picked up sand and bits of rock and grit that peppered his teeth and forced his eyes shut. And echoing everywhere, those voices moaning and screeching and whispering what seemed to be his name. It became a real, full-blown sandstorm that whipped and howled and blasted everything in its path. It carried an odd half-light about it that created shadows and shapes and forms in a murky, surreal illumination. It forced him to his knees next to the wagon and he pulled his neckerchief over his eyes and that was okay, that was just fine.

Because the sand was peopled now with lurching, angular forms that reached out for him, clutched at him. The wagon rocked and seemed to be pushed gradually by the force of the wind. Longtree held on, figuring it was his only link to the real.

The wind subsided a bit and he could see no forms through his squinted eyes...save for one.

In the maelstrom of raging, spitting sand, there was a shape—tall, skeletal, ragged. Bits of it flapped and shredded in the wind. It seemed to be looking in his direction and there was something about it that seized up his heart and made him want to wail like a child. It stood so still in that churning sand, impossibly still. Nothing living could withstand this, even the horses had been hammered down now.

Yet, it stood there, perfectly still and Longtree could almost feel its eyes on him, feel that remorseless, glaring hatred that ate through him like acid.

Then it was gone.

Gradually, almost casually it seemed, the shape stalked off into the wind and tornadic sands until it faded away and became part of them. A few minutes later, the storm abated. Longtree lay there, skin raw from the kiss of pulverized rock and sand granules. He pulled himself up, his legs and boots buried in dirt. Shaking himself off and seeing to the horses—they were all right, just frightened and skittish. He soothed them and dragged himself back to the wagon.

The clouds were gone.

The stars and moon were out. But the crazy thing, the thing that stomped him down hard and would not let him up was the fact that he was miles away from where he last remembered. And not two or three, but twenty or thirty, possibly more. The landscape by moonlight proved it. Flat, empty desert. No mesas or cliffs or towers of sedimentary rock carved by ancient seas.

In the bed of the wagon, the box was open.

The chief was gone.

15

Longtree told Moonwind the story. Despite the blazing fire and Moonwind's warm body pressed to his own, he was shivering.

"You ask me if I believe in the supernatural," he said, rubbing his tired eyes. "And I guess I'd have to say yes. The white man in me conjures up all sorts of rational explanations for what happened that night, but none of 'em fit."

Moonwind held onto him, looked upon him with great compassion.

Longtree just shook his head. "I know what you must think— either that I'm totally crazy or that I pissed-off that ugly old chief and he taught me a lesson. And maybe you'd be right on both counts."

This elicited a short, but welcome laugh from her. "You weren't crazy. You ran up against a medicine so powerful it reached out from the grave. Such things are not unknown to our peoples, Joseph."

"I suppose. Since I came to Wolf Creek, I been thinking about that old chief and how they said he was part of some ancient race. It gives me pause to think. Food for thought, don't you think?"

But Moonwind pulled him down next to her and would hear no more.

16

The next morning, Dr. Perry spent an hour or so with the cadaver of Dewey Mayhew.

With forceps, scalpel, and post mortem knife, he urged the body to give up its secrets. What it told him was nothing he didn't know or suspect: Mayhew, like the others, had been killed by a large predator. He was, for the most part, less mauled and mutilated than the others, given the fact that the beast had been surprised as it plied its trade on him. Mayhew's abdomen had been opened from crotch to mid-chest, but none of the viscera were disturbed. Death had been caused probably from massive bleeding and trauma brought on either by the abdominal wound or the wedge of flesh and muscle bitten from his throat. And given such injuries, shock had played a major part.

"That's about it," he told Wynona Spence.

Wynona nodded and draped a sheet back over the body.

Perry packed his instruments back in their respective cases. He'd brought his microscope along for minute examination of fluids and tissue. This told him nothing new either. The only interesting, but not surprising, thing was the discovery of several coarse hairs lodged in the wounds. They matched the ones Perry had taken from Nate Segaris' house exactly.

"Tell me, Wynona," he said. "How is Marion getting along?"

Wynona looked at him, then looked away. It might have meant nothing...but it might have meant everything. "Oh, fine, just fine."

"She ever come down?"

"No, she prefers solitude. I tend to her needs."

Perry just nodded. He supposed it was none of his affair. "I see."

She cleared her throat, fell into character. "I'll have to leave you now, Doctor," she said. "I have an appointment to keep."

Perry badly wanted to ask with who, but he knew it wouldn't be polite. She was an odd woman, yes, but her affairs were her own business and no one else's. So he bit his tongue and said, "Go on, I'm pretty much done anyway."

Wynona grinned slightly. "If any of my customers get restless," she said, "do calm them...they've already been paid for." She laughed a morbid cackle. "It's my motto: 'No one gets out of here alive'."

Perry just stared at her.

If anyone else had said it, he would have jumped down their throat. But Wynona? No, he couldn't bring himself to do it. He had known her since she was a baby. Her father had been one of Perry's few friends and one hell of a chess player. Wynona had always been a deadpan girl, buttoned up tighter than a corset. It was only in the past few years she'd developed this morose and aberrant sense of humor. Something her father always practiced so well. She was finally showing some life and Perry was not about to crush it. No, let her have that. Maybe, like her father, it made the grim nature of the business go down better. Merely human nature, he supposed. The same way medical students (even himself, once upon a time) made unwholesome and sometimes downright gruesome jokes about the cadavers they dissected.

Whatever it takes, Wynona, Perry thought, just do it.

"On your way, Wynona, you damn ghoul," he said.

She chuckled. "As you wish, sir."

Perry managed a smile himself, but it didn't last long. Too many things worried him these days. Just too many things.

Wynona hadn't been gone but a few minutes before Reverend Claussen came in, looking disturbed. "I think it's time we had a talk, Doctor."

Perry's drooping mustache seemed to droop a bit lower. "What could we possibly have to talk about, Reverend?"

"The well-being of our flock," Claussen said in all seriousness. "You tend to their physical necessities, I to their spiritual wounds and wants."

Perry wasn't a religious man. After his wife died during an influenza outbreak ten years before, he hadn't stepped foot in a church. "I'm listening."

"What do you know of the supernatural?"

Perry sat down, sighing. His eyes swept the shelves of chemicals and instruments. He didn't look too happy. "Not a damn thing."

"But you're an educated man," Claussen argued. "Surely you've read of such things."

"I have, Reverend, but it doesn't mean I know a damn thing about it. The supernatural is your province, not mine."

"Something is killing people, Doctor. Something inhuman."

"I'm aware of that, Reverend."

"Word has reached me that the Sheriff has decided to post a bounty on this beast," Claussen said. "To have it hunted down like a common wildcat. What do you think of that?"

Perry shrugged. "It's worth a try, I guess."

"I don't believe any hunter can hope to outwit this beast."

"I see." Perry pursed his lips and said, "You think we're dealing with something supernatural? Is this what you're getting at?"

"Yes. I believe this beast is no normal animal."

"I've already figured that much. But the damn thing's flesh and blood, Reverend. It's no ghost."

Claussen, a small and petulant man, stabbed a finger at Perry. "Ah, I never said anything of ghosts, Doctor. I'm referring to an old pagan superstition concerning the transmutation of man to animal." He stalked around as he said this, as if he were delivering a sermon. "Shapeshifting, it is called. The Indians believe in such things, it forms part of their pagan worships."

"Werewolf?" Perry said incredulously.

Claussen nodded. "That is the European term, I believe."

"Christ in Heaven, Claussen, have you lost your mind?"

"Not in the least."

Perry shook his head. "I'm a man of science. Men cannot transform themselves into animals. It's a physical impossibility."

"Regardless, Doctor," Claussen maintained, "history is full of the lore of shapeshifters. I studied the matter in some depth at the university. It forms a portion of the legendry of all cultures."

Perry grunted. "Of course it does. You're talking pagan religions, primitive peoples. Is it that odd that a man from a primitive society would consider himself in league with a creature he admires?"

"No, not at all. Unfortunately, we're not dealing with only backward cultures here, but advanced ones as well."

"I can't buy any of this." Perry just wasn't in the mood. His back was acting up and it felt like the muscles were knotted and tied. "It's ridiculous."

Claussen pressed his fingertips together, undaunted. "Are you aware, dear Doctor, that our own local Blackfoot tribe has a religious order called the Skull Society?" the Reverend asked. "This is true. An old prospector told me of this. He said that the initiates believe they can transform themselves into monsters."

"Forget about it, Reverend. There are no monsters, no werewolves. If you start spreading this crap around, you're going to stir a lot of people up. Too many in this town are looking for scapegoats for the murders and I don't want to see a lot of harmless Indians getting killed for some damn fool reason. There's been too much of that already."

Claussen looked insulted. "Harmless Indians?" he said. "Those savages? They've done their share of murdering, I might remind you. They've caused dying—"

"There's been a lot of dying on both sides, Claussen," Perry interrupted. "Trust me, we've done more damage to the Indians than they'll ever be able to do to us. We don't need your ghost stories stirring up more trouble."

Claussen looked as if Perry had slapped him. "You, sir, may dwell in your ignorance. I will not. If Hell has unleashed its terrors upon the living, then let no man stand in my way." He nodded curtly to the doctor. "Good day, sir."

Perry watched him leave and sighed. "Damn fool," he said under his breath. "Goddamn pious fool."

17

The sun was well up when Longtree finally woke.

Moonwind was gone and the day was bright, the world warming. He crawled out into the cold and got his fire going again. He had a quick breakfast of coffee and tinned biscuits with jam. Around him, the countryside began to wake, shaking loose the ice and snow and greeting the day. He heard birds singing and animals foraging. It was a good thing to wake to, feeling fresh from a night spent outdoors. Maybe it was his mother's blood in him, but he enjoyed sleeping outside.

He wondered when Moonwind had left.

She had heard his tale and seemed to believe it. Which was good because sometimes he wasn't sure if he did. He had experienced it, but still it just seemed impossible. But had Moonwind scoffed at him...it would have been hurtful. Not only because he was developing strong feelings for the woman, but because he'd never told a soul that tale.

No matter.

Wolf Creek was a distance away through the hills, but already he could hear it, smell it, feel the presence of other men. He fed and watered his mount and wondered what this day would bring. Something told him nothing remotely good.

And he believed it.

18

"I guess I never expected to see you alive again," Deputy Bowes said when Longtree walked into the jailhouse later that morning. "I thought I'd be forming a posse one of these nights to retrieve your body."

"I didn't have any trouble with 'em," Longtree admitted. "Where's Lauters at?"

"At home, I suspect. Haven't seen him yet this morning."

"Good."

"Those injuns tell you what you wanted to know?"

Longtree took off his hat and set it on the desk. "You know a fellow up there by the name of Herbert Crazytail?"

Bowes nodded his head. "You could say that. His people got themselves a little worked up about a year ago after his son was lynched. Vigilantes forced themselves into the jail, overpowered the sheriff, and strung the poor bastard up." Bowes looked as if this was something he'd rather forget about. "Things got a little tense after that."

"How so?"

"Crazytail's son—Red Elk—was accused of raping and killing a local white girl." Bowes pursed his lips. "You can imagine how folks around here felt about that. Well, Red Elk swore he was innocent. Vigilantes didn't believe him, I guess. After the hanging, trouble started." Bowes stared into his cup of coffee. "A few prospectors were killed out in the hills, a schoolmaster by the name of Penrose was murdered. A few other killings followed. Retribution by the Blackfoot, I suppose. A few Indians got shot. It looked like all hell was about to break loose. Government sent an Indian Agent down here. He smoothed things out with the tribes and business settled down. But I'll tell you something, Marshal," Bowes said, giving Longtree a warning look, "only a damn fool goes up into Blackfoot lands now. They never had much use for us whites and they have a lot less now after that thing with Red Elk. I think that goes both ways."

Longtree chewed on this for a few moments. "Were any Indians arrested for those murders?"

"No," Bowes sighed. "As far as the prospectors went, they're always getting themselves killed jumping each others' claims. No proof there. And that schoolmaster…again, no proof, just a lot of hearsay."

"But you think the Blackfoot were guilty?"

"It seems mighty coincidental," Bowes said. "But…hell, who knows?"

Longtree poured himself a cup of coffee. "The night the vigilantes raided the jail, Lauters was alone here?"

The deputy looked pained. "Yeah. I was delivering a prisoner to Virginia City. I didn't get back till early the next morning." He reclined back in his seat, locking his fingers behind his head. "What does any of this have to do with why you're here?"

"Maybe nothing, maybe everything. I have to look at this business from every side."

"Are you thinking these murders might be some revenge by the Blackfoot?"

"It's a possibility I can't overlook." Longtree sipped his coffee and asked the question that was really nagging him. "Who was this prisoner you took to Virginia City?"

Bowes scratched his beard. "Fellah by the name of Carson. He was a miner, worked at one of the silver camps. Word reached us he was also wanted for murder in Deadwood, Dakota Territory. We took him in. Marshals Office wired us, said to deliver him to Virginia City and lock him up there until one of their men came by train to take custody of him."

"Was there any urgency in getting him to Virginia City?"

Bowes narrowed his eyes suspiciously. "You asking why I took him that night and not another?"

"Yes."

"Sheriff told me to. That's all. There was no hurry. Jail wasn't crowded, the marshal from Dakota Territory wasn't expected for a week or so. Sheriff just up and told me to deliver the prisoner one morning. Nothing more to it than that. Just what are you getting at?"

Longtree swallowed. "I just want to know what was so urgent about getting that prisoner to Virginia City, is all. Why that night?"

"You're thinking the Sheriff was involved in that lynching, aren't you?" Bowes asked pointedly. "Well, if that's the case, Marshal, I'd say you're listening to too much local gossip. I would think after all this time them rumors would've died out."

"Rumors about Lauters being mixed up with the vigilantes?"

"You know what I mean."

Longtree suppressed a grin. If nothing else, their little talk here had established the basic facts of what Moonwind had said: Red Elk had been lynched and there were rumors about Sheriff Lauters' complicity.

Bowes fixed him with a lethal stare. "I'll tell you something, Marshal. I'll tell you something right here and now. I'm loyal to Bill Lauters and I don't want to hear that kind of talk. You investigate these murders all you want and I'll gladly help you all I can, but I don't want to hear you insulting that man. He might not look like much now, but once, once he was a fine lawman."

Longtree nodded. "Don't get yourself upset, Deputy. Nobody's insulting him. You have to remember that my job is to look into every possible motive for these killings. And if I start thinking the Indians are involved, I have to ask myself *why.*" Longtree told him sincerely. "And if you tell me this Red Elk was lynched and there was bad blood following that business and rumors flying around, well then, I'm going to get suspicious. I wouldn't be worth a shit as a lawman if I didn't."

"Okay, Marshal, I understand. And I think you understand me."

Longtree studied Bowes with narrowed eyes. "Tell me about these cattle rustlers."

Bowes laughed. "Damn. Not too much you don't hear about is there?"

"It's my job."

Bowes shrugged. "Nothing much to tell. In the past three, four years, during the warm months, we've had some rustling. No one was ever caught, few were questioned. No leads, no nothing. Just a lot of hearsay."

"Tell me the hearsay."

"Folks say there's a ring involved here, a group of men who are responsible. Some say they're based here in Wolf Creek, others say Virginia City or even Bannack. Take your pick. Nothing's ever turned up, I'm afraid. Folks in these parts call 'em the Gang of Ten. I don't know why. That's it."

Longtree was listening to this and remembering all Moonwind had said about the vigilantes being the rustlers and Lauters being involved. He was also thinking that if it was this Gang of Ten that were the vigilantes, that possibly eight of their number had been murdered. There was no proof of this Skullhead or that the Indians were out for revenge, but Moonwind had certainly wanted him to think so.

He needed proof.

Any kind of proof. But how could he get it? Getting something on Lauters would be tough. But what about the Indians? Also tough. Moonwind had said Red Elk, her brother, was a shapeshifter. It sounded crazy, impossible, but...

"The Blackfoot bury their dead, don't they?"

Bowes looked at him as if he were insane. "Yeah, they do. They put 'em in the ground same as us."

"Where would Red Elk be buried?"

A shadow crossed Bowes' face like he didn't care for where this was leading. "Up in the hills. There's a burial ground up there. But get any crazy ideas out of your head, Marshal. That cemetery is sacred ground to them. You get caught nosing around up there—won't be enough of you left to bury."

"Let me worry about that," Longtree said. "How can I find it?"

Bowes looked upset. "It's in a little valley, hard to find." He sighed heavily. "I could show you, I guess. I went up there once as a kid. On a dare. I could take you. That is, if you're determined.

"I am."

Bowes just shook his head. "What do you want up there?"

"I want to examine Red Elk's remains."

19

"Yes, I do think we're looking at a banner year, Marion," Wynona Spence said, beaming. "We shan't see a year like this again."

She sipped her tea and thought about the killings and, though she did not take pleasure in anyone's untimely death (as if death were ever timely), she couldn't help but feel a certain satisfaction in the money she was taking in. And that was just good business sense, nothing more. When she had taken over her father's operation, people treated her as if she were crazy. A woman undertaker? Good God, who'd ever heard of such a thing and what woman in her right mind wanted to while away the hours processing the dead?

The general consensus in Wolf Creek was that she would not last.

She would certainly fail.

But she had not failed—she had prospered. She took command of the business her father had built, working it and oiling it and crafting it carefully with nimble fingers until it was a sure success. So successful that she had branched out and now owned considerable stock in a silver mine and controlling interest of some three businesses in Wolf Creek. Gone were her father's charming, old world country boy idiosyncrasies—embalming and burial on credit, coffins on a promise of future reimbursement, gravestones and plots given to friends at cut-rate prices. Such things were not only bad business, but self-defeating. The mortuary business was no different than any other: it existed to make money, to show a profit, not to engender the proprietor to the locals with reams of homespun compassion.

Perhaps she wasn't well-liked in general, but she was a very shrewd businesswoman.

And regardless of all the gossip she inspired living with another woman that no one ever saw, they couldn't take that away from her.

She set down her teacup and swatted at a fly. "Flies and at this time of year, Marion. Can you believe such a thing? Must be that sun warming 'em up in the windowsills. Do you suppose?"

Marion, dressed-out in a fine and flowing bedroom gown of fine lace and spiderweb satin, said nothing. The coverlet was pulled up beneath her armpits and her hands were folded over her bosom. She did not stir. She did not do anything.

Wynona added a touch of Irish whiskey to her tea, sipped it, approved. "Yes, I do think father would be quite proud of me. Wouldn't you agree, Marion?"

Marion just laid there, eyes shut, lashes resting against her sallow cheeks like the fine and feathery legs of a moth. A fly lighted off her hair and landed on her face. It walked a tickling tread down and across her lips.

Marion did not move.

20

Sheriff Lauters was at Dr. Perry's, sitting in his little study, thinking over all the mumbo-jumbo Claussen had told the doc and the doc had told him. And every moment, he got a little angrier.

"Damn that Jesus-spouting fool," he said. "If he was here now, I swear to God I'd ring his scrawny neck. Stupid sonofabitch."

"Take it easy, Bill," Perry said, stretching his back and wincing. "Claussen doesn't know any better."

"Yes, he does. Goddamit, he does. He's an educated man. He should know better than to be spreading around old wives' tales like that. Werewolves, monsters...my ass."

"Hopefully, he'll keep it to himself."

The sheriff grunted in disgust. "That's a whole hell of a lot to be hoping for, Doc."

Perry shrugged. It was his back he was concerned with at the moment. Not murders. Not Claussen. Not werewolves and bogies. His lower back was knotted up with a raw, twisting pain. It was not getting better. One of these days he wouldn't get out of bed at all.

"You mark my word, Doc. Come Sunday that damn ass will be spouting off about werewolves and devils and God knows what in his sermon."

"Nothing we can do about that, Sheriff."

"We'll see about that." Lauters strapped on his guns and took off out the door. "We'll just see."

"Sheriff—" Perry started to rise, but the pain in his back pushed him down again, his forehead beaded with sweat. Licking his lips, he opened his lower desk drawer and took out a small black box. In it was a syringe and several small bottles of morphine.

Alone, Perry injected himself.

21

Reverend Claussen sat in the rectory and heard only silence. He was alone today. He was alone and on the desk before him were about a dozen books on folklore and the occult. A portion of his personal collection. He scanned the spines. *Man into Beast, De Lycanthropia, Der Werewolf, De transmutations hominum in lupos, Uber die Wehrwolfe und Thieverwandlungen im Mittelalter, Demonolatry.* There were others. The one he was most interested in was called, *Indians of the Upper Plains: Common Beliefs and Myth-Cycles.*

Everything he needed was here.

Everything with which to do battle against the evil that had taken Wolf Creek in its foul jaws. Claussen didn't care if anyone believed him or not about what was happening. He'd tried the doctor first, simply because Perry was an educated man. And that had been a mistake.

Now he would have to hunt down the evil himself.

The door suddenly swung open. Standing there, was a young woman without a stitch of clothes on. "I feel sinful," she said.

22

Sheriff Lauters stood across the rutted dirt road from the church. Looking around, he fished out his pint of Rye and guzzled down the remainder, tossing the bottle. He wiped his mouth with the sleeve of his sheepskin coat and waited to see if anyone was around.

He saw no one.

He had business with the good reverend, the nature of which necessitated that they be alone. It seemed that he'd come at a good time. There was no traffic whatsoever in and around the church. No old ladies from the various church groups. No sinners seeking forgiveness.

A good day for a little discussion.

A good day to straighten out Claussen once and for all.

Lauters saw no one in either direction on the road and quickly crossed the hard-packed snow and went into the church. It was silent inside. He peered out the door to see if he was being observed. He was not.

He walked down the aisle between the polished pews. He moved slowly, his footsteps landing without sound. And this was a great accomplishment when you consider that since he'd left Perry's house well over an hour before, he'd been doing nothing but drinking. He had a taste for Rye. In his coffee. With water. Straight out of the bottle. It didn't matter. He only knew that without it, he was miserable. A hopeless wreck. But with it…well, he was a man of means, a lawman who could face down any gunman in the Territories without a hint of fear.

He took his own sweet time approaching the altar.

On the way, in the shadowy stillness, he took note of where the carpet was thinning, which prayer books lacked covers, which pews needed replacing.

He was, his head swimming with alcohol, a confident man. He had a job to do and he would do it.

Claussen wasn't in the church itself, which meant he would be in the rectory. This was the place in which he slept and took his meals, Lauters knew, and also the place in which he plotted out his little games.

"Not anymore," Lauters said beneath his breath. "Not anymore."

He had been waiting for this day for a long time. He'd said nothing when Claussen had rolled into town, reeling with self-importance and holiness. He said nothing when Claussen had condemned honest men from his pulpit with sermons of hell-fire and everlasting torment. He even said nothing when the Bible-thumping crazy had turned his own wife against him. He accepted it. But when Claussen had begun criticizing the job he did as sheriff and his lack of progress with the murders…that had been it. And now, this superstitious horseshit about spooks.

He would take no more.

It was time for Claussen to pay for his sins.

Lauters had no intention of letting that goddamn Holy Joe drive Wolf Creek, his town, into panic with these horror stories. No, what was going to happen now was long overdue.

Lauters passed through the vestibule into the rectory.

There was a little sitting room with a fire blazing in the hearth. The sheriff warmed his hands for a moment. He looked in the kitchen and into Claussen's cramped study. The reverend was nowhere. That left only upstairs.

Lauters moved up the narrow stairwell and froze on the second step.

He could hear sounds.

Moanings.

A thrashing of bed springs.

Either Claussen was in lot of pain or he was being killed or…

Well, Lauters decided, the other alternative was *impossible.*

Not Reverend Claussen. Pious, self-righteous Claussen.

Lauters moved slowly up the stairs, pausing at the top. He could hear two distinct sets of moans now. Those of Claussen and those of a woman, heated, breathless. Lauters grinned and moved up the short hallway to the first door which was ajar slightly. He stood there a full minute before kicking it in all the way.

When he did, no one noticed him at first.

Claussen was on the bed, quite naked, his wrists tied with leather straps to the bedposts. On top of him, also naked, was Nell Hutson, a young whore from Madame Tillie's parlor house. Her back was wet with sweat, her ample hips pumping with a ferocity that threatened to drive the good reverend straight through the mattress.

"Well, well, well," Lauters said. "What do we have here?"

23

Up in the hills, at the Blackfoot camp, Laughing Moonwind peered out through the flaps of her lodge. She was watching the sweat lodge in the distance. Her father, Herbert Crazytail, and the other members of the Skull Society had just stepped out of it. Their faces were set and grim, painted a deathly white with black streaks under their eyes. They were dressed in wolf and bear pelts and nothing more, as was the way of the Society. They were pallid, dead-faced spirit warriors now heaped with skins. One of them wore the hideous mask of some grinning demon fashioned from the huge skull of a grizzly and strips of tight-fitting leather.

One by one, the others put on similar masks.

These were actually fashioned from the stretched and cured heads of wolves, painted up with ritual colors.

Crazytail in the lead, they started off through the forest to the sacred grove on the mountainside where they would begin their rites.

Tonight would be a bad night.

The smell of death was already on the wind.

24

Deputy Bowes stood before the window of the jailhouse, looking down the rutted, frozen drive that cut through Wolf Creek. The sky was overcast, threatening snow. The temperature was up in the lower forties today, turning the world into a melting, wet swamp of filthy snow and mud.

It wouldn't last.

Within a few days, the winds would start to scream down from the mountains again, driving the mercury down towards zero.

Bowes was wondering where the sheriff was. He hadn't seen him all morning and it wasn't like Lauters not to show up. At least for a little while before he went about his business of

(drinking)

policing the town.

Bowes stood there a moment longer and then sat behind the desk, sipping coffee. There was no one in lock-up today. No meals to fetch or piss pots to empty. Ezra Wholesome had been released earlier, agreeing to pay for the damages he'd caused. Beyond that, it was a quiet day. If nothing else, the murders had certainly made his job easier. There'd been few arrests since this all started with Abe Runyon's mutilated corpse. Even the miners were quiet, most of them preferring to stay up at their camps, not caring much to be caught on those lonely mountain roads after dark.

Bowes wondered where Longtree was and what he was nosing into.

If Lauters found out what he was up to, Longtree was a dead man. And if he was killed, the Marshals Office would spare no expense in bringing in the man responsible.

Wolf Creek was in deep shit any way you looked at it.

25

Longtree was just riding down the slope from the nondenominational cemetery outside town when he saw the smoke of a campfire in the hills. He'd gone up there to examine the graves of the murdered men for no other reason than he thought he should.

There wasn't much to see.

The markers had all been hewn from wood being that none of them were men of means. Snow had fallen since their burials, covering the graves. The markers were blanketed with melting ice.

Then he saw the smoke and thought he should investigate.

Maybe it was from the fire of some freelance prospector who might know something of the murdered men...or the rustlers. It was worth a shot.

After leaving Bowes that morning, he had talked with some of the widows of the victims. He learned nothing new. They were in mourning and he wasn't about to push them for seamy details concerning the dead.

He urged his black up a rise and through a stand of pines. He could smell the air—fresh, cool—and the smoke of the fire. He also caught hints of bacon and coffee.

He approached the camp slowly, cautiously.

It paid to be careful, particularly with a murdering beast on the loose. People tended to be quick with their guns when they heard someone or something coming.

The closer he got, still out of visual range, he could hear the steady whacking sound of an ax splitting wood. The chopping kept up as he got closer and closer, moving the black along at a slow trot over the slushy ground. He came to a small opening in the trees. A jackrabbit darted off into the brush.

The chopping stopped.

The world fell silent.

He could see the fire and a team of horses picketed near the treeline. An old mud wagon was pulled up near a small army tent. There were a few rifles leaning up against it—a Winchester and a Sharps "Big Fifty". Steel-jawed traps and pelts of every description hung from it. There was a woodpile and enough kindling to last for a week.

But there was no one in sight.

Longtree grimaced. "Rider coming in," he called out.

He stopped the black by the wagon and tethered it. He warmed his hands by the fire and looked around. He knew the owner of the camp was hiding in the trees, getting a bead on him. But the fact that he hadn't shot yet meant he probably wouldn't.

"Who are you?" a voice called out and it was familiar somehow.

It came from behind him, but the marshal didn't turn around. "Joe Longtree, deputy U.S. Marshal," he said.

He heard the man swearing as he came out of the trees. He didn't seem too happy to have the law visiting.

Longtree snaked a hand inside his coat and withdrew one of his pistols. He made no menacing moves with it, he just kept it handy, his hand on the butt.

"What the hell do you want?" a gruff voice asked.

Longtree turned very slowly.

He found himself staring at a bear of a man, his shirt open, his chest gleaming with sweat. He was bearded and carried an Army Carbine. It was pointed at Longtree's head.

"I only came to warm myself," the marshal said.

"Warm yourself somewheres else, Longtree," the man told him.

The way he said it made the marshal sure this man knew him. But from where? The voice was familiar, but nothing more. Maybe without that beard. Then it came to him. This was Jacko Gantz.

It could be no other.

Ten years ago, before Longtree was a lawman, he'd been hunting men for money. There'd been a five-hundred dollar bounty on Gantz for robbing stages in the Arizona Territory. Longtree had caught up with him at a saloon in Wickenburg after three months on his trail. There'd been some shooting. Longtree took a bullet in the shoulder, Gantz caught one in the leg and one in his gun hand.

This took the fight out of the road agent.

Longtree cuffed him and got the both of them to a doctor. Three days later, he delivered Gantz to Phoenix and placed him in the custody of Tom Rivers, then just a U.S. Marshal before his appointment to chief marshal. Gantz, after his trial, had been sentenced to ten years in the Arizona Territorial Prison at Yuma.

"When did you get out, Gantz?" Longtree asked.

Gantz kept the gun on him. "Two years ago, Longtree. I did eight long years in that fucking hellhole. Thanks to you."

Longtree's face betrayed no emotion. "I only did my job."

"Yeah, you sure did, you sonofabitch," Gantz said angrily. "Eight years of my goddamn life. *Eight years.* And what happened to you in that time, Longtree? You became a lawman, a federal marshal. How the hell did a breed like you swing that?" He laughed through clenched teeth. "Rivers got you that appointment, didn't he? He's a big wheel now, so I hear."

"I'd appreciate it, Gantz, if you'd lower that rifle."

Gantz kept it where it was. "Oh, I bet you would, Marshal, I just bet you would." His eyes never left Longtree for a moment and in them was a hatred that burned black. "I thought about you a lot in prison, Longtree. Didn't a day go by that I didn't think about killing you. And now, look what's happened? I got your sorry hide in my sights."

"Drop that weapon," Longtree said.

"Or what? You gonna shoot me down unarmed like you did—"

"You weren't unarmed, Gantz. I took a bullet in the shoulder as proof of that."

"I oughta shoot you down like a sick dog," Gantz grumbled.

Longtree's eyes narrowed. "Drop your weapon, Gantz. Now. This is a U.S. Marshal ordering you to drop your weapon."

Gantz just stared at him. Longtree had his Colt aimed at the man's belly. They stood like that for a few moments, neither saying a word. Longtree squatting by the fire and Gantz standing with his carbine pointed at the marshal's head.

"You must be a real fool, Longtree," Gantz said. "Badge or no badge, I pull this trigger and I'll scatter your brains for a hundred yards."

"Maybe. But the second you shoot, so do I. And my bullet goes in your belly. And if you think you can make it down to Wolf Creek gutshot, then you're a bigger fool than you look. You'll bleed to death long before."

"Maybe it's worth it."

Longtree raised an eyebrow and stood up very slowly. "Maybe. But even if you live, you'll spend your days as a hunted man. Killing a federal officer is a serious offense, Gantz. The law'll hound you to an early grave."

Gantz said nothing. The barrel of his carbine was still pointed at Longtree's head. He licked his lips.

"If you're gonna shoot, then shoot!" Longtree shouted in his face. "Pull that trigger, boy! Shoot, goddammit, shoot!"

Gantz looked uncertain. He lowered the carbine, smiling. "Never said I was going to."

Longtree made like he was going to holster his pistol and then brought it up in a vicious arc, cracking Gantz along the side of the face with the butt. Gantz went down with a cry, blood running from a gash in his cheek. Longtree pulled the carbine from him and kicked him in the ribs.

"I could have you back in prison for this, Gantz." He ejected the shells from the rifle and tossed it in the woods. "Do it again and I will."

Gantz sat up, moaning and pressing a trembling hand to his wound. "You sonofabitch," he gasped. "You didn't have to do that."

Longtree ignored him, lighting a thin cigar. "Why are you here?"

"To get that animal. To get the bounty."

Longtree spat in the dirt next to him. "All you're going to do is get yourself killed, hear? If you're smart, you'll haul ass out."

"No law," Gantz murmured, "against hunting a dangerous animal."

"Nope. But there is one against endangering the life of a federal officer."

"I didn't mean nothin'."

"Keep out of my way, Gantz. If you fuck with me again, I'll kill you deader than deerhide."

Gantz nodded.

Longtree untethered his black and climbed back on, riding off. He knew this wasn't at an end. Not by any stretch. He had a killer beast on his hands. A sheriff who was a violent drunk. And now Gantz.

There'd be some dying before this mess was wrapped up.

26

"Get your clothes on, Nell," Sheriff Lauters said. He didn't watch her dress; he gave any woman that much respect, even a prostitute. "You too, Reverend. It turns my stomach some to see *you* in the flesh."

Claussen was beyond embarrassment. He was mortified. There was no color left in his once ruddy face. His self-righteous pomposity had crumbled to ash. He was a beaten, broken man whose filthy little secrets had been exposed and this by the man he despised most.

"Sheriff..." Nell began.

"Just get out of here, child, and don't let me catch you plying your trade around a house of worship again. Understand?"

She nodded. Her blue eyes were tearful as if she'd been caught in the act by her father.

"Forget about what happened here today," Lauters instructed her. "Forget about seeing me, forget about the reverend. Nothing happened here today. Got it?"

She nodded, sobbing.

"Now, git!"

She took off down the stairs, not looking back. Lauters knew she'd say nothing of this. Not ever. If she did, she'd be in serious trouble and she knew it.

Claussen was sitting on the bed, staring at his hands. They shook. As did the rest of him. Lauters just glared at him for a moment, not bothering to mask the disgust on his face. He took off his sheepskin coat and hung it on the door.

"My Lord," Claussen whimpered. "My Lord."

"Shut the fuck up," Lauters snapped. "You and God have parted company, Reverend. And being that this probably isn't the first time you've done something like this, I'd say you parted company some time ago."

Claussen said nothing more, he sobbed, his entire frame shuddering.

"Jesus wept," Lauters said. He fished out his tobacco pouch and wedged a chunk of chew between his cheek and gum. He polished his badge and took it off, setting it on the nightstand by the bed.

"Now I'm no more a man of the law than you are a man of God," he said.

"Sheriff, I—"

"Shut up," Lauters said. "How long have you been deceiving the good people of your church?"

"Not long, I swear. Sin overcame me—"

"You piece of shit," Lauters grumbled, taking the reverend by the shirt collar and tossing him to the floor. He tried to get up and Lauters kicked his legs out from under him.

"When you were a man of God," the sheriff began, "I had to take a certain amount of guff from you. After all, it isn't proper to strike a man of the cloth. But now that you're just a sinner like me, there's no reason not to."

He hooked his arm around Claussen's elbow and pulled him to his feet.

They stood eye to eye.

Lauters spat in his face and the reverend only trembled. "Sinner," he said, slamming a fist into his belly. Claussen doubled over with a gasp. Lauters grabbed him by an ear and pulled him back up, striking him in the face with one massive closed hand. Claussen stumbled over a chair and went down, blood streaming from his broken nose. Before he could rise or even recover, Lauters was on him. He grabbed the back of his shirt and planted his knee in the reverend's face.

Claussen's head shot back and struck the wall. He slid down into a heap.

"You turned my wife against me," Lauters said.

Claussen, tears streaming from his swollen eyes, shook his head and Lauters slapped him across the face. Then he did it again, laughed, and backhanded the man. Red, hurting handprints were imbedded in the reverend's face. Blood and drool ran from his mouth.

Lauters pulled him to his feet, patting him on the shoulder. "You would have turned the whole town against me in time." He slammed Claussen against the wall and held him there with one meaty fist. "I've fought worse enemies than you, Reverend. I've beaten and killed the meanest, ugliest men this vile country has thrown against me. Did you think you had a chance?" He slapped him in the face. *"Answer me!"*

"I never...I didn't..."

Lauters kneed him in the groin and then in the stomach. Claussen doubled over, going to his knees, gasping and wheezing, and Lauters struck him in the face with a series of upper cuts and tossed his bleeding, broken body out into the center of the floor.

The reverend lifted his head up. His face was an atrocity. His left eye was swollen shut and puffed red. His nose was smashed at an angle towards his cheek. His lower lip was bulging and gashed. Blood was smeared over his chin and cheeks. His remaining good eye studied the sheriff with a raw hatred.

Lauters kicked him in the face.

With a drunken, psychotic rage, he pulled the reverend to his feet and hammered him in the face with his right fist while holding him up with his left. He kneed him in the stomach again and watched him fall, pounding the back of his head unmercifully with a savage series of blows from both fists.

Claussen dropped to the floor and didn't move.

Lauters, panting with exertion, alcohol sweating out of his bloated face in rivers, rubbed his cut, bleeding fists. "This isn't over yet, Reverend." He took a china pitcher from its stand and filled a basin with water and dumped it on the still, broken heap of the minister.

Claussen came to, his good eye focusing and unfocusing, his head swimming with dizziness. Lauters picked him up and dropped him on the bed.

"I want you out of this town, Reverend. If you're still here day after tomorrow, I'll kill you. Is that clear?"

Claussen attempted a nod.

Lauters patted him on the chest and put his badge back on, then his coat. He stood in the doorway and smiled. "School's out," he said.

Wynona was doing what she did best.

After she had stitched up the gaping wounds in Dewey Mayhew's hide (just so nothing would spill out, mind you), she dressed him in an old suit provided by his widow. It was no easy task. Mayhew had curled up in a semi-fetal position as he lay dying behind the smithy's shop. Rigor mortis and a nasty wind out of the north had done their best to freeze up his ligaments and muscles permanently in that position. They'd straightened him out some when Doc Perry had done his little autopsy...but not enough.

It was Wynona's job to force things into their proper places. Otherwise, Mayhew wouldn't fit in the box. Dressing the cadaver was one thing, but making him lie flat was quite another.

"Come on, Dewey," Wynona grunted, "work with me, old man."

She was up on the slab with him.

She'd gotten his legs straightened and one arm flat, but the other was no easy task. Every time she pressed his shoulder down, the arm swung up from internal stress and slapped her. She was kneeling on his bicep and bearing down on his wrist with everything she had. Handling the dead had made her strong. She could toss around 200 pound cadavers like a farm woman handling feed sacks.

But sometimes, the dead were not cooperative.

Dewey was every bit as stubborn in death as he had been in life.

"Come on, you sonofabitch," she groaned. "No need for this now...just help...me out here...unhh..." Wynona gasped for breath. She'd moved the arm enough to fit it in the box, but she wanted to lay it over the breast with the other. It was the traditional position. "You're going in that coffin whether you like it or not...so, please, cooperate..."

She mopped her brow, pushed aside clumps of hair that hung in her face, took a deep breath, and waded back into battle. With a gruesome snap, she got Mayhew's other arm into position. "There," she panted, "that wasn't so bad, now was it?"

"What in the name of the Devil are you doing?"

Wynona, not accustomed to anyone speaking in the preparation room, nearly jumped out of her skin. She turned and saw Mike Ryan standing in the doorway.

"Oh, Mr. Ryan... " Wynona giggled. "Why, you scared the death out of me!"

"What in blazes are you doing, woman?"

She smiled, straddling the corpse, very much aware of how positively undignified it looked. How indecent it might have seemed. "Why, Mr. Ryan...what do you think I was doing?"

"Well, it's just that..."

Wynona giggled again, slid off the slab. "Sometimes you have to straighten them to fit them in the casket. Unpleasant, but necessary. Every job has its unpleasantries, does it not?"

Ryan ignored her, staring at the body. "That Mayhew?" It was hard to tell. He had known Dewey Mayhew for years, but this...this was only vaguely human. It was a bloated, discolored, stitched-up grotesquerie out of a sideshow.

"Yes," Wynona said, covering the body quickly with a sheet.

"My God, he looks worse than they said."

Wynona looked hurt. "There's only so much that could be done."

Mike Ryan was a big man with bushy eyebrows, a hard face, and an intense glare that looked right through a man. He was a local rancher and a very rich man. He dressed in fine vested suits from St. Louis, owned hotels in both Virginia and Nevada Cities, and controlled stock in several copper and silver mining companies. He was a man to be reckoned with. If he liked you, you were set; if he didn't, he could destroy you, being that he owned just about everything and everyone in and around Wolf Creek. He was a good friend of Bill Lauters and had been the primary mover in getting Lauters his current post. He was also the mayor and the city council all rolled into one.

Wynona washed her hands in a basin and dried them, powdered them. "What can I do for you this fine day, Mr. Ryan?"

"Fine day?" Ryan said angrily. "What's fine about it, Wynona? Men are being killed out there!"

"A figure of speech."

He looked at her with complete loathing. He didn't care for undertakers in general and a *woman* undertaker…well, it was just plain unnatural. "Yes, well, I didn't come here to chat with the likes of you." He pulled out a gold pocket watch. "I need a headstone."

"Oh, I see," Wynona said, putting on her best sympathetic demeanor. "Has there been a death in the family?" She controlled her voice carefully, not wanting to sound excited.

"No, no death," Ryan said. "Not yet. It's for me. I want a headstone and a coffin. The best you can get. When people see my stone, I want them to stop and think, 'Here lies a man of worth'. Got it? The very best."

"I know of a fine sculptor and mason in Virginia City, Mr. Ryan. He can create something befitting a man of your station."

"Marble. The finest marble money can buy. Get the very best. Imported. Can you do that? I have imported Italian marble in my bathhouse. I fancy it."

"Oh, you can be assured—"

"Don't assure me, dammit, just do it!"

"Yes, sir. It will be done."

"Fine," Ryan said. "Get on it, woman. I'll be back day after tomorrow to discuss the particulars."

Ryan stormed out, leaving Wynona with a widening grin on her pale face. Whistling a happy tune, she went about pressing Mayhew into his cheap pine casket.

Life was rich.

And so was death.

28

Dr. Perry, his back a catalog of discomfort from the sudden change in the weather, made his way to see Claussen. He moved up the rutted road, cursing as he slipped and slid on the melting pockets of snow.

"If I fall," he said under his breath, "God knows I'll never get up again."

Wagons rolled past him, riders and people going about their business. Everyone waved at him. More than a few wanted to chat. But Perry wasn't in the mood for any of that. He'd been trying to keep his injections of morphine to a bare minimum and such was the way of the drug that, what was enough to blot out the pain a week ago, was only enough to tease him now.

But he had to be careful.

Narcotics were nothing to fool with.

Dependency came easily and he was already beginning to exhibit the signs of it: loss of appetite, euphoria after injecting, a building need that demanded more and more.

Damn, he thought, *but I'm a fool.*

He knew better than to be fooling around with narcotics. He had seen countless men turned into addicts during the War Between the States, and yet he'd willingly started a progression of dependency that could only end in disaster. But his lower back troubles—which had started after he was thrown from a horse five years before and slammed against a rock outcropping—had gotten progressively worse. It had reached the point in the past few months where he could barely function. Getting out of bed was a task, examining a patient with all the bending and turning required, was agony.

If it hadn't been for the drug, he would've had to give up his practice some time ago. That and live the doubtful existence of an invalid, confined to bed for the remainder of his years.

He couldn't let that happen.

People depended on him and the lifestyle of the aged and infirm would've killed him faster than any drug could hope to.

He came to the church and forced himself up the steps. Inside, it was dark and quiet. He called out for Claussen a few times, but there was no answer. He made his way to the rectory and looked around. Claussen didn't seem to be there. Perry thought once of looking upstairs, but he had no intention of invading the man's privacy. That and the fact that it would be hell on his back.

In Claussen's study, Perry found the books he was looking for. He wasn't about to accept any of this monster nonsense, but only a fool dismissed something without a thorough study. He wrote a note to the reverend and took as many books as his back would allow.

As the doctor left, he thought he heard a moan from upstairs.

He dismissed it and went on his way.

29

Some time later, Abigail Lauters, the sheriff's wife, and her cousin, Virginia Krebs, came to the church and couldn't find the reverend. It wasn't like him to miss their bible study meeting.

"My God," Abigail said, "I don't like this. Not one bit."

Virginia looked around the dim church and shivered. "Maybe he's in the rectory. Poor dear's been working himself sick."

So they went to the rectory.

"Where do you suppose he could be?" Abigail wondered.

"I do hope nothing's happened."

Abigail touched the broach on her throat. "I better tell Bill about this. He might know where he is." She said this with a certain amount of distaste for she had precious little use for her husband these days. A drunk. A sinner. A poor father to their children. Reverend Claussen remonstrated him from the pulpit on Sundays and Abigail agreed completely. Something was killing people and all Bill did was drink. Shameful.

Virginia said, "This is a bad omen. I'm sure of it."

Neither of them thought of looking upstairs.

30

The reverend heard people come and people go, but he was in too much pain and suffering, too much humiliation to call out. Lauters had beaten him good. Beyond his shattered nose, nothing seemed to be broken but his pride. But he hurt all over. His face was a swollen purple and yellow mass of bruises. One eye was closed. He was missing two teeth. There was a lump on top of his head the size of a baseball and his nose was a bloody flap.

He didn't want anyone seeing him like this.

He heard the doctor come and go. He heard Lauter's wife and her cousin come and go. He was thankful that neither tried to look for him. To be seen like this...it was unthinkable. They would ask questions and how could he answer them? If he said who did it, Lauters would expose him for what he was.

The reverend couldn't allow that.

There were only two possible choices: Either get out of Wolf Creek and give up all he had worked to build for so long or get rid of the man who had done this to him.

Kill Lauters?

It was unthinkable, yet it was exactly what he was thinking— kill the bastard. But how? How in God's name could he kill a man who was both handy with a gun and his fists?

The reverend wasn't sure. But it had to be done.

31

Longtree caught up with Lauters at the livery.

"I'd like a word with you, Sheriff," he said.

Lauters grumbled. "I ain't got nothing to say to you, Marshal. Just get out of my way."

But Longtree wasn't moving. He was blocking the door. "I wanna talk about the rustling ring. The Gang of Ten."

Lauters wiped his mouth with the back of his fist. "That's a local problem," he said calmly. "It's none of your damn business. You came to stop these killings, so get to it and keep your nose out of the rest."

Longtree hadn't expected cooperation. It was the farthest thing from his mind. The only reason he'd tracked down Lauters was to put him on the spot, to hammer him with questions about the ring and the lynching and their possible connection. And see just what kind of reaction he would get.

"I'm thinking, Sheriff, that these murders and the ring are connected."

Lauters licked his lips. "If you think that you're just a damn stupid breed like I thought all along."

"I wanna know about the Gang of Ten."

Lauters' colorless face was touched with red now. "About all you're going to know is a bullet in the belly if you don't get out of my way."

Longtree ignored him. "I've been hearing talk that these rustlers might be mixed up in a lynching a year back."

"Out of my way, you sonofabitch." Lauters' eyes were bulging now.

"Folks are saying you might know more than you're telling."

Lauters' hand was on the butt of his gun. "You little—"

"Why'd you send your deputy away that night?"

Lauters was trembling. "Shut up! Shut up or I'll kill you! I swear to God I will!"

Longtree had to suppress a grin now. Not because he liked any of this, but because he was pushing Lauters' buttons and the man was reacting accordingly. He had been a lawman for too long not to see that the sheriff was hiding a few things.

Then the ultimate question: "Were you involved with the rustlers?"

Lauters took one step forward. "You're a dead man, Marshal…"

Longtree pulled his coat aside so the pistol on his right hip was exposed. It wasn't a threat, just a warning. "If you're planning to shoot me, Sheriff, you'd best think again."

Lauters glared at him. There was a tic now in his lower lip. His huge hand was shaking on the butt of his Colt.

Longtree stood his ground. "Go ahead, Sheriff, slap that leather. If this is how you deal with your problems, then I guess all my questions have been answered, haven't they?"

Lauters made to turn away, then he launched himself at the marshal. Longtree was caught off guard. Lauters' fist caught him upside the head and he went down.

"Big mistake," Longtree said.

Lauters yelled something and reached down for Longtree. Longtree went back on his elbows and thrust out with his leg, catching the sheriff in the stomach with his boot. Lauters staggered back, but didn't go down. It was enough of a diversion to allow Longtree to get to his feet.

The sheriff came at him, spit running down his chin. "I'm going to kill you, breed! With my bare hands!"

Lauters swung roundhouse and Longtree dodged the blow, coming back instantly with two straight jabs to the face. Lauters fell back, looking shocked, blood running from his nose. With a war cry, he came on again, his punches wild. Longtree kneed him in the midsection, blocked a punch with his left and took another fist on the ear, spilling him sideways.

"All right, you injun bastard, now you're going to get yours," Lauters said, wading in again.

Longtree ducked two more roundhouse blows and smashed Lauters in the face with three lightning quick left jabs, followed by an upper cut that snapped the sheriff's face skyward and sent his hat pinwheeling through the air. Longtree kicked him in the stomach and spun around delivering an elbow to the bleeding wreck of his nose. Lauters went down on one knee, coughing and gasping, arms cradling his belly.

"You want some more?" the marshal asked him.

Lauters shook his head slowly and then drew his gun.

Longtree saw it coming, but there was no time to draw his own weapon. He threw himself sideways just as Lauters' Colt barked. The bullet ripped across Longtree's ribs with a raw and real explosion of pain that made black dots dance before his eyes. He hit the ground, clenching his teeth, unable to draw.

Lauters took aim, his face smeared with blood, his eyes rolling in their red-rimmed sockets.

"SHERIFF!" Bowes screamed from the door. "DROP IT!"

Lauters looked like some wild, insane thing. One of his eyes was swollen nearly closed and his face was painted up with streaks of red. He was puffy and red and panting. He looked from Bowes to Longtree, muttering under his breath.

"For the love of Christ, Sheriff!" Bowes said, pulling his own iron. "Drop it! Drop it now! You can't shoot a man who hasn't drawn...it's murder!"

Lauters grimaced. "I'm gonna kill that redskin bastard!"

Bowes kept his pistol on Lauters. "Please, Sheriff...*Bill*, for goddsake drop it! I don't wanna shoot you!"

"Injun...just a goddamn half-breed—"

"He's a deputy United States Marshal, Sheriff! You'll hang!"

Lauters cursed and spat, dropping his gun. "Look what he did to me, goddammit!" Lauters cried. "Look what he did!"

Longtree moaned and sat up. "I came...to ask him questions...he attacked me...I only defended myself..."

Bowes helped him up. "All right, the both of you, we're going to see the doc. And I don't want any trouble."

"Your time's coming, breed," Lauters said, marching ahead of them.

Longtree swore at him.

"Shut up," Bowes said through clenched teeth. "The both of you."

32

Later, in the jailhouse, Bowes looked disgusted. "It ain't safe to have you two in the same town together," he said. "I stopped it today, Marshal, but tomorrow…"

Longtree took a drag from his cigarette. "He's out of control and you know it."

"Don't you tell me what I know!" Bowes slapped a hand flat on the desk and ground his teeth together. "I can't have this, Longtree, you know I can't. Goddamn, I've got enough trouble without nursemaiding the two of you. This fucking town is like one big cauldron of shit cooking up hot and filthy. It's gonna boil over, goddammit. See if it don't."

Longtree sighed and placed a hand lightly against his ribs. They hurt considerably, but the wound wasn't serious. Lauters' bullet had cut a trench there, but did no real damage. Longtree had been shot before and knew from experience that flesh wounds were often no less painful than taking a bullet in the belly.

"I'd get the hell out of here if I could," Longtree told him, "but it's not that simple. Not now."

"What are you getting at?"

"Do you really want to know?"

Bowes stared at him. "I wouldn't ask if I didn't."

Longtree butted his smoke and rested his hands in his lap. "All right, I'll tell you. Lauters flew into an absolute rage when I asked him about the rustlers, about the lynching—"

"Do you blame him, man? He took a lot of heat about that." Bowes shook his head. "This town went crazy. It's something we'd all soon as forget."

Longtree nodded. "I understand that, Deputy. But why did he fly off the handle about the rustlers?"

"Same reason," Bowes said, as if it was all-too evident. "He's taken heat about that, too. He's never been able to stop the Gang of Ten."

"Do you think that's the reason?"

"I do."

Longtree said nothing. Bowes was unflinchingly loyal. You had to respect that in a man even when the loyalty in question was extended to a rat like Lauters.

"Those rustlers have always been a sore spot with the sheriff." Bowes looked unhappy as he said this. "He's done his damnedest to bring them in."

"Has he?"

Bowes lifted an eyebrow. "What do you mean by that?"

"You know damn well what I mean. Lauters is one of them."

"Bullshit!" Bowes cried. "Are you drunk, Marshal? He's a good...was a good lawman."

Longtree showed no emotion. "Even the best of us get corrupted."

"I don't wanna hear that crap, Mister, I just don't. The sheriff is not mixed up with the Gang of Ten."

"Or should you say Gang of Two?"

Bowes just stared across the desk, drumming his fingers.

"Yes, Gang of *Two,* Deputy. Because I think eight of their number have already been killed off. There's only two left."

Bowes stood up, getting himself a cup of coffee. "You think that all you want, Marshal, but I don't wanna hear it. Understand? If word gets around, Lauters *will* kill you. And I got enough trouble without the killing of a federal officer and the arrest of a man I've known for years."

"That's fine, Deputy," Longtree said. "Since we're on the subject, I got some more trouble for you."

Bowes sighed. "Yeah, I need that, Longtree. You're just a prize package, ain't you?"

"That bounty the sheriff posted," Longtree said, "it's drawn in someone. A fellow by the name of Jacko Gantz. Bounty hunter. I had a little talk with him earlier. He's camped outside town."

"I don't see that as trouble."

"Ten years ago *I* was a bounty hunter, Deputy. I took Gantz in. He spent a stretch in prison. He holds a grudge against me." Longtree explained the rest and what had happened in Gantz' camp that afternoon.

"Well, you just got friends everywhere, don't you?"

Longtree smiled thinly. "The point being, Deputy, that if I was to turn up missing, you know where to start looking."

Bowes laughed. "You're wrong there, Marshal. Lots of men want you dead."

Longtree couldn't argue with that. He had a way of making serious enemies whichever way he turned. But Lauters...Christ, he topped the list. Tom Rivers had said he was an ignorant, violent bastard, but that didn't even begin to tell the story. Longtree figured if he somehow managed to get his scrawny ass out of this particular mousetrap, he was going to have something to say to Tom Rivers. And most of it would be of the four-letter variety.

"I'm just making you aware of what could happen," Longtree said. "Gantz is a killer and he's gonna try for me. Believe that."

Bowes looked disgusted. "And let me guess, you're gonna sit on your ass and wait for him."

Longtree smiled.

And outside, Lauters slipped away, his ear cold from being pressed against the seam of the window.

He knew all he needed to know.

33

It was night by the time Lauters made it out to Jacko Gantz' encampment. He saw much the same things Longtree had—the wagon, the traps and pelts, the rifles, the army tent. There was a smell of coffee and roasted meat in the air. Lauters tethered his horse to the wagon and went to the fire.

"Anyone about?" he called out.

He closed his eyes and winced. Talking above a whisper made him wince. Longtree had put the boot in on him but good. He was sore everywhere. His nose was bandaged. It had been broken and Doc Perry had to twist it back into shape. Lauters had never known such pain. Once, he'd tracked a Cheyenne horse thief up into the Tobacco Root Mountains and had gotten a bullet in his belly out of the deal. He'd had to dig the bullet out with his knife and even that hadn't been quite so painful.

Goddamn Longtree.

Goddamn half-breed sonofabitch.

"Who're you?" a voice called from the darkness.

Lauters didn't turn. "Lauters. Sheriff of Wolf Creek."

"What the hell do you want? I ain't done nothing."

"I know. I just wanna talk a spell with you. That's all."

Gantz sat across from him at the fire. He was a big, bearded man with dark eyes. "There was another lawman here," Gantz spat.

"Longtree?"

Gantz nodded.

"Well, he ain't the law around here—I am. Don't you pay no mind to what that breed says, Gantz."

Gantz smiled. "You know my name?"

"Word travels fast. I heard Longtree talking to my deputy about you."

Gantz spat a stream of tobacco juice into the fire. It sizzled. "Yeah, well, I was just minding my own business, Sheriff. That bastard hit me with his gun for no good reason."

"I don't doubt it a bit. What's the story between you two?"

Gantz, sensing he had an ally here, told the sheriff in detail. His version was a bit different than the one Lauters had heard Longtree tell. "He's a sadistic bastard, Sheriff. I wasn't exactly a law abiding citizen…but he didn't have to shoot me."

Lauters touched his nose. "I know what he's like, just like I know he hides behind that badge and the U.S. Government."

"He do that to you, Sheriff?"

Lauters nodded. "He did."

Gantz' eyes narrowed. "He's a rough one, that Longtree. How well I know that. He's fast with an iron and faster with his fists. He was a scout for the army, you know that?"

Lauters shook his head.

"Pretty good one from what I hear. Not surprising with that Crow blood in him. I heard tell he was a fighter out in San Fran before turning bounty hunter and lawman."

Lauters didn't doubt this. There were few men he couldn't lick, but Longtree fought like a possessed man. "A professional, eh?"

"Yep. Back in the early sixties. They called him Kid Crow out there. He barefisted with some of the best, made a roll of cash I heard. Went ten rounds with Jimmy Elliot, I'm told. Got his plow cleaned pretty good, but he held up."

Lauters took this all in. "He's trouble, Gantz. We gotta get rid of him."

"A federal marshal?"

"Don't matter," Lauters explained. "Like I said, I'm the law around here. If a man was to say, shoot him in the back, there'd be no questions asked. And there might be some money to be had for the man who did it."

"Keep talking, Sheriff, you interest me…"

34

"Strange him not being around, wouldn't you say, Bill?"

Lauters was at Dr. Perry's house. After he struck his deal with the devil, he rode back into town and stopped by Perry's for some dinner and conversation. The dinner was good—smoked ham, roasted potatoes, apple pie—but the conversation was lacking.

"Everything about Claussen is strange to me," he said, lighting one of the doctor's cigars. "If he ran off it suits me just fine."

Perry stroked his mustache. "But did he? That's the question."

"What're you getting at, Doc?"

Perry licked his lips, thinking it out carefully before speaking. "You rushed out of here this afternoon saying you were going to take care of him. Remember? And now no one can find him. Claussen's not one to miss services. He takes his religion a might serious, if you know what I mean."

"Are you saying I had something to do with it?"

"Did you?"

Lauters frowned. "Goddammit, Doc, what do you think I did, kill him?"

Perry sat back in his chair, staring at the darkness outside the window. "I hope not, Bill, I truly do. But when you left here today you looked, well, like a man capable of just about anything."

"I didn't kill him," Lauters maintained.

Perry looked at him with steely eyes. "Then what *did* you do?"

35

Longtree and Bowes rode up into the hills at an almost leisurely pace. They moved quietly, trying to stay in the shadows. To be caught on Blackfoot lands like this would not have been good. They paused in a thicket to make sure they were alone.

"What in Christ made you come out here on a dare?" Longtree said.

Bowes just shook his head. "I don't know…young…stupid…who can say?"

"What happened?"

Bowes' face looked to be cut from bloodless stone in the wan moonlight. But you could see his eyes and they were wide and unblinking. "I was ten years old at the time. Couple of the local kids talked me into it and I felt I had to prove myself. Now, you know Crazytail—he's not a bad sort, you can deal with him, anyway. But his old man? Shit, he was a real spook. They called him Ghost Hand and the name fit. He was a big shot Blackfoot medicine man and folks around here, both white and red, were scared of him. He was our local bogeyman. You grew up around these parts, you were spoon-fed stories about him. Crazy stuff, sure. They said he once put himself in a trance that lasted for six weeks. That he did it another time for twice that long and they even buried him and one night he came walking back into Wolf Creek like Lazarus, thin as a skeleton, his face all white like death and his eyes like silver moons, dirt and roots still clinging to him. Our local minister at the time was the first to see him. He screamed, they said, fell right off his horse and broke his leg. The whole town thought Ghost Hand had come back from the dead and, who knows, maybe he did.

"They said he could pull down the stars and create storms and winds with a single thought. That he could blight your crops and call up devils to tear your head off if he didn't like you. All sorts of crazy shit like that, you know, like pulling rattlesnakes from his sleeves and conjuring up spirit warriors. That he spoke with wolves and hawks. Folks around here used to go see him when kin were sick and he'd brew up some herbs and weeds and crap and more often than not, the cure would work. He could sort through the innards of a buffalo calf and tell you if the hunt would be successful, if your cattle would get screw worm, if your crops were gonna die. They said he told a miner the day he would die and how…and it happened just like he said on the very day.

"You get the idea. I only saw him in the flesh once. He came into town with Crazytail and a few of the others to buy some provisions. He sat in the back of the wagon and I tried not to look at him, but I felt his eyes crawling over me like spiders. I turned and he was staring holes through me and those eyes, damn, like steel balls, like glass mirroring the sun. Those eyes caught and held you and they told you things, Marshal, showed you things. Told you that Ghost Hand knew all there was to know about you— all those things you didn't dare confess to nobody but yourself. He knew your nightmares and dreams, exactly what scared you. And all your dirty little secrets? Yeah, he was privy to them, too.

"Anyway, Ghost Hand had been dead maybe four, five months when I came up here. Damn. It was night and filthy black and the wind was howling and I could hear things moving in the darkness around me. And I swear to God I could hear footsteps crunching through the dry grass and voices whispering. I got up by Ghost Hand's grave and, Christ, I swear I saw him standing there all done up in his funeral finery—fur robes and beads and bones and his hair squirming around like worms and his eyes were yellow like a rattlesnake's by firelight and…shit, I was just a kid all worked up and all. I screamed and ran all the way home."

Longtree thought about it. He wasn't about to tell Bowes he'd been imagining things. The very quality of his voice was very convincing. It made Longtree's hackles rise. So he said: "Some of them shaman…they're pretty damn spooky."

"You have no idea," Bowes said and his voice was filled with dread.

36

"If we're caught here," Bowes said, "we're dead men."

Longtree nodded, saying nothing. They were in the foothills of the Tobacco Roots, in Blackfoot territory. They brought with them shovels, pickaxes, and enough extra ammunition to turn back the Sioux Nation.

They were taking no chances.

"You come here much?" Longtree asked.

"Just the once," the deputy admitted, "when I was a boy. On that dare...scared the life out of me. And I don't care for it much now."

The Blackfoot cemetery was located in between two forested ridges in a little, moon-washed valley of dead, clawing trees. This was sacred ground. This was where the Blackfoot buried their dead and had for countless centuries before white men walked this land. Longtree and Bowes were astride their horses in a copse of dark pines, waiting.

"You sure you want to do this?" Bowes asked one final time.

"Yes."

"Are you going to tell me what we're looking for?"

"In due time. Let's go."

Bowes nodded. "It won't matter if we're caught digging or not, just being here and being white is enough reason to be killed."

Longtree pulled his hat down over his brow. "Let's get it over with."

The moon brooded high in the hazy sky, illuminating everything, casting crazy, knife-edged shadows everywhere. A cool wind whistled out of the north, skirting the jagged peaks of the mountains.

They picketed their horses at the foot of a rock outcropping. If they had to get out fast, the horses would be hidden from view. Course, if they *had* to get out fast, it was unlikely they'd get out of this country at all.

Collecting their rifles, ammo belts, and digging tools, they started into the graveyard. Longtree wasn't sure what it was, but he had an awful feeling in the pit of his belly...a crawling apprehension. He had gone white and cold inside and something had pulled up tight in his belly. He could not adequately put a name to what he felt. It was a mixture of fear and anxiety and irrational terror. And it was very old. An ancient, primal network of horror.

They didn't belong here.

No living thing belonged here.

Longtree thought: *Imagination, that's all it is.*

But he didn't believe it for a second. No more than he'd believed it when he was caught in that sandstorm in Oklahoma Territory.

Bowes was pressed up close to him and when Longtree stopped, he bumped into him. "Quite a place, eh?" the deputy said, his voice thick like tar. "Anytime you've had enough, you let me know."

Longtree assured him that he would.

Despite the fact that the temperature was hovering just above freezing, there was a stink on the wind, like salts and spices and dry things locked in moldering cabinets. Longtree tried to swallow and couldn't...he didn't have any spit.

Certain they were alone, Bowes lit the lantern. It cast wild, leaping shadows over the graves and mounds. The wind began to pick up, sounding at times like cold, cackling laughter. Vines of mist tangled at their legs.

"Think you can find the grave?" Longtree asked.

"I can find the site," Bowes told him. "I know where Crazytail's people are buried...once you see it, you won't forget it. He's part of some society, some weird group. Something funny about it all, if you ask me. I came here on that dare just after sunset that time. And I saw, I saw—"

In the bleak, shivering distance, a wolf began to howl. It was a low, drawn-out, mournful baying.

Longtree's skin went cold. The back of his neck went rigid with gooseflesh. "Just a wolf," he said dryly.

Bowes licked his lips. "I surely hope so."

Longtree fed a cigarette into his mouth, lit it. Bowes joined him. They were in a bad place here and they needed very much to steel their nerves. Longtree was used to trouble, he fed off it like a leech off blood. He was not scared of it; it was part of who and what he was. But this...Jesus, this place...the atmosphere was simply noxious, rotten and pestiferous. He felt for sure they were not alone, that cold and malefic eyes scanned them from the mists. He couldn't seem to shake it. A hush had fallen over the surrounding hills and woods. Shadows rose up and paraded around them.

Longtree felt like he was carved from wood.

"You feel it don't you?" Bowes said.

"Yes."

The images of that burial ground at night were locked hard in Longtree's mind where, he supposed, they'd linger now forever, showing up in nightmares and at four in the morning when he jerked awake with the sweats. The moon gleamed sickly off the graves and cairns of stones, casting huge, nebulous shadows. Crooked, black trees rose up from the frozen, cracked ground, their skeletal limbs like dead fingers scratching at the sky. There were great towers of rock and broken slabs fringed with frost and carved with grotesque images of animals and nameless gods. They raged underfoot and climbed into the dismal sky. And everywhere, a strange mephitic odor of mold and rot.

"Can't say I like this place much," he said.

Bowes looked at him with a cold glare in his eyes and looked away.

There were bones everywhere, animal bones. The skeletal trees were decorated with them. Some were fresh, bleached white with bits of meat clinging to them, others gray and cracked with age. All were covered with frost. They were from large animals. Longtree saw a few horse skulls, half-buried in the uneven ground.

"Why the bones?" he asked.

"It's a custom with these people to kill the deceased's favorite horse upon burial of its master," Bowes pointed out. "Sort of a sacrifice, I guess. That and the Skull Society, maybe."

"Up there," Longtree said, gesturing to a low bluff crowded with dark shapes.

"That's the place," Bowes said.

The graves of Crazytail's clan were set on a long, low bluff of misshapen, craggy trees. Wooden frames—some new, some old, others impossibly ancient and crumbling—were set about, covered in tanned buffalo hides scrawled with drawings and weird letters.

Other frames carried the stretched and sunbleached hides of wolves. There were wooden staffs driven into the hard earth, decorated up with feathers, paint, and beads. On them were the skulls of wolves and men. Dozens and dozens of them. They were all yellowed, cracked, and ancient.

Bowes set the lantern down atop a cairn of stones. It was a recent piling. They didn't have the weathered, arid look of the others and they weren't covered in blankets of furry, winter-dead moss and fungus.

"My guess is Red Elk's under here," Bowes said.

Longtree, the tails of his coat flapping in the wind, said, "Let's take a look."

It took them about thirty minutes to remove the stones, most were frozen in place and only a good blow from a shovel would loosen them. Longtree then took the pickax and broke through the frozen ground. None of it was easy. The frost line went down a good ten inches and the earth splintered like flint with each blow.

"That's good," Bowes said. He took the shovel and carefully dug through the soft, sandy earth. "The Blackfeet don't bury their kin very deep. Shouldn't have to dig down," he grunted, "more than a few...feet."

When they caught sight of a flap of cloth, Bowes used his hands to clear away the soil. Red Elk had been wrapped in a blanket. Bowes, with what seemed genuine respect for the dead, gently pulled the blanket open. Beneath, there wasn't a body, but something that looked like a buffalo skin shroud, stitched up and painted with images of the sun and moon.

"We'll have to cut this open to take a look at him," Bowes said, like it was the last thing in the world he wanted to do.

Longtree kneeled next to the body, pulling his knife from its sheath. "Just one quick look," he said. He cut the buffalo sinew stitching as far down as where he figured Red Elk's waist would be. With one look at Bowes, he pulled back the skin shroud.

"Are you going to tell me what we're looking for now?" Bowes asked.

"You'll know it when you see it."

Red Elk had been buried in his finest. He wore a shirt of soft antelope skin and leggings of the same. Both were decorated up with dyed porcupine quills, feathers, beads, and little bells. The women who'd prepared him for burial, as was the custom, had painted up his face with intricate streaks of white clay and earthen yellows and blacks. A war club ornamented with eagle feathers was sewn up in the shroud with him, as were his tobacco pouch and medicine bundle, both of the softest unborn buffalo calfskin.

Longtree examined him minutely with aid of the lantern. His neck was twisted at an odd angle from the hanging and his skin had shriveled to a blotched brown that clung to the skull beneath. Beyond that, the cold and soil had stopped any real decay.

"Well?" Bowes asked impatiently.

Longtree covered Red Elk back up and wrapped the blanket over him. "Nothing. I'm relieved. Very, very, relieved."

"What did you expect to find?"

Longtree ignored the question and filled in the grave. Bowes helped him pile the rocks back in place. In a few days, after the frost settled back in, no one would know the grave had been tampered with.

"Look at this," Bowes said.

Longtree looked where he indicated. Another grave, an ancient one by the look of it, had been opened. Rocks were scattered aside. All that remained of the grave was a four-foot deep trench. But it was gigantic. Far too large for a man. You could've buried a horse in there. Maybe a couple of them.

"That grave was opened recently," Longtree said. He pawed in the trench with his shovel. "Empty. Now why do you suppose the body was carted away?"

Bowes shook his head.

Longtree took the lantern to another grave a few yards away. This one was particularly ornamented with skull poles and painted up hides on frames and slabs of rock covered with drawings and writings that were obscured by the years. There were no less than half a dozen human skulls here and twice that many of wolves. Some of the poles had fallen, the skulls shattering like brittle yellow porcelain. It looked to be very ancient.

"Who do you suppose is down there?" Longtree asked. "Ghost Hand?"

"No, he's farther up on the next hill."

"I'd say whoever it was must have been important."

Bowes licked his lips. "They're all important up here. All big, bad medicine men," he told Longtree. "But this one...shit, he's been in the ground a hundred years or more. Maybe twice that."

Longtree was thinking the very same thing. He wasn't sure why, but he was certain there was an answer up here somewhere. And this grave...it was so ornamented, so well-tended...it spoke to him.

He removed a stretched yellowed skin atop the cairn and it came apart in his fingers like candied glass. He began to loosen the stones with powerful swings of the pickax.

"I'm finished," Bowes said, throwing up his hands. "I wanna know what the hell this is all about."

Longtree kept working. "When we find it—if we find it—you'll know."

"Goddammit, Marshal, I'm risking my neck out here! Tell me what's going on or I'm riding out!" Bowes shook all over. Then, calmer, "Digging up Red Elk's one thing, but this one...Christ, he's been dead for centuries. What can he have to do with anything?"

"I hope nothing," Longtree panted.

Bowes spat. "Damn you, Longtree." He came over and started working.

It took them longer to take apart this cairn. Countless generations of rains, freezes, and baking summers had welded the rocks together as if they'd been mortared in place.

When they were done, both men had long since shed their coats, sweat steaming on their faces. A slab of rock was beneath the cairn. It was painted with things that were neither animals nor men. They had to use the shovel handles like levers to slide it free. And then they had to chop through the frost line and the hard packed earth beneath.

The wind had picked up considerably, howling out of the north. Wolf hides and moldering ceremonial blankets rustled and snapped on sagging willow frames. That wolf started up again in the distance, baying its ancient dirge. The pale moon looked down, piercing the grotesque, dancing shadows.

Longtree found the first tattered remains of something like a skin-tarp and the two of them cleared away dirt and rubble. The tarp came apart in their fingers, rotted and half-frozen.

"Christ," Bowes said, turning away, "that stink."

Longtree smelled it, too: A heavy, thick smell of decay and grave mold. An odor nothing dead for untold years had the right to possess. It was a black smell, a suffocating evil odor of slaughterhouses and disturbed graves.

"This ain't right," Bowes said in a weak voice.

The grave, once completely unearthed was huge. Gigantic.

The body was stitched up in a hide shroud, too, but blackened with age, covered in spots with mildew and damp gray fungi. And it was not buffalo skin. It had a smoother texture, very, very fine. Longtree suspected human skin, but didn't mention the fact. Whatever it was, given the size, it had taken a lot of pelts.

Longtree slit it open, not being too careful. His fingers were trembling. The baying of that wolf took on a high, shrill pitch. Swallowing, he pulled back the shroud. Bowes held the lantern.

"Jesus in Heaven," he muttered.

Longtree backed away, his skin cold and tight with gooseflesh. A nameless dark madness teased at his brain.

Whoever it had been...he wasn't human. *He was a giant.*

The head was huge and distorted, ridged with jutting bone and covered in a tight flaking gray skin that had burst open in spots like badly worn canvas. There were darker patches of mildew stitched into it. The heavy jaw was pushed outward like a flattened snout, the blackened gums set with irregular crooked teeth, sharp as spikes, fragmented and splintered. There were no eyes, just black yawning sockets, one of which was threaded with moss. Tufts of silver hair jutted from the obscene skull in irregular patches, blowing in the wind like strands of cornsilk.

Longtree just stared. There were no words to be said. A flat, clawing emptiness raged in his brain and he knew then what it was like to go insane, how sometimes madness was the lesser of two evils.

"It can't be, it can't be," Bowes kept saying over and over in a silly, defeated voice.

But it was.

Longtree kept looking. The cadaver had been interred in this unhallowed ground in a shroud of skin that had rotted to rags now, through which protruding bone and withered flesh could be seen. One skeletal hand was thrown over the chest, the fingers covered in parchment skin and ending in hooked claws. There were only four fingers on that hand and they were easily twelve or fourteen inches from knuckle to nail tip. Big enough to palm a man's head. The giant also had a tail wrapped around it, a bony thing that looked oddly like vertebrae.

One of the fingers moved.

"Jesus," Bowes whispered, "bury it! For the love of God, bury it!"

Longtree turned away from the horror in the grave. This is what he'd been looking for, what he knew they must find, but in finding it, the revelation was simply too much. He listened to the wind howling, the wolf baying, and could feel the sickly light of the moon on his skin.

It wasn't human, whatever it was. Not in the least. Just a mummy of some ghoulish, perverse tribe, some nameless monster far larger than a man and twice as wicked.

Skullhead.

Yes, of course. Its body was skeletal and chitenous, the head like a huge misshapen skull. It all fit.

Bowes' eyes suddenly went wide and he stumbled back and fell. He was pointing and muttering gibberish, drool coursing down his chin.

"What—" Longtree began, but by then he knew.

A huge and hideous shadow fell over him with the icy kiss of tombs. He heard something like old, dehydrated kindling snapping and popping. The wind carried a musty stink of old bones and wormy shrouds.

He turned and saw what he knew he would. A warm wetness spread in his belly, his head was full of noise. His lips opened and he could draw no breath.

The thing was standing up in the grave, a decayed scarecrow with a grinning, crumbling skull for a head. Its mummified skins flapped in the wind. The jaws parted with a groaning click, a hissing, reptilian noise issuing from the collapsed throat. It stood seven feet if it stood an inch. That tail—like the spinal column of an animal, all spines and bony ribs—whipped around it and thudded against the ground.

Longtree couldn't move, he was paralyzed.

Bowes fumbled for his gun and drew it, his hands trembling so badly he couldn't hold it still. The first shot ripped apart the stagnant night with a thundering explosion, the bullet whistling past its target.

The dead thing shambled over to Longtree, a discordant, bellowing howl rising from its throat and echoing through the burial ground. One atrophied claw snatched at Longtree's hair, yanking his head back, as the bobbing skullish face went in for the kill. The shriveled lips drew back a good inch from hooked, yellow teeth and festered gums.

The next two shots found their marks.

The first took the top of the ghoul's head off in a spray of dust and filth. The second punched in its chest, dirt and sandy fragments blasting from the wound. The jaws opened with a great whining squeal, a cheated sound, the desiccated flesh of the face splitting open with a series of fanning cracks from the stress. It released Longtree, staggering back, more bullets opening it up in more places.

By then, Longtree was on his feet, a shovel in his fist. When he heard Bowes' gun click again and again on an empty chamber, he launched himself at the monster, swinging the shovel like a club. The blade bit into the ghoul's throat and cleaved its head free with the sound of roots being yanked from the ground. The ruined head spun back into the grave. For a few moments, the headless monstrosity stood there, its knotted fingers clawing at the air. Then it went still and fell straight as a plank to the ground, striking with a cloud of dust. It was nothing more than a heap of brittle, broken bones and filthy rags now. There was no life nor semblance of the same.

It was some time before Longtree moved and when he did, it was slowly. He turned from the moldering wreck and went to Bowes. Bowes wasn't moving, just staring with unblinking eyes. Longtree put a hand on his shoulder and Bowes slapped it away.

"Don't touch me, by God," he snapped. "Don't you dare."

"Easy, Depu—"

"Don't touch me, dammit!"

Gently, Longtree said, "Let's bury that thing and get out of here."

Bowes shook his head. "I can't...I can't move."

"Then stay here and I'll do it."

It took Longtree some time to fill in the grave and pile the stones. When it was done, he helped Bowes to his feet.

"What was that?" the deputy inquired.

Longtree looked away towards the mountain. "It's the patron saint of the Skull Society. The same kind of thing that's killing people in your town."

37

Later.

It was nearly two in the morning by the time Longtree made it back to his little camp in the sheltered arroyo. Bowes and he had made it out of Blackfoot country without any trouble. Even the shots fired had brought no attention. They both ate and had baths drawn for them at Bowes' house. If nothing else, this unknotted Longtree's muscles—none of which were feeling too good after hours spent digging in the frozen graveyard. And to add insult to injury, all the exertion made the bullet wound on his ribs ache all the more. Afterwards, he rode back to his camp and found Laughing Moonwind waiting for him. He knew someone was waiting long before he got there—a fire was blazing and he saw the smoke from a long way out. He was glad not to find Gantz or Lauters waiting in ambush. But had they been, it was unlikely a fire would have been lit.

"Have you been here long?" he asked her.

"Yes. I was waiting for you."

Longtree sat next to the fire and warmed himself. She had made coffee and he helped himself to a cup.

"Word has reached me," she said, "that you have made dangerous enemies."

"You don't miss much, do you?"

She brushed a strand of hair from her eyes. "It's not my way."

Longtree rolled a cigarette and lit it with an ember from the fire. "I seem to make enemies wherever I go."

"I think that is your way."

Longtree laughed dryly. "You could say that. No one seems to like the law and I doubt they ever will."

"Sheriff Lauters is a dangerous man to cross, Joseph Longtree," she said, showing little concern. She was simply stating a fact. "I heard you were shot today."

"Just grazed."

"Soon, you will have worse enemies than Lauters."

He scratched his unshaven chin. "How so?"

"The Skull Society knows of you and what you're doing."

"I'm no threat to them."

"But you are. You are here to stop the killings and you might have to stop them in order to do it."

He smiled grimly. "You still hanging on to that Skullhead business?"

She just looked at him with all the knowledge in the world. "I think you know better."

Longtree kissed her on the mouth and told her where he'd been and what he'd done and what he'd seen. She didn't seem surprised by any of it, merely unhappy with him for going to the burial ground in the first place.

"You visited sacred ground," she said in a low voice. "You desecrated my brother's grave. I should kill you. If I was a good *Piegan*, I probably would."

"But you won't."

She shrugged. "But how do you know I won't tell others of what you've done? That you won't be killed as an act of revenge for this sacrilege?"

Longtree took a slow drag off his cigarette. "Because you won't say a thing. If you do, I'll be killed. And if I'm killed I'll never sort out what *really* happened to your brother...and I'm probably the only man who can."

Moonwind allowed herself a thin smile, her dark eyes sparkled in the firelight. "You're right. My brother's honor is more important than any burial ground. Regardless, you committed a blasphemy in doing what you did."

Longtree glared at her. "That thing would have killed me."

"That thing was a *god.*"

Longtree smoked in silence now. God or not, that horror from the grave was nothing remotely human. It was a demon. No more, no less. The dead didn't walk. This was an established fact...or had been until tonight. He doubted there would ever be anything too far-fetched for him to believe again.

"You believe everything I've said," Longtree said. "Why? If anybody told me a tale like that, I'd laugh in their face."

Moonwind frowned. "That's the trouble with you whites— you think you know everything, that nothing exists or can exist that you have not seen or experienced. Well, now you know different. There are many things in this world outside your limited experience."

"Like dead things that walk?"

"It was a god as I have said. And it was not dead...merely waiting."

He sighed. "Bowes told me some stories about Ghost Hand."

"Ghost Hand was my grandfather, a great medicine man, a legend among our people," she explained. "I heard once that he brought a drowned man back to life, that a baby frozen two days lived again when he breathed life into it."

"What did you know about your grandfather?" Longtree asked.

"I knew he was a kind and gentle old man, little else. He died before I was born. He was a medicine man and a Skull Society member."

"And a shapeshifter?"

"Possibly."

"I think we can dispense with that. Skullhead is no man, shapeshifted or not."

"No, he is a god. But you weren't sure, were you?"

Longtree shrugged. "No, I wasn't. I had to be sure. I had to know what I was hunting. The truth, not double-talk. Red Elk was just a dead man when I examined him. He was no beast."

Longtree had been thinking long and hard about what he'd seen in that burial ground. He still didn't buy any of that business about Blood-Medicine, but that mummy *had* risen from the grave and it had been more beast than man. There was no getting around that; the impossible had happened. But whatever else he might believe, he would never accept that the creature he'd seen was even remotely human. Not even a medicine man could look like that.

"These are interesting tales we're swapping here, girl," he finally said. "Very interesting stuff about the Skull Society, Blood-Medicine, and your grandfather. But they're just tales, aren't they?"

"The Skull Society exists," she said angrily.

"Course they do. But do you really expect me to believe these men are changing themselves into monsters? What I saw was no human being. Want to tell me what it was?"

"It wasn't Blackfoot."

"I gathered that," Longtree said.

She fixed him with a steely glare. "This isn't something to joke about."

"Tell me."

She swallowed. "What you saw, Joseph Longtree, was something my people once worshipped. Something from the beginning of time. They were called the Lords of the High Wood. They were here before men."

"Before the Indians?"

"Before anyone." She pulled her robe tighter around herself. "You were digging in a sacred plot. The place where the last of the Lords were interred countless centuries ago."

"There was an empty grave—"

"And I think you know why. What was in there, now walks again."

"How?" he asked incredulously.

"The Skull Society once worshipped them, ages ago. They would have ways to resurrect them. I know nothing more."

"Don't you?"

She looked angry, mellowing then by degrees. "I commit a sacrilege against my ancestors. I hope they will forgive me. The white man tells us that the Blackfoot Confederacy has only been in this part of the world for three or four hundred years. But that is wrong. We have been here for untold millennia. Our oral traditions reach back thousands of years. Long ago, in what is called the Dark Days, our people came to these mountains. It was so very long ago that the mountains were hills. There were other mountain ranges then that are no more than foothills now. In the Dark Days, the Blackfoot came here following herds of beasts upon which they hunted. What they found was a huge forest, a gigantic forest that covered the world. The trees were so tall they touched the sky. And beneath those trees, in the sacred groves and hollows, there was darkness and shadow in which many strange creatures lived. Tradition tells us our ancestors discovered the ruins of ancient cities of stone, all crumbled and collapsed. But these ruins and the dark woods beyond were the hunting grounds of the Skullheads. There were hundreds of them. They were known not only as the Skullheads, but as the Cannibal Giants, The Mountain Lords, Kings of the Hunt, the Eaters of Men.

"Our people made war with them, but the Skullheads were fierce, they were devil-warriors. The only way we were allowed to live and hunt in their forests and glens was by making sacrifice of our children. A dark practice administered by priests who were to become the Skull Society. It went on like this for many, many centuries.

"Eventually, the forests thinned, the swamps dried-up, sunlight penetrated the lairs of the Skullheads. The ruined cities were dust blown away by the winds. Things had changed. Our people grew numerous and strong, but the Skullheads weakened and died. By the time of the dog days, there were but a handful. And these were laid low by our medicine men, bound by the old ways, held and imprisoned. They were buried alive. But they never died. They could not know death as we do. They only waited as the centuries passed. Whenever our people were wronged, one of them was resurrected to dole out punishment, to seek justice. And this is all I know. There is only two or three of them now up in the burial ground. And one of those walks."

Longtree found it all compelling, a glimpse of prehistory, of the antediluvian world handed down for thousands of years from father to son, mother to daughter.

"Those ruins you spoke of," he said. "The cities—who built them?"

She shook her head. "They were dust long before the Blackfoot came, but the Skullheads did not build those cities, it was another race."

Longtree figured none of that really mattered. "The Skullhead who walks...it'll have to be destroyed."

"I wish you luck."

Longtree nodded. She said he would soon have bigger enemies than just Lauters. And what did that imply? Was this Lord of the High Wood going to come after him now? He put this to her.

"Possibly," she admitted. "If the Society learns you have opened the grave of one of their gods..."

He sighed. "Then I'd better get him before he gets me."

There was no more to be said.

Longtree pulled Moonwind to him and kissed her forcefully. She didn't refuse his advance, her strong arms pulled him closer and held him in a tight embrace. She pulled open her buffalo robe and pushed his lips onto her jutting breasts. Before the fire, he made love to her with his mouth, teasing out her secrets and passions with his lips and tongue. Then she did the same for him. When he entered her, he did it slowly with a gentle rocking motion, urging moans and cries from her. As he pushed into her harder, faster, her legs locked around his hips, she panted in his ear, whispering her desires, and biting at him tenderly. They were like two animals at the end, lost in the heat and need, swimming burning seas, their hips slamming together with raw hunger. The beast with two backs, as it was known.

When it was over, she said, "I am your woman now."

They held each other before the fire, their lips brushing in soft kisses and caresses. Moonwind stayed with him until just before dawn. When she left, she kissed him and rode off quietly, so as not to disturb his sleep.

With what came next, it was better she wasn't there.

38

Just before first light, Longtree heard a horse coming. He was half awake at the time and the slow trod of the horse's hoofs told him danger was near. Whoever was coming, they were coming very slowly. He worked himself quietly from his bedroll, donning his coat and strapping on his pistols.

The rider stopped just outside the weave of trees that ringed the little arroyo. The horse was tethered and the rider approached now on foot. He was being very quiet, pushing his booted feet down in the snow very slowly so as to make little sound.

But Longtree heard him, all right. He'd been a scout and he knew all the tricks of stealth—how to use them and how to know when someone else was using them. This fellow wasn't especially good. If he had been, he would've picketed his horse a half a mile away and come on foot, sneaking into camp to do whatever it was he'd come to do.

But he hadn't. Longtree decided he was no professional, much as he might have thought he was.

Longtree hid in the same outcropping of rocks he'd hid in the night Lauters and his posse had come. It was an excellent place to hide during the night, but now with day breaking...it was less than desirable. It was defendable, all right, but there was no escape route if things turned bad. Behind him was sheer rock rising twenty feet and much the same to either side. Longtree didn't like it. He always sought a place with cover and a backdoor to slip through if it came to that.

In the grainy, pre-dawn light, he saw the man ease through the trees into camp. He suspected it could only be Lauters or Gantz.

It was the latter.

Gantz carried a shotgun and pistols on either hip. There was no question as to why he'd come. He approached Longtree's bedroll cautiously and, when it was in plain sight, aimed the shotgun at it. Cursing, he lowered the barrel, realizing it was empty.

"Drop it, Jacko!" Longtree called out, knowing it was a mistake.

Gantz threw himself to the ground and fired in the direction of the marshal's voice. The blast loosened some debris over Longtree's head, but did no real damage. Longtree shot back, his own bullet kicking up snow and dirt inches from Gantz' head. Gantz rolled away behind a tree.

"Give it up, Jacko," Longtree called out, "before this gets any worse."

Gantz' only reply was another round from the shotgun that exploded more debris from the outcropping. Longtree didn't shoot back. He wasn't going to waste ammunition until he had a clear shot. This was about to become a lethal cat and mouse game, a waiting game. Longtree wasn't going to say anything else; let Gantz believe he'd been hit if the man was fool enough to think that.

"Throw out your weapons, Marshal," he said. "I just wanna talk..."

Somehow, Longtree didn't believe that.

He kept quiet and said nothing.

This affair could end only one way and both men knew it. If Gantz was taken alive he'd be going back to prison and he wouldn't let that happen. So, one of them had to die. It was an ugly situation. Gantz had the upper hand here. He was in the treeline and he could move around in there at will, under heavy cover, while Longtree could go nowhere. And there was nothing stopping him from slipping around the other side of the arroyo and shooting down on his nemesis. Nothing at all. But if Longtree tried to escape, there was no cover until he reached the trees. Easy pickings either way, it seemed.

It all depended on how smart Gantz was.

Longtree could see part of the man's elbow sticking out from behind the tree. At this distance, hitting it was unlikely, but worth a chance. At the very least, it might scare him out into the open for a split second...long enough to put a bullet in him.

Longtree took aim and squeezed the trigger.

The bullet missed its mark by a few inches, gouging free bark and making Gantz dart for fresh cover. The next bullet Longtree fired caught Gantz in the leg and solicited a howl of pain from him. It probably wasn't much more than a flesh wound, but it was something.

Within seconds after the bullet had hit, Longtree came charging from his hiding place, both pistols drawn and firing, slugs ripping apart the brush Gantz was hiding in.

But Gantz was no fool.

He saw what the marshal was doing and he wasn't about to let it happen.

Dragging his injured leg, he hobbled from the trees, bullets zinging past him, shotgun held out and firing. Longtree hit the dirt, feeling the first burst of buckshot scream over his head, the second erupt snow and dirt in his face. He rolled and came up firing. The first and second bullets punched holes in Gantz' stomach, blood gushing from the wounds. The third and final bullet ripped into his chest.

Gantz staggered forward, dropping the shotgun, trembling fingers reaching for the pistols at each hip. His bearded face was pale, compressed into a rictus of agony and hatred. He tried to speak, but blood sprayed from his mouth and froze on his beard. His gasping breath frosted in the air. He staggered and went down on one knee, his eyes rolling back white. With a final coughing, gagging wet gasp of air, he fell forward into the snow. His blood steamed in the chill temperature.

He was dead when Longtree reached him, the crunchy snow red with his fluids.

"Shit," Longtree said, flipping the dead man over with his boot.

He'd wanted very much to take Gantz alive. He wanted to ask him why he'd let this happen, why he'd been pushed into such action. These were questions Longtree never tired of asking and the answers were often less than satisfying. But he always asked them, good or bad.

With a sigh, Longtree turned away.

He'd killed more men in his time than he liked to think about. And each time, death left him feeling the same—empty, hopeless, physically ill. There was never anything to be gained from violent death, only pain and suffering and guilt. But that was the way of this land; it respected nothing else.

He went up into the treeline and retrieved Gantz' horse. He slung the dead man over the saddle and roped a blanket over him. That done, he broke camp and packed up all his things and led Gantz' horse into town.

He wouldn't be coming back here again. Tonight he would stay in town and every night after. Next time when a gunman came after him, he might not be so lucky.

But, ultimately, it wasn't men that worried him.

39

"You should've known better than to be up there," Sheriff Lauters said to Bowes. "You should've known better than to listen to that damn breed."

Bowes hung his head. "That's not important, Sheriff. Because what happened up there—"

"Enough!" Lauters snapped. "I ain't listening to your goddamn ghost stories no longer. *Christ,* Deputy! What's come over you? Before this you were the most level-headed man I knew!"

"I saw what I saw."

Lauters sighed and popped the cork from a fresh bottle of rye. He upended it and gulped, stopping only when he began to cough and gag. "I don't know," he gasped, "what you and that marshal are up to, but it had better stop. Monsters rising from the grave...*shit!"* He pulled off the bottle again, his hands shook and he made gagging sounds, as if he could barely hold the liquor down.

"I'm sorry, Sheriff, that you think I'm a liar, but I saw what I saw. And the last thing I'm going to say on the matter is that these murders are more than we can handle."

"This country can't throw anything at me I can't handle," Lauters insisted. "Not a goddamn thing."

There was a blast of cool air and both men turned to see Longtree standing in the door. "Nothing a bottle can't help you with, eh, Sheriff?"

"You sonofabitch," Lauters growled, his hand sliding down to his gun. "You started all this mess, you—"

"I wouldn't draw that unless you wanna die," Longtree said calmly. "Never met a drunk in my life I couldn't outdraw."

Lauters hand stopped. "You threatening me, breed?"

"No, sir, I'm warning you. I'm warning you that if you ever again try anything as stupid as you did yesterday, I'll fucking kill you. And be within my rights."

Lauters clenched his teeth. "Maybe we ought to settle this out back."

Longtree opened his coat, fingers tapping the butt of one of his Colts. "If you've got the stomach for it, Sheriff."

"All right now," Bowes said, stepping between them. "None of that here. You're both lawmen and you're both doing the same job, so knock it off."

"What do you want here, Longtree?" the sheriff asked.

"A fellow by the name of Jacko Gantz tried to kill me today," Longtree announced.

Lauters just stared, his eyes bulging. A touch of color spread into his cheeks, then fled. He said nothing. He touched his tongue against his lips.

"That's the fellah you were telling me about, wasn't it?" Bowes asked.

Longtree nodded. "His body's outside."

Lauters licked his lips. "You killed him?"

"He didn't give me much choice."

Lauters pushed past him and went outside.

"If I didn't know better," Longtree said, "I'd think the sheriff was disappointed Gantz didn't succeed."

40

There was a light, cool mist in the air by the time Lauters made it out to Mike Ryan's ranch. Ryan had one of the largest ranches outside Wolf Creek and he was, without a doubt, the richest man in that part of Montana Territory. He had some seven hundred head of cattle at present and twice that amount in another ranch near Bannack. He owned several hotels in Nevada and Virginia Cities as well as a variety of dance halls, saloons, and gambling houses. He was a major stockholder in several copper and silver mining companies and sat on the board of directors at the Union Pacific Railroad.

Ryan was waiting for Lauters as he rode up.

"What happened, Mike?" Lauters asked.

"Hell broke loose, Bill."

Ryan had dispatched a rider to fetch the sheriff. At the time, Lauters was at Spence's undertaking parlor with Longtree and his deputy, having a look at the man Longtree had killed. He was glad to be called away. He had an ugly feeling Longtree knew damn well that he'd had something to do with Gantz' attack.

A ranch hand brought the two men mugs of steaming coffee as they walked through the grounds. The ranch was like a little city. Ryan's huge white house sat serene and omnipotent on a hill overlooking everything, its great carved pillars and fancy latticework gleaming in the weak sunlight. Below, was a sprawl of buildings—bunkhouses for the men, livery barns, log barns, outbuildings, a fine insulated ice house set in a low hill, a smithy's shop, a cookhouse twice the size of Lauters' home, and an intricate network of working corrals stretching off towards the horizon.

It was all very impressive.

"Tell me what's been happening in this town, Bill," Ryan said. Ryan had only arrived back in Wolf Creek the day before after some six weeks spent touring his various holdings.

Lauters laid it all out for him. About the killings and the inhuman nature of them, putting special emphasis on *who* the murdered men were. He spoke of Longtree and Bowes and the death of Gantz.

"That injun's gonna be trouble, I take it?" Ryan said.

"More than you can imagine, Mike."

Ryan nodded. "A federal officer, too. That could make things difficult for us. He's not some sodbuster no one will miss."

Lauters nodded, knowing this all too well.

"But every problem has its solutions." Ryan said this with total conviction.

They came to a corral near the house and Lauters saw the reason he'd been called...or one of them. This was where Ryan kept his racing horses. These animals had been, once upon a time, his pride and joy, but now...now they were so much meat. Lauters was looking at the slaughtered remains of some five thoroughbred horses. They had all been disemboweled and decapitated, the flesh stripped down to muscle, the hides ripped free and draped on the fence. They were partially eaten, but food didn't seem to be the primary reason for this carnage. The heads lay in the frozen mud, staring up with bulging eyes.

"I loved these animals," Ryan said calmly. "I truly did. Much as a man like myself *can* love. Whatever did this…is as good as dead."

"Looks like the work of an animal, but…"

"But with a man's twisted intelligence behind it," Ryan interrupted. "An animal will kill for food, to protect itself, but only a man kills for the sport of it. Only a man does something like this."

"Longtree's got it in his head that we're dealing with something that might be a little of both, so I hear."

"Tell me," Ryan said. He wasn't asking, he was demanding.

Lauters told him everything Bowes had said, even the bit about what they'd seen up at the burial ground. "A load of crap, if you ask me."

"Deputy Bowes doesn't strike me as the sort of man who makes up tales."

"Yeah, but—"

"But nothing, Bill. Longtree might be a pain in the ass, but he's right about one thing—we've got ourselves a monster here."

Lauters just stared.

"Don't look at me like that, Sheriff," Ryan snapped. "The evidence speaks for itself. I was in Virginia City last night and…that *thing* must have come for me. When it couldn't get me, it got what I loved best—my horses. Tonight it'll probably come again, maybe for me, maybe for you."

Lauters swallowed. These were things he had thought about quite a bit, but had dismissed as fantasy. Hearing another man say them made it all that much harder to brush them aside.

Ryan turned away from the bitten, clawed horses. "It came last night…and no one heard a thing." He threw his mug of coffee into the snow. "I have nearly a hundred men here, Bill, and no one heard a goddamn thing. I've heard horses die, I've heard the sounds they make when a hungry wolf pack sets on them…it carries for quite a distance. Anything that can slaughter five horses and do it silently, is no mere animal, no man."

Lauters looked skeptical. "But a monster…"

"Look," Ryan said, leading the sheriff into the corral. There were prints in the mud and snow. "It was warm last night. Our beast left tracks that froze hard this morning."

Lauters examined them carefully. The prints were huge, splayed out. Exactly like the ones in Nate Segaris' house: immense, unnatural, triple-toed like a lizard with a thick spur in the back.

"Physical evidence, Sheriff. We need no more proof." Ryan crossed his arms and glared at the mountains in the distance. "Eight men are dead, Bill, and not just any eight men. I don't have to tell you what you and I and those men have in common, now do I? This creature is killing selectively, very selectively. And, if my memory serves me, exactly one year since that injun was lynched."

Lauters shook his head. "This is all crazy."

"Yes, it is," Ryan admitted, "but it's happening all the same. That injun was lynched and now his people have called up something to take revenge."

Lauters looked beaten. "What can we do?"

"First, we take care of Longtree."

"How? Hire gunmen?"

Ryan shook his head. "No, this is something you and I have to do. We don't want anyone to wag their tongues about this down the road. We take care of that marshal tonight and plant him somewhere he'll never be found." Ryan grinned. "And then we'll take care of Red Elk's clan."

Lauters looked suspicious. "We'll need a lot of men."

"I have thirty men right here that have done jobs for me in the past, all of them handy with guns. I can raise another thirty from the mining camps, men who need money and are just looking for a reason to spill injun blood."

Lauters nodded. "Tonight, then."

"Your man Gantz failed, Sheriff, but I guarantee you, we will not."

41

Longtree was with Moonwind again at the Blackfoot camp. They were in the lodge of Herbert Crazytail. Longtree rode into camp and requested a meeting with the old man. And after some wait, it had been granted.

"My father says you are wasting your time," Moonwind translated.

Longtree was a stubborn man and he fully intended to get what he came after: answers. He didn't bother bowing his head in respect to the medicine man, because he no longer had respect for him. Crazytail sat on a bed of dried grasses covered with buffalo hide and tended the fire. He was wrapped in a Hudson's Bay blanket, his right arm and shoulder uncovered. Strips of buffalo meat were cooking on wooden spits. He was gnawing on bits of pemmican.

"Tell your father to stop the Skullhead," Longtree said. "If the killings continue, soldiers will come. His people may be killed."

It was a lie, but neither the old man nor his daughter knew it.

Crazytail turned the spits in the fire, mumbling something.

Moonwind said, "It is too late. What has been set into motion cannot be stopped. Even soldiers cannot stop the Skullhead. He has been called."

"Who called him?" Longtree asked pointedly.

Moonwind translated, but the old man just shook his head.

"I don't think he wishes to talk any longer," Moonwind said.

"He doesn't have a choice," Longtree said, getting angry. "If these killings aren't stopped, soldiers will come and your people will be killed. Those that aren't will be taken off to prisons and distant reservations. They will never see this land again. Tell him that."

Moonwind, sighing, did so.

For the first time since his arrival, Crazytail looked at the marshal. There was hatred in his eyes, the hatred of an entire race. He began talking loudly now, jabbing his finger at Longtree.

"He says our people have a right to vengeance, we have been wronged. The whites must be taught a lesson." Moonwind cleared her throat. "He also says he is sorry you have involved yourself in this, that you will die also. He says if you are wise, you will leave this place before night falls. The Skullhead will not stop killing."

"Tell Crazytail that I want to know where the Skullhead is. I can stop him."

Moonwind translated. "He says no man can stop what has been set into motion. Once the Skullhead is called, he cannot be put down."

Crazytail, the fire reflected in his narrow eyes, began speaking again.

"After the guilty ones are killed," Moonwind translated, "the Skullhead will begin killing indiscriminately. So we have nothing to fear from the soldiers, for the Skullhead will take us all as sacrifices. Our fate is sealed."

"And after you've all died in vain," Longtree said, "then what?"

Moonwind, looking very unhappy, translated: "Then the Skullhead will go down into the town of the whites and kill everyone."

PART 3: LORD OF THE HIGH WOOD

1

Longtree had himself a room now at the Serenity Hotel in Wolf Creek. It wasn't much, but the bed was comfortable and there was a livery stable across the street for his black. There was a saloon just off the lobby and the food wasn't bad. The door bolted from the inside and the window was painted shut; it was very unlikely anyone could sneak up on him whilst he slept. And while he was awake, he didn't see that as a problem. All things considered, it beat the hell out of sleeping outside…particularly when there were men trying to kill you and maybe something worse. He enjoyed the outdoors, found it spiritually refreshing, but the white man in him often yearned for material comforts.

He got a pint of rum from the bar and lay on his bed, sipping from it. He'd come to Wolf Creek under order from Tom Rivers. As a special deputy U.S. Marshal, he had no actual territory to call his own. He was merely sent wherever Rivers thought he was needed, where his skills as a lawman and former scout and bounty hunter would come in handy.

And Rivers had thought Wolf Creek needed him.

But Longtree wasn't so sure.

There'd been nothing but trouble since he'd arrived—with Lauters, with Gantz. And even without those two, this entire situation was well out of his experience. As a bounty hunter and then lawman, he'd brought in nearly every man he'd been sent after. There were few who'd escaped Joe Longtree. He brought them in alive, dead, and nearly dead. He was a hunter of men and he played that hand well. There was no one better at it. He'd taken in murderers, robbers, renegade Indians, road agents, bootleggers, and even entire gangs in his time. He'd had some of the most vicious men (and women) in the west come at him with guns, knives, hatchets, clubs, even their bare hands. He'd been in a hundred near scrapes with death and escaped every time. Oh, he'd been shot several times, stabbed, beaten, and even hanged (that injury still pained him some, but he'd survived). As a scout, he'd even been tortured for three days after capture by a Cheyenne war party.

But this...this business was too much for even him.

It was a complicated affair. First, there was the Gang of Ten, the rustlers, of which he was pretty certain only two still lived and Lauters was one of them. He was sure of this now. He even suspected Lauters had something to do with Gantz trying to kill him...but there was no proof. The rustlers, Longtree was sure, had been found out by Red Elk and before the Blackfoot could speak his piece, he was blamed for the murder of that Carpenter girl. But Longtree didn't think Red Elk was guilt...one of the rustlers had been. Arresting Red Elk and then lynching him killed two birds with a single well-thrown stone: the real murderer could go free and Red Elk's tongue would be forever silenced. The rustlers were probably pretty proud of themselves at the time for how easily they'd covered their tracks...until a year later.

Longtree took another drink, the rum filling him with warmth.

And what had happened a year later? He wasn't entirely sure. The Blackfoot had sought revenge via the Skull Society which had called up some beast to kill the vigilantes. He wasn't sure what this beast was, not really. According to Moonwind, some primeval monster that had once been worshipped by the Skull Society centuries and centuries before. Bowes and he had seen something like it at the burial ground that night. But the one on the loose was no zombie, no hulking mummy, but a creature very much alive. Now Crazytail said that once the guilty parties were all killed, this Skullhead would continue killing. So who, Longtree wondered, were the real victims here? Red Elk and his people or all the innocents that would suffer because of the actions of a group of criminals and the resultant actions of some blood-hungry Indians?

There seemed to be only one course of action: find out who *all* the members of this Skull Society were and arrest them. One of them had to know where this beast was…and if not? Well, then more problems. But Longtree couldn't arrest any Indians on suspicion of something like this. The Indian Agent in the district would go crazy. What did you arrest them for? he'd ask. Because, Longtree would tell him, one of them is harboring a monster.

It was ludicrous.

There was, really, nothing he could do. Nothing at all. His only hopes were to find this beast and destroy it. And when that was done, he was putting Lauters under arrest, too. If he could convince Tom Rivers to issue the warrant, that was.

Longtree corked the bottle. Enough drinking. He strapped his guns on, donned his coat and hat, and left his room, 1873 Winchester .44 in hand. The sun was setting and the beast would be active again.

Time to kill it or be killed.

Outside, he got his horse, saddled it, and rode out of Wolf Creek. Crazytail had said the beast would come after him, too, and the marshal was inviting it to. He started riding up to the Blackfoot camp.

He'd been riding about twenty minutes when he heard galloping hooves. The light was fading fast and he was approaching a little ridge that marked the end of the little valley he was in. He swallowed down hard, knowing it was trouble, and one hand snaked down and slipped the Winchester from its boot.

Who would it be this time?

Lauters? Maybe someone he'd hired? Or maybe Blackfoot braves, out to stop him from nosing around.

He rode up out of the valley and followed a thin, hard-packed snow trail into a stand of pines. Here, he paused. He didn't hear a thing now. He hadn't been able to tell from which direction the rider had been coming, just that he was riding fast.

"Well, show yourself already," Longtree said under his breath.

He lit a cigar and got the black to moving again. Its pace was slow, barely a trot. Longtree's ears were attuned to every sound. He had a bad feeling suddenly, realizing that these trees and their shadowy depths were the perfect place to spring an ambush. He stopped.

There was a hint of movement off to his left.

Longtree threw himself off his horse just as shots were fired. The aim was poor, the bullets thudding into the branches overhead. The black trotted away up the trail, stopping a good distance away, as if knowing what was coming.

Longtree peeked his head out from behind the pine that covered him and there was a crack and a bullet whistled past his ear. He drew back and then darted out again, firing a few quick shots at where he thought the gunman was.

"You over there!" he called out. "I'm a United States Marshal! Throw down your weapon!"

A few more bullets bit into the pine.

I guess it's gotta be done the hard way then, he thought.

He tensed himself and dove to the cover of another tree. More bullets kicked up snow a few feet from him. He hadn't been able to tell from which direction the rider following him had been coming…but it wasn't from in front of him. Which meant there was another one out there, probably getting a bead on him right now. He almost laughed to himself at how slow he'd gotten through the years. The rider following him had forced him into these trees where the gunman was waiting. It was a simple strategy and one that Longtree should've recognized.

He heard sticks breaking on the rise above him. It could only be the rider.

Longtree didn't shoot; he waited. Waited for the assassin to get within visual range. His partner across the trail probably figured this out for he began to pepper Longtree's location with gunfire, trying to make him shoot, warning his partner.

Longtree smiled and waited.

He saw a gray form moving through the trees, down the rise. He couldn't see the man's face: he wore a black hood. Across the trail, the other gunman crept silently from his hiding place.

Longtree let him get close.

Or tried to. The man coming down the rise began shooting and there was nothing to do but return fire. Longtree clipped off a few shots, one of which knocked the hat from the gunman's head, the other went clear as he dove for cover. More bullets from across the trail ripped into the pines around the marshal. Longtree waited until this volley was over and fired two more bullets at the man on the rise and then leaped out from behind his tree, shooting at the other one. This guy wore a hood, too. He fired at Longtree and missed. Longtree shot back, hitting him in the arm. He let out a cry of pain and fell back, stumbling through the brush.

The gunman on the rise pulled back, firing a few bullets as he ran. They screamed harmlessly through the air. As dark settled in, the man on the rise was gone. Longtree heard the other moaning and plowing through the trees. A few seconds later, he heard horses riding off.

He ran down the trail and caught sight of two riders galloping back in the direction of Wolf Creek. One of which was hunched over in his saddle. The marshal figured he could've picked one of them off, but didn't bother.

There was no point.

One of them was winged and it wouldn't be too hard to find a man with a bullet in his arm.

Particularly when he was the sheriff.

2

An hour later, Mike Ryan was back at his ranch.

They'd failed; Longtree was still very much alive. That was bad. And what made it worse was that Lauters had taken a bullet in his gun arm. He'd be of no real use for some time…if he ever was again.

It was quiet at the ranch. Most of the men were over at the cookhouse eating or at the bunkhouses playing cards and snoozing. Ryan could hear a harmonica playing somewhere. It was a nice evening, not too cool.

There were men out riding the perimeters of Ryan's lands, twice the usual number, a good idea Ryan thought under the circumstances. And there were men down in the valley with the herds and half a dozen more walking the grounds. Nothing would come in tonight that wasn't supposed to be there.

He had put together an army of over sixty men that would ride at first light against the Blackfoot camp. That problem would be solved, but as for Longtree…that was another matter entirely. He had to be killed and soon. There wasn't enough time to bring in a professional killer and most of those wouldn't care too much to go after a federal marshal, particularly one with Longtree's reputation for cunning.

No, there was only one man for the job.

Ryan himself.

He considered himself a businessman, not a killer. He wasn't fast with a gun, but he was a good shot. Something he'd picked up in the sixties as a buffalo hunter. And he wouldn't need to be fast...he planned on shooting the marshal in the back. It was the way most professionals did it, he knew. Safe, sure. The accepted method.

But it had to be done tonight.

And doing it would mean leaving the security of the ranch.

That was dangerous. But it was equally as dangerous letting Longtree live. He knew the truth of who the rustlers were and who lynched that injun. It was only a matter of time before he obtained the proper warrants. Ryan was a powerful man and he could probably block said warrants for a time, but not forever, not without looking damn guilty.

He devised a plan.

He found one of the men on watch. Cal Shannon. Shannon was a good man, but he liked the wild life and this is what Ryan needed.

"Cal," he told him, "I need you to ride into Wolf Creek for me."

Shannon's eyes lit up. He knew he could stop for a drink and maybe a round of quick fun at Madame Tillie's. "But the watch..."

"I'll get another man."

"What do you need, sir?"

Ryan told him. He was to go see Wynona Spence, the undertaker, and check on the progress of the monument. Have Spence put in writing the progress she was making. Then he was to go to the Serenity Hotel and procure a case of their best champagne. After that, there were some dry goods needed. But before he did any of that, he was to track down Marshal Longtree and tell him to ride up to the ranch immediately. And after these things were done, he could spend the night as he chose. Ryan even slipped him some money.

"No hurry to come back in the morning," Ryan said. "Have a good time. You need a day off, I think."

Shannon hooked up a wagon immediately and rode off.

Ryan took his guns and rode off a few minutes after Shannon was gone. He found a good spot on the trail to spring his ambush. Then he waited. The spot he'd selected was a shelf of rock rising a good twenty feet above the ground. He could lay up there and shoot Longtree in the back as he rode by. There was no margin for error—if he didn't kill Longtree, Longtree would kill him. He had no doubt of that.

But there would be no error here.

Ryan had a Sharps 1875, .50 caliber. The "Big Fifty" as it was called, a buffalo gun. It could drop a bull with ease. No man would live if hit. And Longtree wouldn't live. It was dark, but the moon was full. Plenty of light to shoot and die by.

Ryan waited.

He figured, at best, it would take a good thirty or forty minutes before Longtree would arrive. He only hoped Shannon could find him. If he couldn't, this entire plan was doomed to failure. It would mean that Ryan would have to go into town himself and shoot the marshal and such an idea was ripe with dangers. But the cold fact remained: Joseph Longtree had to die.

There were no two ways about that.

Ryan wetted his lips and waited for his victim, knowing when the time came, he'd better be damn sure it was Longtree he was shooting and not someone else. The idea of murder didn't sit well with Ryan and if some innocent was killed by accident…no, that was unthinkable.

The wind began to pick up slightly. It was warm. A mere hint of heat to dispel the cold. It wasn't possible, he knew, but there it was blowing on him, driving the chill from his bones and starting a fire of madness in his brain.

It can't be, he told himself repeatedly, just can't be.

But it was. It seemed to burn hotter by the moment with an almost feverish heat. A trickle of sweat rolled down Ryan's temple, his shirt clung to his back, an obnoxious gassy smell filled his nose.

By God, what is this?

Then a shadow fell over him: huge and nameless.

3

Skullhead stood over Ryan, his skin crusted with sores, scant irregular patches of coarse gray fur blowing in the wind. A sickening warmth oozed from his skin in sheets. He'd slipped up the back of the rock outcropping Ryan laid on with a preternatural silence and now he stood at his full height, staring down at the former vigilante with bleeding eyes, his huge skeletal tail whipping like a serpent.

A suffocating stench issued from the beast's hide and it was this, more than anything, that often froze its victims in fear. He drew in sharp gasps of breath, his head reeling with savage appetite. His stomach growled. His tongue trembled fatly in his mouth.

His lips parted, a guttural bark ripping forth.

He shook his head, momentarily attempting to dislodge the hunger that burned in him like a fever dream. He clawed out for the intelligence to communicate, but it was denied him. Eat, his brain said, kill.

His huge misshapen skull was an architecture of bone knitted with poorly-fitting gray and pink skin, rubbed raw and infested with beetles and worms. He flinched each time one of these parasites worked at a strand of nerve.

Ryan moved then, as Skullhead knew he would. He brought up his weapon and pointed the long barrel at Skullhead's huge plated chest. Blinking his eyes, he pulled the trigger. The chamber explosion was deafening, noise beyond noise, but Skullhead had little time to be angered at this as a .50 caliber slug ripped through his chest and exploded out his back. He was thrown from the rocks, an agony that was at once sweet and numbing threading through his chest.

But more than pain, there was rage.

He scrambled back up the rocks with impossible speed. Ryan brought up his weapon and the beast knocked it from his hands with a single lethal blow. Ryan cowered: crying, whimpering.

Skullhead stood over him. Black blood and bile ran from the hole in his breast. His face was twisted up in a ragged sneer, yellow teeth protruding from the gums like knife blades. He was larger than any man, a giant, his arms longer, his skeletal fingers like sharpened stakes. He pressed his face in Ryan's own, enjoying the terror that it produced in the man—making his bladder and bowels void, his eyes roll madly in their sockets. Skullhead licked his cowering face with a spiny tongue, the taste of fear making his loins ache. He drew back his great, bobbing head, lips peeling back inches from slavering jaws.

One fleshless hand gripped Ryan, pulling him up. Skullhead towered over him by more than two feet. With a flick of his wrist, he sent Ryan tumbling through the air. No hurry in eating, a bit of play first.

4

Ryan was dazed when he pulled himself up, his right wrist bent in agony. Skullhead stood before him, bathing him in the acrid heat of his shadow. Ryan made to run and the beast snared him by the head with one immense hand, the fingers of which covered his face. Skullhead drew the spindly, rawboned fingers back, taking Ryan's scalp with them.

Ryan fell to his knees, his scalp hanging by a thread of meat, great furrows dug in his skull. Blood washed down into his eyes and he pushed it angrily away with shaking fingers. He knew he was going to die. There was no question of this; it was only a matter of when. His stomach convulsed at the commingled hot grave odor of the beast and his own rich, flowing blood. He tried to stand, bile squirting into his mouth, and the beast pulled him forward, so he could stare into the merciless face of death one more time.

Skullhead knew it had to be this way. Kill, but take time to savor the fear, to sip it like wine.

His face was huge in the grainy moonlight, the color of fresh cream, a tapestry of abraided flesh pitted with sores. And the eyes...crimson, slitted orbs sunk in bony, angular depressions.

Ryan studied this nightmare in detail. It gave him something other to think about than pain or death. He viewed the face like a map. Here were craters, there valleys, and there occasional matted growths of fur that grew in and out of the skin. The snout was pressed in, only vaguely vulpine, the nostrils flattened and wet, the teeth hooked like sickles.

Skullhead growled with a blast of hot, fetid breath and pulled Ryan's arms free with wet, rending snaps. He dropped the limbs and studied the horror on the man's face. It wasn't enough. He buried his claws in Ryan's groin and slit him up to the throat, marveling at the bounty of glistening jewels that bulged out. Ryan slumped and Skullhead caught him. He chewed his face free from the muscled housing of his skull and broke the dying man on the rocks, slamming him against them with titan force until Ryan came apart like a drenched and running rag doll.

Then and only then, did he dine.

5

Longtree lit a cigarette and exhaled in the wind. "Did he say what he wanted?"

"No, sir," Cal Shannon told him, "he just said how he wanted to see you right away. That it was important."

"I see."

"If you ask me, Marshal, something strange is going on up there. Mr. Ryan's got men walking guard, twice the number of riders with the herds...peculiar, if you ask me. Don't tell him how I said so, though."

"Course not."

"His race horses got slaughtered last night. Boys are saying how maybe it's that beast folks are talking about."

"Could be."

Shannon shrugged. "Anyway, he said to ride up there right away."

Longtree nodded. "I will. Thanks, Shannon."

Shannon jumped up on his wagon and rode off, leaving Longtree outside the livery barn alone. He never made it up to the Blackfoot camp. After the masked gunmen had attacked him and rode off, Longtree found his horse nearly a mile up the trail and returned to town. He'd been planning on searching out Lauters, but that could wait...the sheriff's wound wouldn't heal for some time.

6

By ten that night, the blizzard hit.

It had been threatening for days, finally arriving with screaming winds and blowing snow. About the time the first snowflakes fell, Skullhead was miles away from the scene of his crime, lurking around the outskirts of town. There was only one left now, he knew, and after that…well he decided, for reasons even unknown to himself, he would keep on killing. It was such good sport.

Longtree didn't let the snow deter him from his appointment with Ryan. He'd plowed through many a blizzard and now was hardly the time to cower behind doors. He rode and rode hard.

Sheriff Lauters was at Dr. Perry's getting a bullet dug out of his arm. Despite Perry's repeated questioning, he would say little save that someone had taken a shot at him. But Perry didn't believe a word of this. Not for a minute.

Deputy Bowes stood in the doorway of the jailhouse watching the good and not-so good citizens of Wolf Creek go about their lives despite the wind-driven snow that blanketed the streets. He had a bad feeling in his gut and had for days.

And at the Congregational Church, a battered and bruised version of Reverend Claussen crouched on the altar, praying. He prayed to Jesus, he prayed to Mary, he prayed to any gods that would listen. Things had to be put right in this town, he knew, and couldn't be until Sheriff Lauters was resting in peace in the cemetery outside town. But how to accomplish this? There lie the question. Claussen couldn't do it himself and he refused to hire some sinful gunslinger. Yet, it had to be done. Prayer seemed the only viable answer. He had been praying for hours, his knees aching, his back knotted with pain. But suffering was part of the process, only true discomfort could bring results. So Claussen prayed to any gods that would give him audience. More so, he prayed for his guardian angel to be sent to him.

But there were other things going on in Wolf Creek, other secrets tended in dark gardens of the soul. Many of which were closely-guarded and coveted like sin.

One of them was that Wynona Spence, that shrewd businesswoman with the morbid tongue, kept the body of her lesbian lover embalmed in her rooms above the mortuary. She had died two years before, but Wynona would not let her go. She chatted with her, fixed her hair and make up, read her poetry and took her meals with her. And at night, she slept beside her happy as only a true necrophile could be.

Another was that Dr. Perry had a serious morphine habit which grew worse week by week. It helped with his back pain but often plunged his usually meticulous and analytical brain into a fog of hallucination and dream. And lately, those dreams were becoming nightmares where he was once again a Union battlefield surgeon during the War Between the States. He was in a misty valley during the Shiloh campaign, in a barn which was being used as a field hospital. The injured and dying and mutilated were piling up around him as he performed amputation after amputation, limbs heaped like cordwood. It was a nightmare, yes, but he'd witnessed such a thing firsthand and although a man could close his eyes, some things would never go away.

Then there was the Skull Society.

No white man (and precious few Indians, for that matter) knew exactly how it was to call a primal monster from its grave. They didn't know that for three weeks before Skullhead's first appearance, the Skull Society—all twelve members—had prayed and fasted in the sacred grove, denying themselves any and all comforts until they were purified to a point where they could literally see one another's thoughts, their brains functioning as a single unit. For the last week, not a word was spoken. It didn't need to be—the extracts of certain sacred herbs and roots had amplified their latent telepathic abilities. As a single brain they were able to call up the beast from its grave, resurrect him to full potential via the Blood-Medicine—a heady brew of their own blood, reptile toxins, plant saps, and the juices of a deadly mushroom found only deep within mountain caves. Through this, Skullhead was restored to fleshy vitality, very unlike the mummy Longtree and Bowes had seen. In the sweat lodge each night, they would concentrate on the image of the next victim and transmit it to the Lord of the High Wood. The only drawback being, that if Skullhead could not find said victim, his bloodlust would be sated on anything and anyone he could find. And when the enemies of the tribe were gone, Skullhead would continue murdering, destroying, and devouring until he himself was destroyed.

These were the ways of the Skull Society and they were secret, taken to the grave.

The people of Wolf Creek knew little of the Gang of Ten, but they speculated endlessly as was their way. Sometimes, even the most gruesome speculation paled beside reality.

Abe Runyon, the first victim of Skullhead, was a veteran Indian-hater. Or so he thought until he took a fancy to a Blackfoot girl barely in her teens. She spurned his advances and Runyon decided that was unthinkable. He abducted her and kept her in his little cabin outside town where he repeatedly raped her until, overcome with guilt, he staved in her head with a hammer. He buried her beneath the floorboards of his cabin where she still lay, a skeleton dressed in a rotting elkskin dress, dreaming away eternity in a rage of moss.

Cal Sevens, the second victim, was a quiet man, a loner in every sense of the word. But at night in his room above the smithy shop, he would dream of a prostitute he had known in Kansas City and masturbate fiercely...and then, overcome with guilt, would read from the Bible.

Charlie Mears, the third, was a highwayman who specialized in robbing and murdering miners in the hills. He was perpetually drunk and had been since the night he'd tipped over an oil lamp and his house had burned to the ground, taking his wife and infant son with it.

And Pete Olak, the fourth victim, was thought to be a good father and provider for his little family. But it was he who pulled the noose over Red Elk's head and tightened it, smiling as he did so. The fifth, sixth, and seventh victims—George Reiko, Nathan Segaris, and Curly DelVecchio respectively—had been the ones who had cooked up the lynching of Red Elk and had done so under Mike Ryan's supervision. They dragged Red Elk through the streets, kicking and cussing him all the way. As a final gesture of hatred and disrespect, they had urinated on him.

And Dewey Mayhew, who had pretty much stood by and watched the hanging, lived a cursed and haunted life. Like that nameless miner, he had been told the exact date of his death by

Ghost Hand, Herbert Crazytail's father. And told it would be violent, painful, and unpleasant. It was.

Mike Ryan, the most recent victim of Skullhead, was a very rich and powerful man. Equally respected and feared. But for all his bravado and barrel-chested machismo, Ryan had a taste for young men and, whenever possible, satisfied his urges with a male prostitute in Laramie.

The last surviving member of the Gang of Ten was Sheriff Bill Lauters. He had a fine farm and wonderful family, but he, too, was haunted. Ever since Red Elk's lynching he had been drinking heavily. Sometimes it was the only way he could get the boy's face out of his mind—that distended visage livid as a bruise, those bulging sightless eyes, crooked neck, and lolling blackened tongue. Sometimes Lauters would dream that Red Elk came to him, a dead thing with a shaft of bone jutting from his broken neck. He would carry a noose in his hands. His own. Lauters would wake in a cold sweat and immediately hit the bottle. Sometimes, he prayed for death.

There were worse things in the town, but they would never be known. For as Deputy Bowes had commented, Wolf Creek was a seething cauldron ready to boil over.

This, then, was the scene before the slaughter.

7

Longtree found the body about half a mile from Ryan's ranch. It was covered in a light dusting of snow, the world's oldest shroud. He would've missed it save that it was sprawled over the trail, twisted and flayed, a cast-off from an abattoir. It was still warm.

Lighting the oil lantern he always carried for times like this, Longtree investigated.

The face had been torn free as had the throat. The body had no arms and one leg was missing. It had been eviscerated, plucked, bitten, clawed, and chewed. Longtree, nausea like a plug of grease in his stomach, searched the surrounding area and found the arms, some bloody meat that might have been a regurgitated face, much frozen blood, but no leg. A snack carted away for the trail, he decided.

In the snow and the wind, his horse whinnying with displeasure, he made a fairly through examination of the crime area. He found nothing there he hadn't seen at the others: carnage, simple and brutal. Nothing more.

Yet, he knew there was always more to be gleaned than what struck the eye. This was the work of the Skullhead, the marshal full well knew, an act of revenge perpetrated with an animal's hunger and an inhuman, sadistic imagination. This man, whoever he might have been, had to be one of the Gang of Ten. Unless the Skullhead had allowed a serious slip in methodology, it could be no one else. The mysterious ninth member. But who?

He searched the corpse for signs of identification and found none.

It was no easy task. Such was the degree of atrocities performed on the cadaver that its clothes and flesh were threaded together. Both were frozen stiff with blood, it being hard to determine where one started and the other left off. After a few minutes of this with nothing to show for it but filthy gloves, Longtree gave up.

His horse had pawed through the snow and was happily munching some tender grasses. But he heard whinnying. He looked around. The snowfall obscured everything. The lantern's light was growing dim, fuel running low. It sputtered and spat. He set out on foot, trying to pinpoint the direction of the sound. Noises were broken up by the wind, scattered, and set back upon themselves so it was impossible to trust his ears. He found a rifle in the snow, a Sharps buffalo rifle, .50 caliber. It had to belong to the dead man. From the smell of powder on the barrel, it had been fired recently. Maybe at the beast.

Longtree searched the area in ever-widening concentric circles that slowly brought him out of range of his own horse. Had he not been a scout at one time, he would never have attempted this. It was dangerous to wander off in a blizzard in such desolate country, but his sense of orientation was flawless.

He found the horse some time later, picketed behind a high shelf of rocks. It was a fine muscular gelding, sleek and proud. A rich man's horse. He searched the saddlebags and found some papers of a business nature, all bearing the signature of Mike

Ryan. He also found a Springfield 1865 Allin Conversion in the rifle boot, finely customized. A brass plate on the butt identified it as Mike Ryan's weapon. There was no doubt then, the body was either that of Mike Ryan or someone who had robbed him. Longtree decided on the former.

Mike Ryan had been the ninth member.

But why was he out here? Shannon had said he was expecting him at the ranch. So why would Ryan be out here?

Then it came to Longtree. It was all too obvious, a child's leap of logic. Ryan had asked him up here in order to kill him. He had hidden on the trail, probably atop the rock outcropping, waiting for Longtree to ride by, the Sharps rifle at the ready. But the Skullhead had found him first.

Another assassination attempt thwarted. This time by the killer himself...or itself.

Quite by accident, Skullhead had saved the lawman's life.

Longtree laughed grimly in the wind, taking Ryan's horse back to the body. He now knew who all the rustlers were. Only one remained alive. Lauters. Ryan had probably been the other masked rider with him. It all fit together seamlessly. If Longtree wanted to stop the beast, it was only a matter of sticking close to Lauters.

Because the beast would come sooner or later.

And as unpleasant as it was, Longtree would have to follow the sheriff wherever he went.

8

Sheriff Bill Lauters had a little farm outside Wolf Creek. And as the storm picked up its intensity, the eldest of his three sons—Chauncey—was sent out into the cold. As the eldest, he was considered man of the house when his father was away, which was often. More often than not, Chauncey, with the assistance of his brothers, pretty much took care of the place. They milked the cows, fed the chickens and slaughtered them, slopped the hogs, tended the grounds—everything. When their father was around, which was seldom, he was often too drunk to do more than sit on the porch or collapse in bed.

Tonight, Chauncey braved the elements to drive the hogs into the barn where they'd be safe from the cold. His brothers were supposed to do it when they got loose and do it before sundown, but as usual they'd forgotten.

"Git!" Chauncey cried, kicking the sows towards the barn, snow hitting him in the face like granules of sand. "Get a move on, will ya? If you think I like being out in this cold, yer damn wrong!"

The barn door was open, swinging back and forth in the wind. Another thing his brothers had forgotten to do. No surprise there. Chauncey wrestled the hogs through the door, knowing they'd be paid in full for their treachery once slaughter-time rolled around.

"And I'll enjoy it this time," he promised them.

The last time he hadn't. It was hard to care for an animal for years and then kill it, particularly when the animal in question didn't die easy but fought and screeched till the bitter end.

The hogs safely in their pen, Chauncey froze. There was a stink in the barn. A viscid, rotten odor of spoiled meat. It hung high and hot in the air despite the chill. Swallowing, Chauncey lit the lantern that hung on the wall and checked the horses on the other end. They were silent. They usually started snorting when someone came, thinking it was feeding time, hungry for attention.

"Old Joe?" he called. "Blue Boy?"

The first thing Chauncey's brain took notice of was that their stables were broken open, the wood shattered as if by an ax and cast about. The next thing it took notice of brought him to his knees and stopped his heart.

Oh, God, no...

The horses had been killed; more so, butchered. There was blood everywhere, the straw red with it. They'd been taken apart like dolls a child had grown tired of—bits of them scattered everywhere. They were gutted, decapitated, stripped to the bone. The head of Old Joe was impaled atop a corral post. Blue Boy had been skinned, his hide driven into the wall with spikes. The wet, still steaming intestines of both were strung like Christmas garland through the stable fencing and up into the rafters.

Chauncey went down on his knees, vomiting, his head spinning. This couldn't be, this just couldn't be. Nothing could do this…nothing. No beast was this savage, no man this deranged. When the dry heaves had subsided, Chauncey looked upon the atrocities once more, tears in eyes, bile on his chin.

Something wet struck him in the back of the head.

Chauncey turned. There was a clump of damp warmth in his hair. With a cry he pulled it free. A piece of bloody meat…no much worse: a tentacle of flesh connected to a single swollen eye. Blue Boy's. Chauncey threw it aside, his guts churning. Another object came whirling out of the darkness, flipping end over end. It came to rest against a stack of hay bales. The remains of Blue Boy's head…skull cracked like an egg, brains scooped out, tongue chewed free, eyes licked from their orbits.

Chauncey screamed.

Something else whistled from above: A femur stained red, shattered, a hunk of bloody meat and white ligament trailing from the knob of bone like a pennant. He ducked and it missed him.

Chauncey went red with anger, gray with fear. He glared up at the hayloft. *"Who's up there?"* he croaked. *"Who the hell's up there? I've got a gun…"*

A lie, but it gave him strength.

There was a low growling sound, then a wet ripping followed by chewing. Nothing more. A segment of vertebrae was dropped into the hay. It had been sucked clean.

Chauncey's brain was telling him to run; anything that could take apart two draft horses with such ease would make a nasty mess of him. But he couldn't run. He wanted to see this thing, look it in the eye and make it feel his raw hate.

There was a groan from up in the loft and a blur of motion.

No time to run now.

The beast landed about seven feet away. Chauncey stared at it, drinking in every hideous detail. Chauncey was nearly six feet tall, but this thing dwarfed him. Its flesh was scarred and raw. And that face, lewd and colorless and revolting.

The beast took a step forward. Its huge, misshapen head quivered with grotesque musculature, scant, threadbare tufts of fur bristled. Its jaw was thrust out almost like a snout, its eyes red as spilled blood and slitted, covered with a shiny transparent membrane.

Chauncey turned to run and promptly slipped on the horses' entrails, stumbling forward and catching a coil of intestine across the neck that put him promptly on his back.

The beast had him by then, one huge hand locked in his hair, bending him back over the bony ridge of its knee. Chauncey opened his eyes and saw the mouth opening, the shaft of the black throat. Crooked teeth jutted from discolored gums which were pitted with wormholes. Chauncey smelled the charnel odor of its breath, saw the flickering lantern light gleam off those needled teeth and then they were in his throat, buried to the hilt. When they came away, he had no throat, just a bleeding flap of flesh. The pigs began to squeal.

Skullhead moaned low in his throat, the taste of hot human blood an ecstasy of no slight intoxication. It filled his being with a sense of roaring omnipotence that was almost too much for even him. The horses had been amusing, sweet tidbits to torture then kill, but they were gamy things, they lacked the satisfying richness of the boy. Skullhead ate him slowly, savoring every honeyed clot of marrow, every hot sip of blood, every sweet nibble of gray matter.

And then it occurred to him and he couldn't understand why it hadn't before: He was a god. A king. A lord. Nothing less. And the people, those that had called him and those that opposed him, were his servants, his cattle. He could picture it in the hazy, red confines of his brain. Picking out the tasty ones, killing the others for sport; slaughtering the old ones to relieve boredom, dining on the young ones. It was their destiny—to fill his belly. He'd eat women and boys, pull apart the men like fragile flowers, snack on the heads of infants like candies.

Yes, that was how it had been in the Dark Days and would be again.

Skullhead, caked with dried blood, Chauncey's spine lying across his swelling belly, thought about these things. He knew there was a reason he was brought forth from the boiling firmament of the grave. It wasn't merely to kill the white men, it *was to kill everyone.* Appetite was his destiny and it was enough. What more could he want?

A poet might have said: He ate to live and lived to eat.

It was so childishly simple. Skullhead closed his eyes, belched, and waited for necessity or mere boredom to force him into the house, the dining hall. There were others there...he could smell their parts—hot, secret, wanting. Skullhead dreamed as the wind blew cold and the lantern went out. He dreamed of a fine tanned smock knitted from the soft hides of children. Warm and toasty, covering his innumerable bare spots.

He waited for carnage. It was all he knew.

9

After Longtree had turned over the body of Mike Ryan to Deputy Bowes, he had a look for Sheriff Lauters. No one had seen him. He wasn't at Doc Perry's and Perry claimed he didn't know where he was.

Longtree didn't believe him.

He knew the doctor was a friend of the sheriff's and had been for some time. Perry knew where he was, but he wouldn't tell, not even if Longtree put him under arrest and slapped him around. Perry was a very loyal man. Longtree respected this. Lauters was out there somewhere, holed up in some saloon or whorehouse, drinking himself blind. His career was over and he knew that now. He was in hiding and the only thing that would bring him out was the Skullhead. And sooner or later, this would happen.

Longtree stabled his horse in the livery across from the Serenity Hotel and set out on foot. He had to find Lauters and if that meant checking every saloon in town, then this is what he'd do. He didn't want to arrest Lauters just yet, merely put him under a sort of protective custody. Whether the sheriff liked that or not didn't concern Longtree. He wanted the man behind bars in the jailhouse so Bowes and he could get a crack at the beast when it came for him.

It was a plan.

The snow was still falling, the wind still blowing when Longtree passed the smithy shop. He stopped there. Dick Rikers was the blacksmith and according to Bowes' records, he'd been one of the few to witness the vigilantes actually stringing up Red Elk.

Longtree went in.

It was hot in there, Rikers working branding irons at the forge.

"Marshal. What can I do for you?" Rikers asked, his powerful arms wet with sweat.

"I'd like to ask you a couple questions, if I may."

Rikers nodded, setting aside his work and wiping his face and neck with a towel. "Just fashioning a new set of irons for the Ryan combine. It can wait, though."

"Mike Ryan?"

"Don't know of any other."

Longtree rolled a cigarette and lit it slowly. "Ryan's dead, Mr. Rikers," he said.

"Dead?" Rikers looked shocked.

"Yeah, murdered. Killed by the same thing that's killed the others. The thing you saw, I believe."

Rikers went pale, remembering the night he'd seen the creature run off after assaulting Dewey Mayhew. "Ryan," he said, "Mike Ryan."

Longtree nodded. "I don't think he'll be the last, either."

"Something had better well be done."

"Oh, we're trying, Mr. Rikers, I assure you of this," Longtree said, exhaling a cloud of smoke. "But you see, this is a strange situation, a very strange one indeed. I'm of a mind that these deaths are connected with the lynching of that Blackfoot last year. You saw it, didn't you?"

Rikers swallowed. "I saw it, all right. But there was nothing I could've done for that boy except gotten myself killed, if that's what your insinuating."

"No, you did right, Mr. Rikers. No sense in tangling with outlaws like that."

"I don't know who they were—they wore masks."

"No, that's not what I'm interested in either. I want to ask you about the murder that led to all that."

Rikers features went slack. "The Carpenter girl?"

"Yes. What do you remember of her?"

Rikers sat down, licking his lips. "She was a pretty girl, Marshal. That and a very nice one. She was liked by everyone. Just a nice kid who never did any wrong by anyone."

"Did she have suitors that you recall?"

Rikers laughed. "She had too many, Marshal. Men crawled out of the woodwork when they got a look at her."

"You remember any in particular?"

"Hell, Marshal," Rikers said, "it was some time ago. There were ranch hands, some of the miners, even Liberty, the dentist."

"A real popular girl, eh?"

"Yes, but a moral one, you understand. She never so much as dated a single man that I remember." Rikers laughed again. "She really did have her choice, though, even married men took a shine to her. I recall Sheriff Lauters was pretty sweet on her."

"Lauters?"

"Yeah, Big Bill was in love, I think."

10

Jimmy Lauters, aged twelve, collapsed in the snow outside his house. His head was spinning with dizziness, his eyesight blurred. As he lay there in the snow, trembling with shock, dry heaves wracking his body, he thought only of death.

In his mind, he saw only slaughter.

He tried to will himself to crawl the last few feet to the door, but movement, any movement seemed a chore. He heard the barn door swing open and slam against the wall. It made a great hammering noise as if it had been reduced to kindling. And no wind, Jimmy knew, had the strength to do that. He could hear heavy footfalls behind him and knew that the beast was coming.

He could feel its hot breath on his back.

Let it think I'm dead, he decided with iron nerve. Let it think that.

The beast sniffed a line down his spine and withdrew, just standing above him, tasting the air.

Jimmy launched himself to his feet with a cry, already running by this time. The beast howled and Jimmy felt the tips of its claws rip gashes into the back of his neck. Then he was at the door. A split-second later, through it. He threw the bolt and snatched the shotgun from above the hearth. He broke it open and fed shells into it with numbed fingers.

"What are you doing, boy?" his mother asked, crossing the room quickly.

He said: "The monster." Nothing more.

Abigail Lauters, her steel gray hair pulled back in a tight bun, wasn't impressed with this foolishness. "I told you to fetch your brother," she snapped. "It's bath night…"

He looked at her with crazed, dreaming eyes and the words died on her lips. His face was colorless, vomit smeared down the front of his shirt. His throat was bleeding.

"Dead," he muttered, "Chauncey's dead."

Abigail said nothing for a moment, the impact of those two words weighing in slowly, heavily. She could hear her cousin Virginia upstairs, singing a song as she bathed JoJo, the youngest. Dead? Chauncey couldn't be dead, why that was sheer nonsense—

"The monster got the horses," Jimmy sobbed. "It tore them apart…and Chauncey…it was eating him…"

His mother snatched the shotgun from his hands. There was a thud against the door.

Another.

Then another.

"Get upstairs," she said calmly, but with iron behind her words.

Jimmy had never heard her use that tone before. Mechanically, he backed to the stairway, tears running from his eyes. The door was hit again and again. The plank that held it secure splintered, then split in two. The door seemed to *bulge* in its frame and then it exploded inward.

The beast stood there, breathing with a low, bestial grunting.

Abigail looked on it and decided it was a demon from hell. It could be nothing else. It had to stoop low to come through the door, a horror knitted with tufts of matted fur and scaly skin, stinking of slaughterhouses, dusted with snow. Its huge tail swung back and forth, casting aside tables and chairs. It came forward hunched and bent, but still its skull brushed the ceiling rafters. Ribbons of drool hung from its mouth.

Abigail shot it twice and it reeled with the impact, but never stopped. It came at her like a freight train, the gun slapped from her hands. As Jimmy watched, cowering on the third stair, the beast tore his mother apart. She looked, if anything, like a burst feather pillow stuffed with red. Bits of her rained in the air, sprayed and exploded in every conceivable direction.

Jimmy scrambled up the stairs.

Virginia was standing up on the landing, little JoJo in her arms. She stared, shocked into stillness. Jimmy looked back and saw the beast, its armored torso red with his mother's blood.

"Jesus in Heaven," she whispered.

"Run!" Jimmy yelled. "Run for godsake!"

Virginia scampered down the hall, slamming and locking the door of the children's room behind her.

Jimmy dashed into his father's room and returned with a knife.

The beast came to him, vaulting up the stairs, its massive weight collapsing individual steps as if they were fashioned from balsa. Its obscene, hideous face was hooked in a crooked grin. Its nostrils flared at the boy's smell. It saw the knife and was unimpressed, two bleeding holes already open in its chest.

Jimmy lifted the knife to strike.

The beast's lips drew back slickly from its dripping gums, rows of razored and serrated teeth gnashing together. Saliva spilled down its jutting chin, blood and bits of viscera were dropping from its mouth.

Jimmy threw himself at it, sinking the knife in its throat. Then it had him. The blade still buried in its neck, it brought its jaws together on Jimmy's head, his skull going with a muted wet pop. It ate him this way, feeding him between those rows of teeth until there were only bones, hair, and stringy tendrils of meat to show for twelve years of struggle.

Virginia held no illusions that she was safe in the bedroom. She was next and there were no two ways about this. The door shattered to brushwood and the beast stepped in, squeezing its bulk through and taking most of the doorframe with it. Virginia read from her Bible in a high, shivery voice.

"Thou shalt not be afraid for the terror by night," she read, "nor the arrow that flieth by day; nor the pestilence that walketh in darkness—"

Skullhead stood there, drunk with blood, listening to these words and disliking them for reasons he wasn't even sure of. In two steps, he was on her. He pulled her head free, examined it, turning up his nose at the perfume in her hair, and tossed it away through the door. It bounced down the steps like a meaty ball. He had no use for this one.

It was the child he wanted.

Under the bed, he heard it crying. Such sad sounds were music to Skullhead, a choir of angels. He flipped the bed over and snatched the child up in his arms, crushing it against him.

In silence, he ate, pulling its juicy limbs free like a butterfly's wings.

11

Reverend Claussen heard the doors to the church slam open with a crash.

One was nearly torn off, snow and wind blowing in, but they did nothing to disguise the figure which stood there. Claussen was lying at the foot of the altar, bruised and hurting and filthy with his own urine and excrement. His mind had gone to mush now and he did not doubt what his eyes showed him.

The beast.

It came forward slowly with a raw and vile smell of death lingering about it. Its eyes found and held the reverend and in those eyes, dear Christ, was...*deliverance*. In those red and glistening orbs was a promise of purity. For, Claussen saw, it was no beast, it was a *god*. Not some storybook deity who couldn't be bothered to put in an appearance, let alone speak to and instruct his flock. This was a god in the flesh—huge and pulsing and jutting and stinking and anxious to claim the faithful as his own.

It occurred to Claussen as his mind raged with religious awe, that this was one of the creatures mentioned in the book on Indian folklore. But unlike the phantoms and fairies of Christianity, it was real. It lived and breathed and lusted.

Its stink was like sacred incense to Claussen even though it put his stomach in his throat and made his bowels ache to be voided. It came forward and towered above him. He was on his knees before it, trembling, sickened by the noxious bouquet of its stench. It filled him, roiling his guts, and turning his thoughts to mud.

"Take me, oh Lord," he said in a screeching voice, "take me as sacrifice."

It reached down and grasped him by the neck with one immense hand, hoisting him skyward so his face was in its own. Its breath smelled of decay and vomit and blackness, hot and appalling. Claussen gazed into those unblinking red eyes and jolts of electricity thrummed through him, boiling his blood and filling his skull with white light. He saw—

He saw the world before man. He saw the civilizations that had risen and fallen. He saw things unknown and unguessed. He saw the Skullheads and their kingdom. He saw the world change and the red man come and the great, fierce Lords of the High Wood sicken and die. Their herds thinned as they could no longer bear children. Then there were only a few left that were worshipped, then entombed by the Indians. Where they waited and waited in solemn, suffocating darkness until they were called forth.

Yes, the knowledge had been passed.

Claussen was to become its priest.

To prove this, it bit off his left hand at the wrist and swallowed the meat and bone without chewing. The agony was beautiful. It dropped the reverend and mounted the altar. Its lashing tail shattered and tumbled the effigies of Christ and Mary. It pulled down the cross and urinated over holy relics and missives.

It claimed the church as its own.

Claussen, at last, had found meaning to his existence.

12

Early the next morning, just before light, Dr. Perry was up and about. His back wasn't too bad today, a bit sensitive. His cells were content, having been fed their ritual breakfast of morphine. He made rounds in his wagon, treating two cases of frostbite and mending a shattered leg up at one of the mining camps. When day broke, the sun came out, parting the clouds. There was every indication that today—though cool—would be a lovely day, he decided.

He couldn't have been more wrong.

On a whim, he stopped by the church.

He didn't like to think that Lauters had killed the reverend. It was the last thing he wanted to believe, but, as Marshal Longtree had pointed out a few days before, the sheriff was entirely out of control. And Reverend Claussen *was* missing.

In the church, much to the doctor's surprise, he found Claussen at the altar, reveling in something. He soon saw what. The altar had been destroyed. It was smeared with excrement and worse things. Everything was destroyed and defiled.

"Good Christ," Perry said. The church smelled like an abattoir.

Claussen turned. "Do not profane in this house, sir," he said.

Perry was speechless. The reverend's face was bruised and swollen.

"What happened to you, man?" he demanded.

"Baptismal under fire," the reverend laughed.

Perry went to him, but the reverend pulled away. "I don't need your help, sir."

"Tell me who did this."

Claussen grinned. "Oh, I think you know."

Perry sat down on the first step of the altar. Claussen was right, of course: Perry did know. *Lauters.* The sheriff hadn't been lying to Perry the night before when he'd said he hadn't killed the reverend. He hadn't committed murder, he'd merely assaulted the man. Perry had always known Lauters to be a bit heavy-handed and particularly in the past few years—there'd been more than one feisty prisoner he'd had to stitch up and set—but never anything to this degree. A beating of such magnitude could never be blamed on mere self-defense except in a lunatic's brain—this was a crime and the man who had committed it, a criminal.

"When did this happen?" the doctor inquired. "Did he do this, too?" He indicated the altar, the jackstraw tumble of pews, the shredded tapestries, the ravaged statues.

"Hardly."

"When?"

"In the dim past."

The doctor took a deep, pained breath. "You'll have to press charges, of course."

"Nonsense."

Perry just stared at him. He wanted nothing more than an injection right now; nothing else could hope to sort this mess out.

"Lauters will face punishment, yes, but not by the law," Claussen said with abnormal calm, "but by His hand."

"God?" Perry said without knowing he had.

Claussen smiled again: It was awful, like a cadaver's grin. *"God?* Yes, perhaps, but not the one you mean, not the one I've thrown my life away on."

Perry stroked his mustache. "Easy, Reverend." He had a nasty feeling Claussen had lost his mind. "I'd like you to come back to my home with me," he said, picking his words carefully. "You've been through a shock, you need rest. I can see that you get it. I'll have Deputy Bowes and Marshal Longtree come by."

"For what possible purpose?"

"To arrest the man who did this."

Claussen laughed softly. "I don't need them, Doctor. None of us do. You see, there's only one law now—*his* law."

"Who are you speaking of?"

"You know, you know very well. You borrowed my books—"

"I didn't read them," Perry lied. "There hasn't been time."

"Much to your disadvantage, then, I would think." Claussen went back to the wreckage of the altar. "When *he* takes command, when *he* assumes his throne, he'll need educated men like you and I to help him sort out affairs. But you must read the books, you must know of *his* past..."

Perry just looked at him.

Claussen grinned. "You see, Doctor, he is a king. He ruled this land once. When our relations came from Europe, they brought European gods with them. This was a mistake. They knew nothing of this land, its history, its needs, its course."

"Yes, well—"

"The Indians know they weren't the first race here, that there were older races." Claussen smiled at the idea. "So wise, those people...and we call them savages." He shook is head. "No matter. The old race were called the Lords of the High Wood. When the Indians first migrated into this land countless thousands of years ago, the Lords were still here. Not many still survived, but some. Enough, I would say."

"What does this have to do with anything?" Perry wanted to know.

"I'm instructing you, Doctor, on the new religion which is actually quite old. These are things you'd do well to remember." Claussen touched a finger to his chin. "Now, at present, our lawmen are hunting a beast, a creature that is slaughtering people. But this creature is not new, in fact it is very old. It is a direct descendent of these Lords, the Kings of the Hunt. You see, in ancient times, the Indians worshipped these creatures. They were gods. They made sacrifice to them, offered them virgins to breed with. Eventually the Lords died out—oh, due perhaps to changes in climate, destruction of their habitats—but a few survived."

"You're insane," Perry told him.

"On the contrary, I'm probably the only sane person left," Claussen said, stabbing a finger at the doctor. "I told you once of the Skull Society. Do you remember? Well, this Skull Society is an ancient cult. At one time they were priests of the order that selected sacrifice to the Lords. They were the law-makers, holy men of a cult of barbarity."

Perry sighed. "Are you trying to tell me one of these...*things* still exists?"

Claussen massaged his temples wearily. "Yes, exactly. Most of these Lords, these gods of old, died out long ago, but a few survived into modern times. Certain tribes believe until quite recently."

"Stop it, Reverend. You—"

Claussen silenced him with a look, lost in his new religion. "Do you know what are meant by the 'dog days', Doctor?"

Perry nodded. The dog days referred to the pre-horse period of the tribes when all activities were accomplished with canine assistance: camp moving, hunting, etc.

"Many of the tribes, our own Blackfoot included, believe a few of these Lords survived into the dog days—which would mean within the last four or five-hundred years or so."

Perry's back was aching fiercely now. Claussen explained it all with such cold, compelling logic, it was hard *not* to believe him. But it was fantasy. Had to be. Perry was something of a naturalist himself and he didn't doubt for a moment that the earth had been populated at various times by bizarre animalistic peoples and nameless beasts. But they were all extinct now. To accept, even for a moment, that some primordial horror had survived...

"Nonsense," he maintained.

"Is it?"

"Of course. Even if there were such creatures, they are long gone."

"Not at all, Doctor," Claussen said as if he were addressing a child. "One has survived."

Perry just stared at him. It was insanity; there could be no shred of underlying truth in this.

"Read the books, Doctor. It's all there. What we know comes from legend, tribal memory, but legend is the only glimpse we have of those ancient times and ways."

"You need rest," Perry said.

"The Blackfoot call him Skullhead."

"Why?"

"Because his head is like a huge skull. The Skullheads, you see, wear their skeletons on the outsides of their bodies like insects. Throwbacks to prehistory, Doctor. Lords of the High Wood. Beings whose savage appetites can never be satisfied." Claussen grinned ghoulishly.

It was all madness; Perry did not want to hear it. Claussen had kept his left hand stuffed inside his coat the entire time. Perry had not wanted to ask why. But now he did.

"That doesn't concern you. When the time comes..."

Perry stood up and began walking to the door, silently.

"He's here to feed on us," Claussen gloated. "To destroy all we've built, to take back his lands. And to breed. Blood is his wine...give unto him..."

13

Perry said, "The church has been wrecked. Claussen is out of his mind."

Longtree heard him out and did not like any of it. Lauters had assaulted the man and he had now gone quietly—or not so quietly—out of his mind. That much was true. Lauters needed to be put under arrest.

Perry just shook his head. "He's raving, Marshal. He believes this creature is some sort of god and he is its priest."

"Did he call it by name?"

"Yes." Perry swallowed. "Lord of the High Wood. Skullhead."

Longtree paled. "Maybe he's not as crazy as you think."

Perry just stared at him. "What do you mean by that?"

So Longtree told him everything he knew. Told him in detail even though he didn't really have the time to do much explaining. But it was important that the doctor know.

"Like some sort of ogre," was all Perry said. "A monster from a story book."

"Yes," Longtree admitted. "But far worse."

14

An hour later, the carnage at Lauters' farm was discovered. And as the fates would have it, the sheriff discovered it himself. He was sober when he rode out there, his injured arm bandaged and aching. He knew something was wrong when he'd rounded the little hill that overlooked his spread.

I had a funny feeling, he said later, *a tickle at the back of my neck...*

He'd paused up there on the hill. What he saw was a cold, unnatural stillness enveloping the grounds. The boys weren't out tending to things. No chickens squawked, no pigs squealed, no horses whinnied. No trail of smoke issued from the chimney.

What he found was slaughter. His family murdered.

Longtree put together the rest. Lauters had rode into town and informed everyone, before collapsing with hysteria. He was now at Dr. Perry's, sedated. Perry said he'd sleep until evening.

Longtree toured the crime scene, his stomach in his throat. The remains of Lauters' eldest son, Chauncey, were discovered in the barn, mixed in with those of several pigs, two horses, and a blizzard of feathers from the chickens. In the house, a body ripped like a bag of meat and cast about was thought to be what was left of Lauters' wife, Abigail. Upstairs, were the headless corpse of

Abigail's cousin Virginia Krebs and a collection of pitted bones thought to belong to Jimmy Lauters. The youngest boy, JoJo, was nowhere to be found. The window to the children's room was broken outward, so it was thought the fiend leapt out with the three-year old in tow. Bloody, inhuman footprints nearly covered by snow wound out into the distance.

Alden Bowes was, for all purposes, the sheriff of Wolf Creek now. He knew Lauters' family well and none of it was easy for him. But he had a job to do and do it he would.

"I can't believe this," he kept saying. "What kind of animal does something like this?"

"No animal," Longtree said.

Bowes narrowed his eyes. "These people had nothing to do with that lynching, Marshal. I think...*this* puts your little theory to bed."

Longtree frowned. "Not at all, Deputy. It couldn't find him, so it went for his family."

Bowes paled and walked off, joining Spence and Perry as they examined the atrocities in the barn. Longtree didn't blame the man for how he felt; the other victims were bad enough, but this...this was *obscene.* No other word could be applied here. Women and children. Longtree had seen plenty of killing in his time. Enough to turn most men sick with the awful potential of their fellow man, but never had he experienced the aftermath of such gruesome savagery before.

He joined the others in the barn.

Perry was examining a human femur stripped of flesh. There were huge indentations in it. "Teeth marks," he said in disgust. "This thing must be incredibly powerful. I've seen the leftovers from a grizzly's meal...but never anything like this..." He coughed then, fighting against tears.

"It must be insane," Wynona Spence said, "this beast. Even a pack of hungry wolves stop...they fill themselves and let the scavengers have the rest. But this thing...by God, it eats and eats. It kills for pleasure, for the fun of it."

Longtree lit a hand-rolled. "You better get a posse together, Deputy. You get some men and tracking dogs on that thing's trail, you might find it. Trail's still fresh."

Bowes nodded. "You coming?"

"I'll join you later. Something I have to follow up first."

Bowes got on his horse and rode off.

Longtree pulled Perry aside. "I hate to add insult to injury, Doc, but when this is wound up, I may have to arrest the sheriff."

Perry didn't look surprised. "Why?"

Longtree told him about the masked gunman. "I figure you dug a bullet out of Lauters' arm last night, did you not?"

Perry nodded grimly. "Just wait until this is over, son. Do that for me. I suspect the sheriff is guilty of a great many crimes around here." He looked back at the litter of bodies. "God help him," he sobbed. "Oh, Jesus, Marshal, the children..."

Longtree watched him walk away stiffly, wondering just what the doctor knew and what he didn't know. And feeling for him and this entire town, a great compassion.

15

Skullhead, the last of the Lords of the High Wood, was far away from Wolf Creek by the time the posse was organized and dispatched. He was watching the Blackfoot camp in the hills, his stomach growling. He'd slept off last night's feast on a shelf of rock a half mile from town. He woke just after dawn, realizing he'd fallen asleep, bloated and gassy, while in the process of eating the child. The boy's innards were strung around him like a threadbare blanket. They were quite frozen and unpalatable.

He left the remains for scavengers.

After his long walk up into the hills, he was famished. He still had one more of the white men to kill, but no law stated that he couldn't take his sacrifice before they were all dead.

He approached the camp carefully, being silent as possible. Once the dogs started barking, he'd have to kill them. Too bad there wasn't some way he could simply slip in there and twist their necks without being noticed. But that was impossible. No longer able to contain his lusts, he moved into the camp.

The dogs began to bark.

Two of them ran at Skullhead and he slashed them into ribbons with a single swipe of his claws. A third and forth were torn asunder by a sweep of his bony, jagged tail. No more came.

There was screaming now, crying. People were running about, gathering up children and retreating into the forest. Skullhead let them go. He went from one lodge to the other, tearing them down and stomping them into the snow with childish glee. A few of the tribal elders weren't quick enough to escape their lodges and Skullhead grinned as their fragile bones crunched beneath his step.

There was shooting suddenly and Skullhead grimaced in pain as bullets swept over his back. He turned and chased down the defiant ones. He killed the first by merely tearing out his throat, the second by detaching his limbs, and the third by crushing him in a hug that forced his viscera to exit from any available opening. There was another and Skullhead beat him into submission with ragged, bleeding parts of the others, then opened his skull with a blow from his own rifle.

But this was merely for amusement.

His real interest was the sweat lodge. It was set away from the others at the fringe of the forest. It was in here that would be the men who summoned him, the Skull Society members. They knew their debts and would not run. Skullhead forced his way in, the tanned flap of buffalo skin that served as a door coming apart in his fingers. The men in there squatted on the earthen floor, their naked bodies painted up with streaks of white, black, and red. They chanted and mumbled meaningless prayers.

They did not attempt to hide or flee.

These were the ones that had called him. It seemed so silly to think that these weak, cowering creatures had summoned him from his grave. Of all the absurdities. Skullhead emasculated them one by one, laughing with a dry roaring sound as he did so. He watched them bleed and cry and moan and writhe on the ground. Bored with this display, he crushed their heads to jelly and brought the lodge down on top of them. It was how sacrifice was offered and received.

Outside, he smelled meat cooking on the fire. Strips of it smoking and sizzling on wooden racks. The stench was sickening...yet, he was curious. He snatched a strip and chewed the vile substance, forcing it down the cavern of his throat. When it hit his stomach, the reaction was instantaneous: he went to his knees and vomited. This done, he pulled himself up dizzily, remembering now the ancient taboos concerning cooked flesh.

He would do well not to forget again.

He decided now that these dark-skinned people were not worthy of worshipping him. As he devoured a woman and her child he decided they could only be of use as meat. The white men and their kin…they would be his new flock. They were the ones with power, with imagination. They reared cities like the ancients. A brutal and savage people. Skullhead liked them. They would do well.

Moving into the forest, he found small packs of the dark-skins hiding under the cover of trees and rocks. He took his time in claiming them. When he'd filled his belly to the point of bursting, he staggered back into camp and doused the fire with a stream of piss. Remembering that this was an old way of marking territory, he emptied his bladder throughout the camp. All who came here would know now that this place belonged to a king.

A Lord of the High Wood.

16

As the posse ran in circles outside town, Wynona Spence returned to the body of Mike Ryan. It had been very fortuitous of Ryan to order his elaborate headstone some days earlier. There were various stories circulating about how he had known of his approaching demise—everything from death threats to second sight—but Wynona was of the school that some men just knew when their time was coming. It wouldn't be the first time someone had ordered a stone only to be placed beneath it a few short days later.

Such was life…and death.

Wynona had spent most of the morning at Sheriff Lauters' farm, sorting through the rain of flesh and bone, separating human from animal. The remains of Lauters' family had already been buried in the cemetery outside town in one mass grave. A headstone would be placed tomorrow. It took a team of five men, volunteers all, several hours to dig through the snow and frozen ground and hollow out the grave. Nasty business that. But she was used to death and dying and nothing surprised her anymore.

The money was good, but her heart was heavy. This town was cursed.

She covered Ryan's body with a sheet and settled into her chair, her head aching. She'd always considered herself something of an optimist. Her father had said that both optimists and pessimists were in truth fantasists; that a realist was someone tucked safely in-between. And maybe he was right. Her optimism told her, *assured her,* that this beast, this monster would be caught and killed. Pessimism told her it would never happen: the beast would kill everyone and then move on. And realism told her it would be killed but not before it slaughtered a great many others.

Realism was safe; it avoided the extremes.

Sitting there, thinking of Marion and her love for her, Wynona decided she would be a realist now. Under the circumstances, it was a safe thing to be. A cloak of pragmatism that could be donned and would safeguard against all circumstances.

But she forgot about fatalism.

Until she heard the door to the back room crash in, that was. And suddenly she knew some things were unavoidable. As she peered into the back room, her eyes trembling with awe on the blood-encrusted giant standing there, its massive head brushing the roof beams, she knew it was all at an end. She was dead. No weapons or locked doors would change that. The beast was here and the beast had business with her.

She'd flirted with death for years and now here it was, huge and pissed-off and smelling.

"My God," she muttered.

And the beast advanced, teeth gnashing.

17

Lauters was awake when Longtree walked into Dr. Perry's surgery.

Longtree wasn't surprised; he expected this very thing. Perry had said he'd given the sheriff enough drugs to keep him unconscious most of the day, but somehow, Longtree figured, given the state of the sheriff's mind, he wouldn't be out for long.

"Sheriff," Longtree said, staring down the barrel of his gun, "there's no need for that."

Lauters was a big man. Huge, really, bloated from alcoholism, but still a very large man in his own right. His eyes were red and puffy, presumably from crying, his face damp with perspiration.

"I've taken as much as I'm going to from you, Longtree," he hissed, "you've pushed me around for the last time. My family...oh, Jesus..."

Longtree felt pity for the man. But he also felt the gun on him.

"Put it away, Sheriff. Please."

Lauters gaped at him through tear-filled eyes, his bandaged nose making him look all the more pathetic, pitiful even.

Longtree swallowed. The sheriff had his Colt on him. Even if he drew and drew fast, Lauters would still shoot him and probably in the chest. Such a wound had a high mortality rate.

Longtree held his hands out before him, innocently. "If you're gonna kill me, Sheriff, least you can do is hear me out first. That ain't asking too much, is it?"

Lauters stared at him. "I'm listening."

Longtree eased himself slowly in a chair. "You killed that Carpenter girl, didn't you?"

"Yes." Atrocity had brought honesty at last.

Longtree nodded. "You were part of that ring, the Gang of Ten. You boys set up Red Elk with the murder because he knew about you, then the other gang members lynched him and you stepped aside. Am I right?"

"You are."

"And now you're the only one left, the last of the gang."

Lauters nodded. "You're very good, Marshal. I always knew you were and that's why I didn't want you here. The beast is coming for me now...even the law can't change that. Your badge is useless, boy."

Longtree licked his lips. "What you did was wrong, Sheriff, and I think you know that more than any man could. But you've been punished beyond the limits of the law...I'm not going to arrest you."

Lauters lowered his gun. "Then why are you here?"

"Because I wanted to have this little talk with you." Longtree slipped a cigar from his pocket and lit it up. "You lost your family to this monster, Sheriff. You've suffered enough. Putting you on trial would be pointless, particularly given the fact that the witnesses and co-conspirators are all dead now." Longtree let that sink in. "What happened a year ago happened and we'd just better forget about it. The people in this town have a lot of respect for you and I've got no interest in dragging your name through the mud. Let 'em think you're a good lawman...because down deep, you probably are."

Lauters said nothing to any of this. A single tear slid down his cheek.

"We've got us a real problem here, Sheriff. We've got a monster that's killed a lot of people and it'll keep on killing until it's stopped. I think it's up to you and me to stop it."

"How?" Lauters asked.

"I don't rightly know," Longtree admitted. "But I do know that it'll be coming for you and I'm going to be there when it does."

"All that'll do is get you killed."

Longtree stood up. "It's my job to die fighting this thing same as it's yours. So get dressed. It's time we go hunting."

"You want me to help you?"

"Damn right. We're lawmen. Let's kill this thing or die trying."

It was about this time they heard shooting in the distance.

18

The posse led by Deputy Bowes was made up of eight men. Bowes had gathered the best and bravest shooters from the mining camps and the various ranches outside Wolf Creek. They were tough men, he decided, but more than that they were angry men. They were sick of the killings, sick of being able to do nothing. They lived hard, frustrating lives. They had a lot of aggression to spend and they had been given a target to spend it on.

"There!" someone cried. "The undertaking parlor!"

Bowes turned his head and saw. It seemed impossible in that first second of realization that something this hideous could possibly walk, let alone in full daylight. It moved hunched-over, knees bent, arms crooked, arms dangling limply. Its great tail swung from side to side and when it stooped over (as it did coming through the door of the undertaker's), the tail rose up as if it were part of some fulcrum that balanced the beast. The beast staggered out into the streets, taking the door to Spence's place off its hinges in the process. It waltzed out and stood up to its full height.

The men dismounted their horses. The horses had to be immediately tethered: some vague racial memory had stirred in them and they remembered this thing, its kin, and what they were capable of. The horses whinnied and bucked, some throwing riders before they could hop off. Others ran off down the streets.

And Skullhead, Lord of the High Wood, advanced on his flock.

"All right, you men," Bowes cried out, "hold your fire! Spread out, goddammit! Spread out!"

The men, most of them pale and trembling like babes now, fanned out in a skirmish line as the beast approached. There was a stink of feces and Bowes knew someone had shit their pants. He did not blame them.

Bowes watched the creature. It gave off a sickening, acrid stink. It was tall, bulging with muscularity. Its huge and deformed head bobbed, blood freezing on its lips.

Some brave woman had circled behind it and slipped into the undertaker's. She stormed out now, falling into the street. "Wynona!" she gagged. "It got Wynona...she's...all over the place..."

Bowes motioned for someone to get her inside. A man, presumably her husband, did just this.

"Let's shoot the bastard!" someone yelled.

"Take aim," Bowes told them, knowing if he didn't let them shoot and soon, they'd do it anyway or just run off. "Steady, steady, hold it..."

Skullhead was ignorant to what was happening here. He could remember in the old days, the forgotten days, how the dark-skins would gather around like this and await the blessing of his claws and teeth.

"Fire!" Bowes screamed.

The beast roared.

The first barrage hit the beast and he stumbled back, blood oozing from a dozen holes in his chest. The pain was intense. Pain was something he was used to, but having these white-skins bestow it upon him with no regard for ceremony or sacrifice angered him. They were to be his chosen children. This was unforgivable. He was an animal at heart, a night-stalker, an eater of flesh, a devourer of bones and babes, but he was an intelligent killer with a love of ceremony, a pagan's love of pageantry. He did now what instinct told him he must do.

He charged.

The next barrage of bullets brought him to his knees, the agony intense and irresistible. It had been a mistake doing this, he knew. Their weapons were hurtful. And although his kind didn't die very easy—it was this stubborn survivability that had kept his race alive eons after it should have went extinct with other such species—he was afraid. Afraid that the white-skins he'd underestimated would surround him and fill him with bullets so that even he would have to concede death. But no, he wouldn't let this happen. He would lie still; feign death until they got close. It was an ancient way. Many thousands of years before, when his race was thinning and dying out, and the dark-skins first came, they had waged war on the Lords of the High Wood. Only by killing hundreds of them had the Lords survived, beating the dark-skins at their own game of supremacy, enslaving the newcomers. But before this...there were strategies, ways to draw in the dark-skins, methods to fool their superior numbers.

Skullhead did this now.

And these whites, oh they were easy prey. They waltzed right into the jaws of death. The beast was wise with the ages as a score of victims could attest to. Century upon endless century of hunting and stalking had taught him much.

"You men!" Bowes shouted. "Get away from it!"

Five men were circled around the dying beast, prodding it with their rifles.

"It can't hurt anyone now," one of them said.

"Come on, Deputy, it—"

Then the beast was on its feet. It opened the bellies of two men, and tore the throats from a third and fourth. The air steamed with blood and spilled internals. Listening to cries of agony, Skullhead snatched up the fifth man and tossed his rifle over the rooftops. It was an old strategy and a good one. He held the fifth white before him like a shield, knowing the others with their rampant sentimentality would not attack and they didn't.

"Don't shoot!" Bowes told them. He only had three men left now. Many more had poured into the street, but were cowering well away from the beast and his appetites.

He'd told them not to get too close, by Christ, he'd told them...

The posse had been butchered. There were four men in the street, ripped open, their stuffing scattered in all directions. The remaining members were vomiting.

The beast was in the doorway of the undertaker's again. It slipped through, taking the fifth man with him.

"That's my brother!" someone yelled. *"It's got my brother for the love of Christ!"*

But not for long.

As the remaining gunmen and a few interested civilians slowly approached Spence's, there was a crash and an explosion of splintered glass blew out at them. The fifth man's broken body came out with it.

Bowes kneeled by it. "Dead," he muttered. The neck was broken, probably before he was launched through the window. The beast hadn't the time to properly maul the man, but he killed him for the sake of appearances.

"C'mon," Bowes told his men.

With them at his back, he charged into the undertaker's.

19

Perry was one of the last to arrive.

He did what he could for the injured men which was little more than pray for them. Most were dead when he got there. His mind dead tired and worn to threads from all the killing and bodies and blood, he went into Spence's and viewed the carnage. Had a tornado slipped through there, it could have been no more complete. Cabinets were shattered, chemicals spilled. Vats overturned. Walls smashed to debris from the passage of the beast. And mixed in with that refuse, was what remained of Wynona Spence.

Jesus.

Perry remembered Marion upstairs.

Steeling himself and pressing a hand to his back, he went up those creaking, narrow stairs and into the apartment above which smelled of incense and wood smoke. There was a slightly sickening stench of lilacs, as if Wynona had been spraying perfume liberally.

It didn't take him long to find Marion.

It took him even less to realize that she'd been dead for years. Her skin was tight and flaking, gray as cement. The lips blackened and shriveled. The eyes sunk into dark pits. The fingers were shrunken into fleshy pencils. Wynona had embalmed her, turned her lover into a mummy she could covet and coddle for years and years.

Perry, sobbing, went back downstairs. "Oh, Wynona," he said. "Oh dear Christ, what happened to you?"

The locals would feed off this like leeches. Wynona's father had been a good man and Perry thought that, down deep, she was a good woman. Yes, she had a body up there. But she had harmed no one. Never slandered or hurt a soul.

Perry fired up an oil lantern and got it burning bright.

Then he shattered it against the wall. Flames engulfed the room and, eventually, they would take the entire building. And that was a good thing. For fire purified and Wolf Creek was long overdue.

20

Next, Perry went to see Claussen.

Something dangerous was brewing with that man.

Perry had a syringe with him, loaded with morphine. This one wasn't for himself, however (he'd already had his taste and was swimming in an exotic sea), but for the madman who'd once been a reverend. A madman who now thought himself a pagan priest of some new, yet ancient blasphemous order.

Perry's head was full of fog, but he had a duty and he would perform it.

From all over town he could hear screams and gunshots. He paid them no mind and mounted the church steps. Inside, he stopped. There was a smell in the air. One that told him to run while he still had breath.

"Claussen?" he called. "Are you here?"

"The beast," a voice in the darkness said, "the beast."

Perry followed the voice and found the reverend slouched in a pew. He was pale, his face beaded with sweat. He looked terrible.

"Are you all right, Claussen?"

The reverend smiled, his chin wet with drool. "He returned as I knew he would."

It was dim in the church, a few feeble rays of light bled in through the stained glass windows. Dust motes danced in the beams, thick and clotted. Perry looked around, seeing nothing, hearing nothing. He swallowed dryly. There was only that smell, that gagging perfume of putrescence.

"I think you should come with me now," Perry said.

"Where?"

"To my house. I can care for you there."

Claussen laughed shrilly. "Leave?" he said in a congested voice. "Leave? *This is my church!* The house of God! I can't leave here, not now! God has come, he's here now..."

Perry scowled slightly. "Yes, of course. Spiritually he—"

"Not him! Not that one! Not that false shepherd who I've prayed my soul out to and has yet to honor me with so much as a word, a sign!" Claussen was trembling now, his eyes rolling. *"He has come! The Lord of the High Wood! The beast!"*

"Stop this, Claussen. Come away with me."

"No!"

"You can't worship a mindless beast."

Claussen laughed. "Such blasphemy. You should be quiet about such things...if he hears you..."

"He won't."

The smell was strong now: violent, offensive. A brutal odor.

"Won't he?" Claussen seemed confused.

"Of course not, he's just an animal."

"Heretic! "Claussen cried, springing to his feet. "He is here! He is here now! He came and I made sacrifice to him!"

To prove this, Claussen pulled his hand from the pocket it had been thrust into...except there was no hand. Just a stump wadded up with red-stained cloth bandages. The man was bleeding to death. Slowly...but dying all the same.

"Christ, Claussen, how—"

"Don't say that name in here!"

Perry knew that now, more than ever, he had to give him the injection. Unless the man was drugged, he'd never get him away from this place. The question was: How could he hope to subdue a crazy man even for the few precious moments it would take to empty the hypodermic into his arm? Perry, despite the painless dream-life morphine gave him, was in poor shape. His back was twisted, incapable of supporting more than his own fragile weight. It was in no condition to take the kind of abuse needed to overpower another man. And his age, too, was a factor. The doctor never would again see the good side of seventy.

Claussen hobbled away up to the altar. Perry followed.

"Blasphemy," Perry said.

Claussen smiled. "It has to be rebuilt, this altar, retooled with new and greater meaning."

The altar had been smashed and rent. Boards were pulled up, statues of the heavenly fathers broken into fragments, prayer books were freed of their pages. The altar cloth had been shredded. It was even worse than the other day.

"This is *his* church now, Doctor."

And indeed it was. This was the sort of obscene shrine only a demon of savage appetites would or could appreciate.

"I must commission new artworks," Claussen said, "in his image. Busts of the finest stone, paintings in livid colors...perhaps blood..."

"Where is he, Claussen?"

"I can't tell you that. Not yet. Know only that he is close..."

Perry scowled. "What you've done is blasphemy, Claussen. It's disgusting."

"You're a fool, Doctor. This is *his* house now."

"In the name of Christ, man, get a hold of yourself."

Claussen grabbed Perry violently by the arm. "You shall not revere the names of false gods in this holy place."

"Fantasy…"

"Really?"

"Yes, I…"

Claussen cackled with laughter. "Behold," he said, "he stands at the door and knocks."

The stink had grown omnipotent now.

It dried the words on Perry's tongue, put a frost into his bones. And then, behind him, as his senses reeled with nausea, there was movement. He turned quickly, his back wrenching and crying out. He ignored it for the Lord of the High Wood had arrived. The doctor looked on the beast with no reverence, no respect, only a sort of numbing awe at this mistake of evolution. It was huge, its shoulders twice the breadth of any man's, its head mammoth. A giant. Its gray flesh was stained with dried blood and those eyes…good God, those eyes…bleeding balls that ran with discolored tears.

The beast came closer, moving with a slow grace that was frightening for something its size. Its arms hung limp at its sides, matted with patchy fur, bulging with obscene muscularity, the fingers—impossibly long—ending in hooked claws. Rapiers. Its sex swung with pendulum strokes between the massive thighs proudly. Its skin was ruptured, torn, splitting open with a vile sap in a hundred places. But its eyes, these are what held Perry. And the mouth, the sneering, hateful mouth that opened with a wet smack exposing teeth that glimmered like sacrificial daggers.

"Jesus," Perry managed.

"Not Jesus," Claussen said, stepping between them. "The Lord has chased Jesus from this place on the cowering tails of the saints."

Claussen looked up at his god and made a quick benediction. The beast roared and with a single slap of its bleeding fist sent the reverend sailing over a row of pews.

Perry pulled his gun. "We'll see what kind of god you are."

The beast began to drool.

Skullhead stood on the altar, having finished with the old man and his little gun. He didn't bother snacking on this one—he was far too old, far too tough, stringy, and meatless. No, the old ones served only one purpose and had for ages and that was to be broken by the will of the Lords, killed for amusement. This was all. Murdering the old was tradition amongst the Lords. The dark-skins held the aged in such reverence that these were the first the Lords had killed when they waged war on the little men. After that, the men. Women and children were a different matter.

Skullhead sat down on the altar, fatigued with all the excitement and bloodshed. He was hurting. Pain rolled through his great torso in sharp waves. Bullets. Too many bullets in him. But the agony was good. Often, in the old days, the Lords would cut and slash themselves to bring on pain before a battle. It made them fiercer, more savage fighters. But this pain...though it made him angry, a sadistic conqueror...was not good. There was simply too much of it. It clouded the mind and made the senses reel.

It had to be alleviated.

When the Lords fought the wars against the advancing dark-skins in those ancient, forgotten times, the dark-skins used arrows and spears. Both of these were far more painful than mere bullets—they opened great gaping wounds in the body. Once they were removed, the healing began and went quickly as was the way with the Lords' biology. But sometimes arrowheads broke off inside the flesh and had to be dug out by claws or teeth. If they weren't, the body would fester and rot and death would follow. Skullhead knew the tales of those old days, they boiled in his cells. He knew the bullets had to be removed.

But it was no easy task.

His flesh, usually as tough as a beetle's carapace, was sensitive and hurting from all the abuse it had taken. Still, it had to be done. Groaning, the last of the Lords of the High Wood began to dig the slugs free. Bloody, mangled and mushroomed bullets dropped to his feet. Many were near the surface, others were deeper. He worked his long bony fingers into his belly, searching and sorting through his internals. One by one, the slugs were removed. With a surgeon's finesse, he groped and probed and stroked the secrets of his anatomy.

It was some time before he'd finished.

He removed nearly twenty bullets and there were still four or five left. He didn't think they'd do any harm. There were other foreign bodies lodged in him, tokens of battles centuries gone, and they caused him no trouble.

Lying back on the altar, he rested.

His flesh was resilient and in a short time, his wounds would scar over. He'd lain in that grave for some four centuries before the dark-skins had dug him back out. And though there was no consciousness, only vague dream, a spark of life remained in him. It was the way of his kind. If they weren't dismembered, they could not really die, not totally. A rugged sort of half-life would remain. His kin, with the exception of one or two whose graves were the closely-guarded secrets of the dark-skins, had all been pulled apart after they'd sickened and fell. The dark-skins saw to that. Though they'd worshipped the Lords for thousands of years in one form or another, in the final days when the Lords had fallen ill with unknown infections, they'd risen up and hacked their masters to bits. Skullhead knew those were the Dark Days, the end of his race. A few of his kind, no more than three or four, had proved immune to these new contagions. But the dark-skins, natural born traitors, had rebelled and attacked the remaining Lords. Bound with rope, leather, and twine, the surviving Lords were buried alive. Their graves, a secret to all but a few in the passing centuries.

Skullhead closed his eyes.

Gone were the old days when the children were offered in sacrifice, when virgins were staked out for breeding. The system of service had vanished. It was up to Skullhead now, as the last of his race, to set things right. He would be worshipped again. Meat would be offered. The old and the weak would once again be set free naked and unarmed in the forest for sport. And women would be offered. This last thing was the most important. The race would not survive until women were impregnated with his seed.

Once the white-skins were beat into submission, this task would be the first order of business.

Longtree watched Wolf Creek burn.

It had started for mysterious reasons in the undertaking parlor. But once started, it had found the chemicals therein and exploded into life.

It turned into a major blaze within minutes.

Whether the fire was unleashed by accident or on purpose, it didn't matter—the town was burning. He had arrived with Lauters moments after the slaughter had occurred. By then, the beast was long gone. But the evidence it left was all-too apparent. The beast had broken through the rear wall of the mortuary.

The fire was spreading fast. Almost effortlessly, cheered on by the winds that screamed out of the north. The buildings and houses in Wolf Creek were all packed together very closely and the flames jumped from roof to roof.

Longtree and Lauters were stalking the beast.

There was no posse to be had. All available men (and women) were busy fighting the blaze and this included Bowes. Even the sixty men Ryan had assembled to exterminate the Blackfoot, were helping out.

The trail of the beast was easy to follow, though somewhat erratic. It was only a matter of following the path of wreckage and death. Wherever it went, people were killed, homes or buildings destroyed. It had charged through the wall of a saloon, murdering six people and maiming a dozen others. Then it kicked down the door of a miner's little home and decapitated his family. Next, the trail led to a dry goods store. The proprietor was crushed like a bundle of old sticks and stuffed into a coal furnace. One valiant, though suicidal, man had attempted to stop the fiend as it left the store. They found his shotgun bent into a V and his body driven headfirst like a fencing post through the snow and into the frozen earth. Only his wrenched legs were visible. Wherever the lawmen went, the tale was the same: atrocity upon atrocity.

"It's taking back its lands," Longtree commented as they slipped through the caved-in wall of a dance hall.

Lauters studied the stomped furniture and shattered fixtures. "Its lands?"

"Yes," Longtree said. "Once there were many like it. They ruled this land, the Blackfoot and other tribes worshipped them. Now it's come back and it's taking back its property."

Lauters looked at him like he was crazy. "It's a monster."

"But not a mindless one.''

"You're giving it a lot of credit, aren't you? Maybe it can reason a bit, but it's still a monster."

There was no arguing with that.

Longtree was wondering if the beast was on the run or merely hiding out in one of these ruined structures, awaiting the man he needed to kill. Or had he forgotten now, in the inebriation of massacre, why he'd been called back? What his reason for being was. Anything was possible with this creature, anything at all.

"I take it," Lauters said, scanning the debris for bodies, "that you've been talking with Crazytail and his bunch."

"I have."

"And you believe those tales they tell?" the sheriff said incredulously.

Longtree sighed, realizing he still disliked this man. And why not? He was a rapist, a murderer, a vigilante, a cattle rustler, would-be assassin (and God knew what else) parading as a lawman. "If you have a better explanation about the origin of this beast, Sheriff, I'm all ears," Longtree said. "It came from somewhere."

Lauters spat. "Hell. That's where it came from."

"Regardless," Longtree sighed, "that's where it's going."

They moved along, Lauters in the lead. There was blood in the beast's tracks now. Fresh blood.

"If it bleeds," Lauters said happily, "it can die."

The trail suddenly ended. The only possible place the beast could have gone was the building leaning before them. The church. Together they circled around it. No tracks led away.

"We've got it." Lauters was jubilant. "We've got the sonofabitch."

"We'll need help."

"Stay here," Lauters ordered. "I'll get some men."

Longtree watched him vault away, moving quickly through the drifts. Longtree studied the church. Why had the beast come here? Was it for the obvious reason that it simply needed shelter, a place to mend its wounds? Or was it something else entirely? Did it know a house of worship when it saw one? Did it think in its unflappable egotism that it belonged here, a god to be kneeled before?

Longtree waited. If the beast tried to escape now, he would have to try and stop it...and no doubt perish in the attempt. There was nothing to do but wait for reinforcements. He toyed with the idea of wiring Fort Ellis for Army troops, but getting them when they were needed was like getting a child to open its mouth so you could pull a tooth. Besides, it would take them a day or so to reach Wolf Creek...and the beast surely wouldn't sit still that long.

So the marshal waited, smelling the smoke of the burning town. Like Nero, he fiddled while Rome burned.

23

Dr. Perry was alive.

Despite the abuse put to him by the fiend, he still lived. The spark that burned in his body for seventy odd years refused to be snuffed. Bones were broken, limbs twisted and crippled, blood spilling from a dozen wounds, yet he lived and in living, was awake. He looked down on the fiend below him with a consuming hatred that would smolder, he was certain, long after death had claimed him and the fiend was so many ashes in God's palm.

24

Lauters knew more pain than the doctor could ever dream of in his most anguished moments. He'd lost friends, he'd lost his family, he'd lost his way of life. Much of it was due to the beast, but Longtree was hardly innocent. When that ravaging monster was put to rest finally, he'd have a word or two to say to the marshal. He was beyond caring whether or not Longtree wanted to arrest him. He planned on dying at the beast's hands or with Longtree's bullets in him. Either way, he was going to die. And if he slew the beast and Longtree and lived, then he'd put his gun to his head and end it. Having no reason to live, Lauters took satisfaction in his own coming death.

A third of the town was ablaze now. The conflagration had eaten its way through most of the businesses and was busy blackening homes, hungry for new conquests.

"I need men," Lauters told Bowes when he found him in the mulling confusion. "We found it. I need men to kill it."

Bowes, black with soot, coughed. "The town's burning," he said dryly. "Burning."

"I don't give a fuck about this town," Lauters snapped. "I found the monster and we have to kill it. Get some men."

Bowes efficiently went about the task of rounding up what men could be spared, even though, technically, there were none. He came back with four smoke-blackened men.

"These are the only ones who'll come," the deputy said.

"Shit. All right."

Grimacing as he took one final pull from a bottle of rye in his desk drawer, Lauters handed out rifles and ammunition. His eyes blazing with revenge, he led the posse to their deaths.

25

Skullhead, grinder of flesh and render of souls, lay sleeping on the altar as the dogs of war inched closer. He snoozed and dreamed of the old days of slaughter and barbarity. He was sure these days would come again.

His arrogance would allow him to accept nothing less.

But what he failed to realize in the blood-misted corridors of his brain was that this was a new age and men had little use for the old gods. In these times, men wanted gods that were quiet, that didn't interfere with their own plans and conquests. Advisors, not active participants. The days when men offered up their sons and daughters to primeval monsters were long gone. In the collective psychology of the masses, this was unthinkable.

But none of this would have made any sense to Skullhead.

His was a reptilian brain—a mass of nervous tissue devoted to need, want, and desire. He was hungry, so he ate; thirsty, so he drank. His loins ached, so he raped; his territory was threatened, so he killed. Simplicity itself. The perfect hunter, the ultimate predator. There was logic and reasoning in that brain, too, but it was generally only applied to methods of the hunt, to slaughter, to self-indulgence. The little men existed only to feed, clothe, and worship him. And they should do these things, his brain decided, because he wished it.

So, the beast laid on the altar, beneath ravaged symbols of Christianity, a god in his own thinking, sainted by atrocity, immortal through his own appetites. In God's house he waited, bloated with sin and suffering, his belly fat with human meat. A Christian demon, as it were, in the flesh.

26

Longtree grew tired of waiting.

When the posse was but five minutes away, he entered the church. He was carrying his usual armaments—Winchester rifle, Colt pistols, and Bowie knife. There was death in his eyes as he entered through the main door which was hanging from one hinge as if it had taken a tremendous blow. From the claw marks drawn into the wood, he knew what had struck it. He paused just inside, lighting a cigarette and listening. He could hear movement, but the movement of a man, a sort of limping gait.

He moved up the nave, sighting the man just ahead. It was Claussen or a beaten, bleeding, and bedraggled version of the same. There was a fire going in the aisle, a small one fed by prayer books and shards of wood.

"The marshal," Claussen said. "I wondered when you'd show."

Longtree looked at his arm. There was no hand, just a stump burnt black. "What happened, Reverend?" he asked calmly.

"I was bleeding. The master...he took my hand...sacrifice," Claussen mumbled. "I cauterized it." He grinned madly at the idea.

No sane man could thrust his arm in a fire even if it meant saving his own life. The pain would be unthinkable. "Where is it?" Longtree inquired. "The beast."

"The *master?*" Claussen looked suddenly sheepish, but his eyes blazed with the embers of lunacy. "Have you come to serve? To worship?"

"I've come to kill it."

"Get out of here," Claussen demanded.

Longtree scanned the dimness, eyes bright. "Where?"

"You can't kill him, Marshal. No man can. If you've not come as a brother to him, then run before he discovers you."

There was a glint of humanity left in the man, but little more.

Longtree sighed. "You're ill, Reverend. You'd best leave now, I've got business—"

"You've no business here. Not anymore."

Longtree moved up the aisle. Claussen blocked his path.

"Step aside, Reverend, or I'll shoot you," he said, spitting out his cigarette.

Claussen launched himself forward and Longtree easily sidestepped him. He slammed the butt of the Winchester into the man's belly and snapped it up aside his head. Claussen fell, whimpering.

"Where is it?" Longtree demanded.

Then a sound: a single grumbling moan.

Longtree looked up to the altar. In the shadows...the beast.

And in the time it took him to see the horror, its wretched form, Claussen was on him. The icy fingers of his remaining hand were cutting into Longtree's throat, the stump beating him around the face, eliciting cries of pain from its owner each time it struck. It was as much the insanity of the situation as the attack that made the marshal drop his rifle and stagger back, shielding his eyes. Claussen was on him, kicking, striking, clawing, trying to bite. Longtree shoved him away, kicked him fiercely in his lamed leg and struck him in the face with a series of quick jabs. Claussen, old cuts on his face opening, fell to his knees.

Longtree, picking up his rifle, walked slowly to the altar.

A ghostly, smoky light rained in through the stained glass windows. They had been defaced with perverse drawings now. The pulpit loomed ahead, the defiled altar, and the beast, bleeding and asleep.

Dr. Perry had been added to the fiend's roll call of victims. He had been crucified on the great wooden cross, spikes stolen from the shattered altar driven through his hands and ankles. He hung above the beast, an aged and depraved Christ, rivers of red wine staining the altar cloth below.

Longtree looked down on the beast.

He wondered if it was dead. For just one hopeful, fleeting moment, he thought it might be. Dead or dying. But he knew it was neither. In his mind he saw the butchered faces of its victims, the dead children. Had it visited the Blackfoot camp yet? Were Laughing Moonwind and her folk dead now?

No time to think.

The beast was a blood-streaked, stinking mass of foul intent. It was tight with throbbing muscle and jutting bone. Its shoulders broad, its head huge. Its cavernous mouth open, black spiny tongue stuck to its lower lip. Its eyes were wide and staring, but it did not have lids as such.

It was a horror.

Longtree thought it seemed to be composed of many things. It had bits of fur like a mammal. The thorny, exaggerated flesh of a lizard. The ridged, armored torso of insect. The hooked, yellowed claws of a bird of prey. The spiked and skeletal tail of a saurian. Yet, it resembled a man in that it had four limbs and walked upright. Some bastard, perverse uncle of humanity.

Longtree took aim at its head.

There was a bustle of commotion from the vestibule. Lauters, Bowes, and a few others stomped in, shoving Claussen aside.

"Longtree!" Lauters shouted.

The beast stirred.

Christ, Longtree thought, so close, so close...

The men were charging up the altar now, talking excitedly amongst themselves at how the marshal had slain the monster. Longtree backed away into the chancel.

"It's alive," he muttered.

And it was.

One sheer membranous eyelid opened crustily, then another. Slitted pupils stirred in seas of glowing red. They expanded to take in light. The mouth dropped open, lips thinned and drew away from swollen, black gums, teeth sliding forth like arrows from a quiver. The beast was awake.

It stood up, easily eight feet in height. It was, Longtree decided, his finger tickling the trigger of his rifle, an amazing exercise in lethal anatomy.

It looked to be armored for battle like a knight of old. Like a fleshy, living skeleton. Its arms fed into sockets just beneath the shoulders which were shielded by jutting plates. The legs, the same, plates concealing their origin. Its torso was gleaming with ribbed mounds, knitted with a black oily skin that bled into gray, riddled with numerous lacerations and punctures. It had no neck, the head firmly mounted on the sloping shoulders, jaw protruding in a quasi-snout, nostrils flattened and bulging with each rasping breath. There seemed to be barely enough flesh to cover the protruding architecture of the massive skull. It was drawn tight, scarred and thinning. Silver and gray tufts of fur sprouted here and there like weeds through cracks in rock.

A thing engineered to stalk and kill and take any amount of abuse thrown at it. The ultimate hunter. Built to survive in a savage world of half-humans and monsters that no longer existed.

The beast took one step forward.

One of the men—the one who'd lost his brother to this horror—charged forth, screaming out a battle cry. The beast took his knife in the abdomen and then took the man himself. Before the cowering, helpless eyes of the posse, the man was pulled apart, his viscera decorating the altar. There was nothing to do but watch.

The body was dropped. The beast crushed the head with a grinding of a bony heel, wetting the remains down with a gush of viscous, steaming piss.

Longtree and the others fell back, shooting.

Skullhead felt more bullets pierce his hide. He took them and roared, still standing. He'd been deceived into thinking these white-skins had brought offerings of themselves. But it was not so; they refused to obey the ancient laws. So, great instructor in all things bloody and agonizing, Skullhead would teach them.

Longtree watched the beast move. It had just absorbed no less than a dozen bullets, and here it leaped like an angry child, the great tail thrashing. It knocked Lauters aside and grabbed the first available man. With a grinding, an awful wet snapping, it separated the first man at the hip, tossing his legs one way and his body the other. The man screamed and flopped, legless, blood coming out in a flood.

As more shots were fired, Longtree ran to the small fire Claussen had built and removed a chair leg, the end of which was a flaming red coal. As the monster turned on him, he jumped up and jammed the torch in its face, falling back before he was swatted away. Its left eye and much of the flesh around it was incinerated into a sap of blackened fluid. The beast roared, swinging out madly in all directions, claws whistling through the air seeking life to take.

Bowes got behind it and opened up its muscled back with blasts from his shotgun. It turned on him and Lauters and another assailed it from the front with bullets. The beast howled with rage, pounding dust from the rafters overhead. Its back was ripped wide, glistening vertebrae exposed.

"Its eye!" Longtree shouted. "Shoot out its eye!"

As the men attempted to do this, Longtree turned and saw Laughing Moonwind and Herbert Crazytail coming up the aisle. The old man was dressed out in his finest. He wore a shirt of antelope skin, matching leggings, both ornamented with colored beads, feathers, and dyed porcupine quills. He wore a skull mask over his face and carried a medicine club decorated with wolf fur, weasel skin pendants, and topped by the foot of a wolf, claws extended. He pushed past Longtree and the others, facing the beast.

At the sight of him, Skullhead stopped dead.

Crazytail took items from his medicine bag—bits of herb, pinches of colored powder, feathered talismans—and threw them at the beast. He chanted and sang, circling the beast now, forming a circle of powder around it.

"What's that crazy injun doing?" Lauters asked.

No one answered. The beast had paused now, whether held by magic or by curiosity, it was held all the same.

"It killed everyone in the village," Moonwind said. "Only a few of us escaped…"

"What is your father doing?" Longtree asked.

"Binding him."

"Will it work?"

She shook her head. "No, it's too late for that...but he feels responsible. He and the others brought it back. It should never have seen the light of day again."

The beast suddenly grew bored with the ceremony. It buried its teeth in the old man's head, his skull pulped under the jaws. He fell dead at the monster's feet.

Laughing Moonwind screamed.

Lauters walked right up to it, emptying his rifle into its hide. "No more! Goddammit, this ends now!"

The beast put hands to either side of Lauters' head, lifting him into the air and crushing his skull slowly into mush. Longtree dashed away to get another stick from the fire and saw salvation: pushed beneath a pew was a can of kerosene.

The beast charged him and he uncapped the metal jug, letting its contents wash it down. Skullhead ignored this benediction and slammed into him, sending the marshal sailing through open air. In the process, the beast stumbled into the fire. In the time it took him to feel the pain of the embers beneath his feet, flames had licked up and over him. He spun and danced, trying to shake the kiss of fire.

No good.

Skullhead had never known such pain. He and his kind had no use for fire; it was something the little men used. Cooked meat was repulsive. In the old days when a finger of lightning set a dry forest ablaze, the Lords fled, migrating to safer environs. Fire destroyed. Fire hurt. Fire consumed. He slapped at himself and threw his body on the floor, rolling and rolling. It was no good. The fire ate at his flesh, cremating his will. When all the hair was gone from his skin, the flames died out. He pulled himself weakly to his feet, singed, blackened, blind, his face a distorted running mess.

"Now," Longtree said, directing his remaining troops, "kill it."

Keeping well away from the clawing fingers of the beast, they began to shoot and shoot. Reloading when chambers were empty. Finally the fiend fell to its knees. Its crisped flesh was open in dozens of places, mangled and bleeding viscera bulging forth.

Claussen dragged himself forth now. He had an ax. With a single vicious swing, he buried it in the monster's spine. It went down face first, jerking with convulsions, a sickly mewing deep in its throat. It was beaten now and all knew this.

"Hack into pieces," Moonwind directed. "It can only die if it is pulled apart."

Bowes, Longtree, Moonwind, and the two survivors from the posse went to work on the primal monster that would be a god. As Claussen looked on at his fallen idol, they each took the ax and chopped at the beast. Its hide was incredibly tough, but its assassins worked with an almost superhuman diligence. Soon its torso split. Its arms were severed free, it legs divorced from their thorny housings. Longtree cleaved the head free himself, kicking it away to the altar. To his amazement, the jaws still chattered, the legs still trembled. With a few more blows the skull collapsed, brains emptying at his feet.

"Not a god," Claussen mumbled. "Jesus, help me."

Longtree looked down at the wreck of Skullhead with Moonwind by his side. It was a great butchered slab of meat now, bleeding black blood and yellow fluid. Its guts steamed with a foul odor. The altar was stained with bits of it and would have to be destroyed.

But the creature was dead.

27

Two days later, it was over.

The fire had been contained the same day the beast died. A heavy snowfall drowned the flames. Half of the town was destroyed. The survivors quickly began rebuilding. Reverend Claussen died from his injuries that night and was given a Christian burial along with Perry, Lauters, and the other members of the posse. Herbert Crazytail was buried in the Blackfoot cemetery. Only Longtree, Moonwind, and a few others were present. The remains of the beast were assembled in sacks, tied shut, and buried in another part of the burial ground—the same grave they'd been originally interred in centuries before.

The church was burned to ashes.

"I don't know what I'm going to do about all this," Bowes said to Longtree as they sat and sipped coffee at the jailhouse. "How I'm going to explain this."

"There's nothing to explain. The beast is dead."

"But all the deaths…"

"People know what happened. Let it go. In a year, it'll be forgotten."

Bowes looked at him. "Do you really believe that?"

Longtree didn't answer. He stood and pulled on his coat and gloves. "I guess I'm done here," he said.

"Thanks for your help," Bowes said.

Longtree nodded and walked out into the cool air, listening to the sounds of sawing and hammering as the town was put to right. People wouldn't forget what happened, he knew, but they probably wouldn't talk much about it. In time, the entire experience would take on the connotations of legend. A twice-told tale. A myth. Something to frighten children with on stormy nights. Nothing more. A dark bit of collective memory that would seem all the more unreal as the coming days of normalcy blotted out its darker elements into the stuff of nightmares.

Longtree rode out of town, hoping he'd never have to return. He would ride to Fort Ellis and put in his report. Tom Rivers wasn't going to like the truth about this matter, but the truth was the truth. On the way, he would meet Moonwind. They were bonded now, he knew, from these horrors. Parts of them were linked. He couldn't imagine being without her.

A cigar in his mouth, the wind at his back, Joseph Longtree rode away from Wolf Creek.

-The End-

NIGHTMARE OF THE DEAD
VINCENZO BILOF

In a world of war and mayhem, a twisted nightmare of undead cannibals begins.

The outlaw Neasa Bannan uncovers a horrifying conspiracy engineered by the psychopathic mastermind behind the Confederacy's deadly flesh-hungry weapons. A homicidal gunslinger and a brotherhood of killers emerge out of Neasa's tragic, blood-soaked past while the living dead ravage the land.

With the fate of the country in the balance, Neasa must decide: save the Union from the undead menace, or surrender to Saul's vision of ultra-violence.

www.severedpress.com

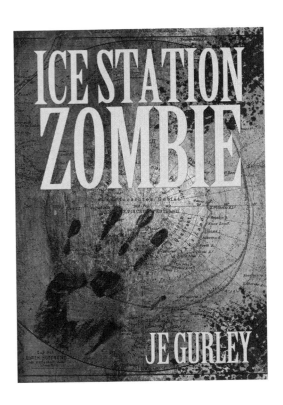

ICE STATION ZOMBIE
JE GURLEY

For most of the long, cold winter, Antarctica is a frozen
wasteland. Now, the ice is melting and the zombies are thawing.
Arctic explorers Val Marino and Elliot Anson race against time
and death to reach Australia, but the Demise has preceded them
and zombies stalk the streets of Adelaide and Coober Pedy.

www.severedpress.com

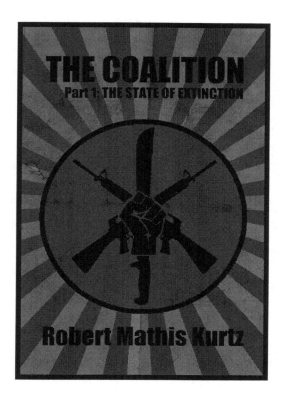

The Coalition

When the dead rose to destroy the living, Ron Cutter learned to survive. While so many others died, he thrived. His life is a constant battle against the living dead. As he casts his own bullets and packs his shotgun shells, his humanity slowly melts away.

Then he encounters a lost boy and a woman searching for a place of refuge. Can they help him recover the emotions he set aside to live? And if he does recover them, will those feelings be an asset in his struggles, or a danger to him?

THE STATE OF EXTINCTION: the first installment in the **COALITON OF THE LIVING** trilogy of Mankind's battle against the plague of the Living Dead. As recounted by author **Robert Mathis Kurtz.**

www.severedpress.com

MACHINES OF THE DEAD

The dead are rising. The island of Manhattan is quarantined. Helicopters guard the airways while gunships patrol the waters. Bridges and tunnels are closed off. Anyone trying to leave is shot on sight.

For Jack Warren, survival is out of his hands when a group of armed military men kidnap him and his infected wife from their apartment and bring them to a bunker five stories below the city.

There, Jack learns a terrible truth and the reason why the dead have risen. With the help of a few others, he must find a way to escape the bunker and make it out of the city alive.

www.severedpress.com

JUDGMENT DAY

Dr. Jebediah Stone never believed in zombies until he had to shoot one. Now they're mutating into a new species, capable of reproducing, and the only defence is 'Blue Juice', a vaccine distilled from the blood of rare individuals immune to the zombie plague. Dr. Stone's missing wife is one of these unwilling 'munies', snatched by the military under the Judgment Day Protocol.It's a new, dangerous world filled with zombies, street gangs, and merciless Hunters desperate for a shot of blue juice. Has the world turned on mankind? Is Mortuus Venator the new ruler of earth?

www.severedpress.com

TIMOTHY
MARK TUFO

Timothy was not a good man in life and being undead did little to improve his disposition. Find out what a man trapped in his own mind will do to survive when he wakes up to find himself a zombie controlled by a self-aware virus.

www.severedpress.com

NECROPHOBIA

An ordinary summer's day.
The grass is green, the flowers are blooming. All is right with the
world. Then the dead start rising. From cemetery and mortuary,
funeral home and morgue, they flood into the streets until every
town and city is infested with walking corpses, blank-eyed
eating machines that exist to take down the living.
The world is a graveyard.
And when you have a family to protect, it's more than survival.
It's war.

Zombie Fallout
Mark Tufo

CURRENTLY IN DEVELOPMENT WITH

Illuminandi Media